PRAISE FOR The Butterfly Cabinet

"An utterly compelling tale of hidden secrets and culture clashes played out against the backdrop of a large country house in Northern Ireland . . . a haunted tale, eerie with recrimination, illicit passion and frustrated motherhood . . . Pitch-perfect in tone, McGill captures, in counterpoint, the voices of the two women as they declaim a melancholy murder ballad."

—*Marie Claire*

"An exquisite series of painful revelations . . . McGill easily recreates the lives of the Castle's owners and servants and the intricate connections between them. As both Harriet and Maddie's stories emerge, the tale becomes a powder keg of domestic suspense that threatens to explode as long-kept secrets surrounding Charlotte's death are teased out."

—*Publishers Weekly*

"An emotionally bracing, refreshingly intelligent and ultimately heartbreaking story."

—*Kirkus Reviews*

"A kind of gothic *Upstairs, Downstairs* . . . Chilling and gripping."

—*Booklist*

"[B]eautiful and languorous and wild . . . in the end, we are caught and held tight."

—*The Huffington Post*

"[C]ompelling . . . a densely textured plot. The interplay of the voices of two exceptionally different personalities is perhaps the book's major achievement . . . While *The Butterfly Cabinet* is an intense exploration of maternal failure and a haunting illumination of cruelty and guilt, it also ... authentic backdrop of defining moments in Iri...

...*ribune*

"An absorbing story of ma...

... *Home*

"Intricately layered . . . McGill's assured debut is an intense exploration of maternal love and guilt. What also distinguishes it is its delicate portrait of a society that, within one life-time, would face unimaginable change."

—*Financial Times*

"A dramatic and haunting novel that tells the tale of two women whose lives are linked by an appalling tragedy. Inspired in part by the true story of events surrounding the death of the daughter of an aristocratic family in Ireland in the late 19th century, this is an enthralling and beautifully written debut."

—*Good Housekeeping* (UK)

"A gripping novel . . . The plot depends on suspense and uncertainty, as the story unfolds gradually up until the very last pages where the last strand is finally revealed. Providing plenty of psychological insight, the intimate nature of these accounts will leave you unable to fully sympathise with or completely condemn any of the characters. The humanity of both the main narrators is striking. It raises the questions of what we can learn from the past, what lies beneath the surface of an apparently simple story, and whether a person's character is developed by nature or nurture. Disturbing and thought-provoking, the story is nevertheless not entirely gloomy; it is an examination of how to deal with the past in the midst of hope for the future. Bernie McGill's writing style involves a combination of poetry and local influence, and this novel is hard to put down; a truly absorbing and cleverly written tale that will send a shiver down your spine."

—*Verbal* magazine

"McGill's rare, hypnotic gift for writing fills every page. The substance of her tale explores class, religion, politics and everyday life in upper-class Ulster toward the latter end of the nineteenth century and brings us well into the twentieth. It has the best nonsalacious description of sex from a woman's point of view that I have ever come across and contains no end of sentences you want to remember."

—Eugene McCabe, author of *Death and Nightingales*

"A haunting, often lyrical tale of quiet, mesmerizing power about the dangerous borders of maternal love."

—Rachel Hore, author of *The Glass Painter's Daughter*

*f*P

The Butterfly

Cabinet

A NOVEL

BERNIE McGILL

FREE PRESS
New York London Toronto Sydney New Delhi

For all the McGills and all the McClellands,
especially Kevin, Mary and Rosie

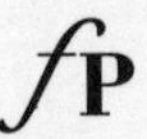

Free Press
A Division of Simon & Schuster, Inc.
1230 Avenue of the Americas
New York, NY 10020

Originally published in Great Britain in 2010 by Headline Review

First Free Press trade paperback edition May 2012

Designed by Akasha Archer

Manufactured in the United States of America

1 3 5 7 9 10 8 6 4 2

The Library of Congress has cataloged the hardcover edition as follows:

McGill, Bernie
The butterfly cabinet : a novel / Bernie McGill. — 1st Free Press hardcover ed.
p. cm.
Originally published: London : Headline Review, 2010.
1. Children—Death—Fiction. 2. Mothers—Fiction. 3. Reminiscing in old age—Fiction. 4. Butterflies—Collection and preservation—Fiction. 5. Secrecy—Fiction. 6. Diary fiction—Fiction. I. Title.
PR6113.C474B88 2011
823'.92—dc22 2010051294

ISBN 978-1-4516-1159-5
ISBN 978-1-4516-1160-1 (pbk)
ISBN 978-1-4516-1161-8 (ebook)

Cambridgeshire
12 August 1968

Dear Nanny Madd,

I am thinking about you today. Do you remember, nine years past, when Conor and I took you out? July 1959, a day of sparkle and glitter. We went for a dip and left you on a wooden bench on the Cliff Walk, with the sun on your face and the light dancing off the water at Port-na-happle. The crags all shadow, and the sea loud around the rocks and a jet plane, like a white threaded needle sewing its way, straight as old Miss Greenan used to teach us, across a washed-out sky. And then, do you remember, Nanny Madd, what we did?

Later you said you had a story for me, and I knew what story it was. There have been enough whispers over the years, enough knowing looks for me to piece some of it together. I wasn't ready to hear it before but I'll hear it now. You're the only one left who can tell it.

We're coming home, to the yellow house. I'll see you in September. Keep well.

Love always,

Anna

Maddie McGlade

RESIDENT, ORANMORE NURSING HOME
PORTSTEWART, NORTHERN IRELAND

8 SEPTEMBER 1968

Anna. You're the spit of your mother standing there—Florence, God rest her—and you have the light of her sharp wit in your eyes. Give me your hand till I see you better. There's not much change on you, apart from what we both know. Ah, you needn't look at me like that. Sure, why else would you be here? I know by the face of you there's a baby on the way, even if you're not showing. It's an odd thing, isn't it, the way the past has no interest for the young till it comes galloping up on the back of the future. And then they can't get enough of it, peering after it, asking it where it's been. I suppose that's always been the way. I suppose we're none of us interested in the stories of our people till we have children of our own to tell them to.

You couldn't have known it, but you've come on my birthday, of all days. At least, it's the day I call my birthday. When I was born, Daddy went to register the birth but not having had much schooling he wasn't sure of the date. If it's not the exact day, it's not far off it. One thing's certain: within the week I'll be ninety-two. If you stay for your tea you'll get a bit of cake.

Sit down, Anna. Can you smell that? Gravel, after the rain. You must have carried it in on your feet. Metallic tasting, like the shock you get when your tongue hits the tine on a tarnished fork. I'll never forget that smell, that taste in my mouth: it's as strong as the day, nearly eighty years ago, that I was made to lie down on the avenue with my nose buried in it. Your grandmother was a hard woman, Anna, brittle as yellowman and fond of her "apt punishments." This was to teach me to keep my nose out of the affairs of my betters, she said, and in the dirt where it belonged. Oh, don't look so shocked; I survived that and many another thing. And, hard as she was, I think I understand her better now. I know something now about what it is to feel trapped and though it's a strange thing to say, with all the money they had, I think that must have been how she felt.

She suffered for what she did. I bear no grudges against the dead. There's none of us blameless.

She was such a presence about the place, there's days I half expect to meet her on the landing, standing up, straight as a willow, her thick auburn hair tucked up tight, her face like a mask, never a smile on it. She went about her business indoors like a wound-up toy, everything to be done on time and any exception put her into bad humor. If the gas wasn't lit or the table wasn't set or there was a spot on a napkin, you'd feel the beam of her eyes on you like a grip on your arm. She was like a dark sun and all the rest of us—the servants and the weans and the master—all turned round her like planets, trying not to annoy or upset her in any way, trying to keep the peace.

I'll never forget the first time I saw her in evening dress. I wasn't long started at the castle, and I came up the back stairs to dampen down the fire in the drawing room because Peig, the housekeeper, said the master and mistress were going out to a ball. When I came back out, she was standing at the top of the main staircase, the master at the foot, and she was in a black satin cape, all covered in black cock feathers, tipped at the ends with green. She looked like a raven about to take flight, half bird, half woman, like she'd sprouted wings from her shoulders. I couldn't see where her arms ended and the cape began. It was stunning and scaresome all at the same time. I've never been so frightened of a person in my life! She stood at the top of the stairs, her arms spread out, waiting for the master's opinion, and when she peered down and saw me she looked the way a hawk might look at a sparrow. I wouldn't have been one bit surprised if she'd raised herself up on her toes and flapped those great feathery black wings and taken off over the banister, swooped down through the house and picked me up in her beak. I went into the kitchen shivering, and Peig looked at me and asked me what was wrong. I told her I thought the mistress might eat me, and she laughed till her eyes streamed and she had to wipe them with her apron. When she finally recovered she said there was that many animals had gone into the outfitting of her that I could be forgiven for wondering if there was any portion left of the mistress that was human!

Don't look like that, Anna. You needn't worry: you have nothing of hers that you need fear. Your mother put me over the story a dozen times or more, and she read all the newspaper cuttings that I'd kept and many's the time she cried sore tears for her sister, Charlotte, that she never knew. She promised to take care of you better than any child was ever taken care of, and she did, for seven short years, for as long as she could. For as long as her lungs allowed her, before the TB took her. She fought hard to stay with you, Anna, she knew what it was to grow up motherless and she didn't want that for you, but she was no match for it. She said to me, after she got sick, that she'd always felt there was prison air in her lungs, damp and cold, on account of where she'd been born. She was only a wean o' days old when the master brought her back here to the castle; she couldn't have remembered anything about Grangegorman Prison, but she had that notion in her head. "Prison air," she said, trapped in her chest, and her body only then trying to cough it up. I'd have taken over from her, Anna, looked after you myself if I'd been able, and I did try for a while. But your father could see it was a struggle for me and that was when he hit on the idea of the Dominicans, and sent you away to school at Aquinas Hall. I think he was trying to do what your mother would have wanted for you.

You have her sweet nature, Anna. You've waited for a child nearly as long as Florence waited for you. You must be, thirty-two? Am I right? Not far off it. September babies, the pair of us. What does that make us? Virgo and Libra: that'd be right. I remember the night you were born, the Big Sunday, September the twenty-seventh, 1936. The place was full of day-trippers, pouring into the town from the crack of dawn, taking their last chance at the weather, putting a full stop at the end of the summer. The Parade crammed with stalls selling ice cream and minerals, and the spinning pierrots, and the bay full of dancing boats: green and yellow and blue. Your mother and father were living in the yellow house where you are now, at Victoria Terrace, only yards away from the harbor. The young fellas started as usual to push each other out onto the greasy pole, and every time one of them fell in, there was a splash in the water and a roar went up from the crowd, and poor Florence gave another groan out of her and another cry. Ten hours, she was in labor with you. Poor Mrs. Avery, the midwife, was exhausted. And your father, pacing up and down the hall outside, drinking one pot of tea after another, smoking a whole packet of Players, and then going down to switch on the wireless as if there'd be some news of you on there. The psalm music was coming up from below: the BBC Chorus and then "Hallelujah!" and one last cry, and there you were. Little Anna, with a rosy face and a smile that would melt an unlit candle. You were born into love the like of no other child I've known. You've heard that story before, Anna, but you never tire of it, do you? Everyone should have a person in their life to tell them stories of their birth.

Florence got shockin' upset, a month or so before you were born. A baby was got in the river, up at the Cutts in Coleraine. A baby girl, it was, or part of one: she'd been in the river a long time. The coroner couldn't tell if her lungs had ever drawn a breath, the paper said. Your mother walked about for days after it, cradling her belly, talking to you. She mourned for that baby like it was her own, took it severely to heart that someone could do such a thing to an innocent child. And I was thinking that somewhere up the country, near where the Bann runs fast, there was a girl, standing in a farmhouse kitchen maybe, or behind a counter in a shop, a girl who had been waiting for that news, a girl with the paper in her hands, reading, knowing that was her baby that was got in the fishing gates, a girl with the insides torn out of her.

It's an odd thing I ended up back here after all these years. You know, it is a kind of home to me, for when you add up the time I was here as a servant and the time I've been here as a resident, I've lived here longer than I've lived anywhere.

The first time I came, Anna, the first time I set foot over the door of this house, I was fourteen years old. I'd never seen anything like the castle. Oh, I'd seen it from the outside, sure enough, you couldn't miss it. Grew up in its shadow, you might say, the way it stands on the headland looking down over Bone Row and the Parade and the harbor and the Green Hill at the far end. On a day like this, you can look out over the sea to the hills of Donegal in the west, Scotland to the east and the Atlantic as far north as you can see. It was never what you would call a pretty building. There's always been a touch of the fortress about it: gray, nothing heartsome. But inside, it was a palace. Rooms the size of churches, not all divided up like they are now, everything light and airy, full of fine-looking furniture but spacious, you would say, nothing too close to anything else. And smelling of lilies, the mistress loved lilies. I hated them, still do, those white petals like curled tongues when they open, the choking way they catch at the back of your throat, the rusty pollen that stains your hands for days. Give me a bunch of snowdrops any day, or bluebells, bluebells from Knockancor Wood. But your grandmother loved the lilies, would have filled the house with them if she could. She thought they cloaked the smell of the gas. Better than the smell of the place now, anyway: Jeyes Fluid and boiled spuds. Washable surfaces, that's what's important now, lino and emulsion; the smell of disinfectant everywhere. Why is it that people come to the sea to die? Is it the sound they're after? The first sound? Mistaking the crash and suck of the ocean for the swill of warm blood in their ears? Is it a return?

Do you see that, Anna, that little mark above my wrist? I saw that same mark on my mother's hand not long before she died. It would put you in mind of a swift in full flight: two dark wings, a divided tail. I know where that little bird is headed: swift by name and swift by nature, straight to the blood. I've been hiding it up my sleeve; I don't want the doctor near me. Let the hare sit, that's what I say. What's the point of rising it now? My time's near as well, but in a different way to yours, thank God. I'm glad you've come.

There's Nurse Jenny, Anna. Do you see her, in her lovely white uniform? She can smell death on a person. She's never said anything, but I've seen her face change, one day when she was helping oul' Mrs. Wilson up out of the chair; another day when she was spooning Jimmy's dinner into him. There's a gray look comes over her round face; a furrow comes in her brow, and then she's very gentle, gentler even than before. Oul' Mrs. Wilson was dead within two days, Jimmy that very night. It'll not be long now, I'm thinking, till she smells it on me.

There's something I want to show you, up in my room,

behind the door. Do you know what it is? It's your grandmother's butterfly cabinet: I've had it these years. The keeper of secrets, the mistress's treasure. Ebony, I think it is, very solid: four big balled feet on it. The darkest wood I've ever seen. There was never any warmth in it, not even when the light from the fire fell on it. Twelve tiny drawers, every one with its own small wooden knob. None of us was allowed to go near it; it was the one thing in the house that the mistress saw to herself. I'll never solve the problem of her: what's the point of keeping a dead thing? No luck could ever come of it. Mammy used to say that a white butterfly was the soul of a child and that you daren't harm it or the soul would never find rest.

The cabinet ended up in Peig's house, and when I opened it all those years ago and looked inside there was nothing left but dust and mold and rusted pins where the butterflies would have been. It was one of the saddest things I'd ever seen and for the first time ever—I don't know why—I felt sorry for the mistress and I cried for her. I cried for her loss of Charlotte and her loss of the boys and her loss of the master, and for the days she spent in prison and for the misery of her sad lonely life. And most of all I cried that she didn't know what she had and what she'd lost. Every drawer was the same: dust and mold and the dried-up bodies of carpet beetles and spiders, a waste of small lives.

But when I went to close it up again, one of the drawers wouldn't slide back in; I could tell there was something behind it. I slid the drawer out and reached in and felt a book and when I pulled it out, I thought it was a missal, bound in black leather with a metal trim. I opened it and saw the date in pencil on the first page and then I knew straightaway what it was: the diary the mistress had kept in prison. Her writing was very neat always, small and careful, but here and there, there'd be a stumble forward to the loop of an "l" or an "f," like the pencil was trying to get away from her and start some jig of its own.

I read three lines, and I closed it up again and put it back. You might find that hard to believe, Anna, but it wasn't meant for me. Maybe she put it there that first visit back to the house. Maybe she meant to come back. Maybe she intended to destroy it. Maybe it was for your mother. Who's to say? But, I think, it was her chance to speak, and she must have wanted someone to listen and she wouldn't have wanted it to be me.

After Peig died, the cabinet and the diary passed into my hands. I decided I'd give them both to Florence someday, when you'd grown up a bit, when she'd proved to herself that there was no curse, that she was deserving of the name of "mother." But I waited too long. And now I'm giving them to you. You are the true heir to the story. You can decide for yourself whether to read it or not, but you're its rightful keeper. Who better than you?

I'm tired, daughter. You'll come back? I could tell you more, maybe, another day. There's more to tell. But the story runs away from me, the like of a woolen sleeve caught on a barbed wire fence. It unravels before my eyes. I am trying with my words to gather it up but it's a useless shape at times and doesn't resemble at all the thing that it was. It's hard to do, to tell one story, when there are so many stories to tell.

Harriet Ormond

Inmate, Grangegorman Prison, Dublin

Saturday 16 April 1892

There is someone who looks just like me, who wears my clothes and brushes my hair, who rises when I am lying on this mattress in the early morning and goes about her business as if she were me.

The cell is eight by five. I have had time to measure it with my steps. The damp of the flags creeps up my legs despite my woolen stockings. There is a small barred window of ground glass above the height of my head. I have a view of a square of sky the size of a handkerchief. On a good night, when blessed sleep comes, I dream that I am stretching toward it, the silken square, and that when I am about to grasp it, it flaps its wings, a chalk-hill blue, and all that dusty color falls down around my face. The irony of the situation has not escaped me. To be locked in a room like the room into which I put Charlotte appears indeed to be an apt punishment.

I have learned to be thankful for small mercies. They have permitted me to wear my own clothes. I must wear mourning, of course, and I am mocked for doing so since, as I was told by the papers, I myself am the cause of having to wear it. I am sick at the sight of black crape. I had only just left off wearing it after Father died, and then Mother, and now here I am sheathed in it again. As if there were not misery enough to be had, without looking down on it every day.

I confess that I was unaware of the subtleties of degrees of punishment. I was a believer in absolutes. If one were dying, there was no comfort to be had. It was all the same, I thought, to die in a ditch or to die in a soft bed. What difference did it make? The choice of location did not alter the outcome. And if one were incarcerated, then there was nothing to be added or taken away. Nothing, I believed, could ease or exacerbate the truth that one's freedom was gone. Now, though, I can see that to have one silken square of sky is everything. To be able to see a glimpse of the world that is outside the horror of the place where one is confined, to see the sky change, to observe clouds pass overhead (once, I am sure of it, I glimpsed the flutter of a tortoiseshell): that means everything.

On a bad day, a sound like a hornet's wings shoots past my ear and I raise my hand and swipe at the air, at nothing. Tiny specks flit about at the corners of my vision. When I move my eyes toward them, they dart away, a silver-backed shoal of light, always just on the edge of what I can see. They herald the pain and when it comes, it is directly behind the eye like a splinter of light, like something that has been left behind from too much seeing. I feel that if I could reach in and touch it I would find it lodged there, jagged and solid. Then nausea, a heaving, emptying stomach, and each time I put my head down to find the pail, the jag of pain stabs forward again and again. I should recognize the signs by now. Yesterday, I bent my head over the copper basin, scooped the chill water into my hands and over my face, threw up my head to prevent the water dripping on my dress, then felt myself flung backward against the door of the cell, a sound like the beating of small wings in my ear. I found myself seated on the stone floor, staring back toward the window, and it seemed to me that the wall before me had tapered in, had narrowed a good three or four inches toward the ground. When I picked myself up my face and dress were dry. Afterward, in the yard, it was as if I had been blinkered, as if I were seeing everything down the barrel of a telescope. As I walked, the flagged ground, the wall, the inmates, the warders, the scraps of moss the crows had picked off the roof and dropped, the entire scene jolted up and down to the rhythm of my steps.

And all the time, I am lying here, eyes open, not moving, watching the square of barred light creep down the wall and cross the floor and vanish into darkness. A new skeleton has formed inside the old: it is she who walks about and mouths the words, and I, the split skin, am left discarded here, opened at the seams. There is nothing the prison doctor can prescribe for the headaches, he says, for fear of damage to my unborn baby. My ninth child: what will it be?

I consider my roll call of children: Harry, the eldest, who is honorable, who will always do the right thing, who takes after Edward in character, who resembles my father in looks. Thomas, whose eyes are green as marram grass and who bends with every breeze, who cannot settle at a task for more than a minute at a time, who in this, as in other things, takes after Edward's father, Lord Ormond. James, I think, a little like my mother, stern mouthed, somewhat self-indulgent. If he continues to favor her in looks he will never be tall but fine framed and pale, much like my sister, Julia. Gabriel and Morris remind me of Edward's maternal grandfather, or at least of what I know of him: bluff, red-faced, matter-of-fact chaps, hands-on, curious, practical. Freddie and George, too young, too early to say, though Freddie shows signs of Morris's temper when his teeth are coming through—as if firing his rattle against the wall will make them come any sooner or easier. They are none of them alike, my children: dark, fair, red haired; gray eyed, blue eyed, brown; tall, heavy framed, fine. I see nothing of myself in any of them. They have come through me from Edward, from his ancestors and mine, but they seem little to do with me. And that is especially true of Charlotte, my sixth, my only girl. What can I say about her?

She had a gesture that was all Edward's: a way of tilting her head when she was listening carefully, a strange fully-grown tic that seemed entirely at odds with her small frame. It did not seem copied: it appeared that she had inherited it, as surely as those serious gray eyes, those blond curls that had been his too as an infant. And she was wise, like a child, as they say here, that had been before, would be again.

She could never take an object by its handle. When she was given a cup she immediately wrapped her fingers around the bowl. She was contrary to the bone and entirely comfortable in her own skin. She had no interest in mounting a horse but would have fed carrots to my gray, Caesar, the whole day long. And she did not like the sea. It was loud, she said, a monster. She was plagued with dreams. Once, she woke up crying and I went to her and said, "It has gone away now. Go back to sleep," and she said, "That is why I am crying." She dreamed she could fly, she said. She had sprouted strong white feathered wings on her shoulder blades—she could feel them—and she was soaring high up in the blue looking down on the house and the strand, wheeling through the air, turning and gliding, being borne up on the warm currents that rise off Inishowen and Binevenagh, and she did not want to come down.

Why so many children? Too indelicate a question for anyone to ask, but it was on their minds, I am sure of it. I saw the looks they gave me in church each time my condition became apparent. Why not lock the door against Edward? Surely I had provided him with heirs enough. Surely my duty was done. How can I describe the way I am with him, when we are alone together? It has something to do with touch, and something to do with ache, and something to do with living, and something to do with freedom, and something to do with loss, and something to do with a return to oneself, and something to do with fear, and something to do with relief, and with color, startling color, and with harmony, and with rhythm, and with abandon. A thrumming of parts, a butterflying, a dancing. And at the end of it, often, there is a child. It is a price to pay.

I loved Charlotte—that could not be helped—but she was a difficult child to like. She was willful, disobedient; nothing particular in that, but her misbehavior had a quality that I could not fathom. She was so unlike the boys. Their mischief was impulsive, uncalculated, soon ended by a punishment that befitted it. I insisted on breakfasting with the children several times a week, a peculiarity that my defenders chose to view as dutiful and my detractors held up as an example of tyrannical control. On one such occasion I caught Harry emptying his morning porridge into his napkin. He loathed the taste, complained it was like swallowing warm frogspawn. I had him sit at the table at every meal for two days without a morsel on his plate. He ate his porridge on the third day, and every day thereafter. I caught Morris unpicking the wallpaper in the dining room, trying to set fire to it with a lucifer, the room adrift with black floating ash, an experiment, he said, to discover if a wall would burn. I held his hands on the hot-water pipes until he cried, and never once did he venture near a flame again. But with Charlotte nothing was ever simple. She repeated the same offense time and again, and nothing I did appeared to have any impact. She was not unintelligent—precisely the opposite in fact—but she would not see the consequences of her actions, she would not be turned. She was entirely stubborn, would not bend her will to anyone, and in the matter of her toileting, I was utterly defeated. I have found myself, since she began to walk and talk, remembering moments I had forgotten from my own childhood with my sister, Julia—the sudden hatreds, the mind games, the jealousies. There have been times when I have felt

Charlotte to be my senior. She had something over me the way Julia always had.

There was nothing straightforward, direct with Charlotte. If she wanted more bread she would ask if everyone else had had enough; if she wanted to feed Caesar she would ask if he was likely to be hungry; if she wanted to draw with Julia she would ask if she was busy. Every question was leading somewhere, nothing to the point. She seemed to want to consider any given matter from every angle available, to examine the reverberations on the entire household. She knew what she wanted but she would not ask for it outright. No one else seemed troubled by this, indeed Julia found it charming, but her circumnavigation drove me to distraction. I often felt with Charlotte that an interpreter was needed: someone who could sift through the emotional entanglement of her language, translate to me a clear intention. Julia, on the other hand, appeared to understand her perfectly.

Charlotte loved Julia, and Julia loved her, and why would they not? Julia does not discipline the children, never speaks a cross word. She is in the privileged position of the indulgent aunt who can spoil them at will and then leave them since they are not her responsibility. It is not to her they come with stomach cramps in the night for having overindulged in ice cream, it is not at her they snap in the mornings for having been put to bed too late. Julia is softhearted. She would not outwardly cross me, not anymore, not since we exchanged words on the matter. She feels her position in my household keenly. But if she could find a way to soften a punishment, without appearing to go against me, she would do it. She has grown predictable, can be depended upon to bring bread and water to the children when I have said they are to have no supper, to slip in and read to them when they have been put to bed early for some misdemeanor. I have never acknowledged this subtle interference and she has never referred to it. And this, our unvoiced agreement, worked well enough for a time. I feigned ignorance of her temperance, never sanctioned it, and her discretion was complete; she did nothing outwardly to flout my authority. That I came to rely on it was my mistake.

My see-through sister, Julia, pale faced, light haired, fine, nothing dark, nothing hidden, nothing deep. It was always made clear to us that she was the one to be educated; I was to be married. Neither of us questioned our father's will. She went to Girton, not long after it opened, where she read the classics and came back full of talk about the equality of the sexes, and how there was no reason on God's earth (she did not use the phrase in front of Father) why she should not be awarded a degree the same as her male counterparts. She was going to be an artist, had had two of her paintings accepted by the Royal Academy. I wanted to view them but was told they were "accepted but not hung," which meant they were in line for a place. I never heard of them being exhibited, as I am sure I would have done, had they been.

Julia's offer to stay at Oranmore and take care of the baby when it comes has shocked me. I had not thought she was interested in growing up. She has been the petted child for so long I had believed her incapable of taking responsibility for herself. Her brief sojourn as nurse to Mother and Father must have terrified her: I could see her relief when we invited her to live with us. I wonder how she will fare when the novelty of Oranmore has worn off, when she grows tired of playing at mistress of the house, when the tedium of those hours in the kitchen with Peig, managing the household, becomes apparent: the perennial dilemma between mutton and lamb; the controversial question of whose job it is to break the sugar or order the coal. She must be excited at the prospect of having free rein in the house without me in it, but I doubt that that will be enough to sustain her for very long. Her enthusiasm over new projects is generally short-lived.

She will not have much time for her newest interest. Aptly, she has decided to become a photographer, a thief of time and light. She has no idea how ridiculous she looks. She insisted on photographing the family, of course, returned from a visit to London with her apparatus in tow, boxes and baskets of mysterious chemicals and bewildering equipment. Explained the whole process to Edward over dinner. How glass-plate negatives have revolutionized photography, made it possible for her to traipse about the countryside photographing out of doors. She might as well have been speaking Greek for all the sense she made to me. She planned to visit Dunluce Castle and the Giant's Causeway, to capture them for posterity, she said. And people, too—she wanted every face in the house. Edward humored her. He had a soft spot for my dark-lashed half-suffragist sister.

"With every new preoccupation of Julia's I thank God it was her sister I married," he used to say.

I wonder if he still feels that way. She had me sit for her. She wanted me with my hair loose, in a silk dressing gown of hers, under the tulip tree in the garden. I came down in my Busvine, red and green herringbone, dressed for the hunt, my hair pinned tight under my riding hat. "Oh, Harriet!" she cried when she saw me. "If you must wear a hat, why not the hummingbird? Put it on, dearest, do. It would be perfection!"

I ignored her, took up position behind the green leather chair in the library. She has made her views on my jewel of a hat perfectly clear—a real hummingbird, ruby throated, quick eyed, every feather a surprise of beaten metal, green and silver and blue. It is mounted, as if still hovering above a head of wild columbine. I have never seen anything so lifelike. Edward brought it back from Paris. When I showed it to her first, expecting admiration, she said, "How exquisite, Harriet, did you stuff it yourself?" She will grant me no pleasure. I will not defend it, and I will not be guilted out of wearing it by Julia, but I will not wear it in her company.

She positioned herself to my right-hand side, asked me to look to my left. In the photograph, one can clearly see the dusty old boar's head on the wall behind me. She had the likeness hand-colored to her own instructions but the studio assistant made a poor job of it. My color is too high, and the shade of my costume a dull red. I look a fool in it, dressed for the hunt, leaning over the back of the library chair, the boar leering behind me. Julia made Edward a gift of it. She said every man should have a "revealing" portrait of his wife. Honestly, "revealing"! Buttoned up to my throat. How is it possible to make one look a fool in a photograph?

Pretty Julia with her kitten's teeth. And she is pretty, when her face is at rest, which is infrequent now. She is slight and pale, was the type of child that adults patted on the head, the type of woman men wish to protect, I believe. Her nose is a little wide, however, and her mouth somewhat too expressive, and her head, I always think, seems a little too big for her body. We are nothing alike: me, with my dark features and long limbs, a jawbone too strong for a woman's, large hands; one would never take us for sisters. Mother was beside herself when her lovely Julia showed signs of developing eczema. It is not serious, but when the light catches the side of her face, little raised sores are sometimes visible just under the skin that occasionally become infected. When she came to us, I recommended American syrup of bloodroot, advised her to pull her hair forward to hide the marks, but she said a doctor friend had prescribed exposure to the sun in order to energize the skin. I commented that she had no eczema on her chest and that she ought, at least, to cover that. She gave me that peculiar look of hers, said, "Harriet, you were born a century too late," and flounced off to walk in the garden.

I hurt her hand once in a wardrobe door. We were children at the time, nine and five: she was standing beside me, prattling as usual, and I closed the door with her hand in it. A blue line appeared, running below the knuckle on her little finger to the edge of her hand. The finger turned white beside the pink of the others: it looked quite dead. When I looked at her face, her mouth was open wide, soundless.

"Ssshhh," I said, "it will be all right. Ssshhh, Julia, do not cry."

Her face grew redder and redder, and still there was no sound. The silence was terrifying.

"Ssshhh, Julia," I said, even though she wasn't making any noise, "I will fix it. I will make it better. I will get some water."

Then came the cry, one long, loud howl. Good God, one would have thought she was being mauled by wild animals.

I was still trying to soothe her when Father came into the room, his first words "What have you done to her, Harriet?"

"Nothing," I said. "It was an accident. She put her hand in the door."

He was looking at Julia's hand, then scrutinizing my face. "You could have taken her finger off, Harriet, do you understand? You could have really hurt her."

"I did not see her put her finger in. I did not know it was there."

He picked Julia up, carried her to the basin, called Lily to bring water. He sat on the end of my bed with her on his knee, pouring cold water on her hand, massaging color back into it, speaking softly to her, rocking her gently. I do not think either of them noticed me leave.

I have been photographed since, my first day here. I was made to sit in front of an oval-shaped board with my name and admission date chalked upon it. Afterward, the warder commanded me to cross my hands on my breast, palms in, she said, thumbs pointing up. I looked at her blankly, momentarily unable to translate the instructions into actions. "Like a bird's wings," she explained, not unkindly. They were on the lookout, it seems, for any identifying marks. A square mirror hung on a chain on the wall behind me and cast my image in profile. It was an odd gesture to be asked to make, to sit, with hands butterflied, left under right. I wonder what Julia would make of that portrait.

Julia insisted on capturing the entire household, caused havoc carting that three-legged wooden beast of a camera about from the kitchen to the stables. She was preparing to exhibit, she declared, and she wanted the pulse of an Irish house, the servants and the farm workers, all human life. There was sudden mayhem when an itinerant tailor arrived in the stable yard and all had to be dismantled and taken outdoors so he too could be captured au naturel. If she had been able to mesmerize the dogs I believe she would have photographed them as well. I saw those images later: Peig, the housekeeper, her face like a skull, looking out from the paper with her deep-set eyes, a century of misery creased on her brow; the tailor, tousle headed and wide eyed, in fear of his life but immobilized by the glass eye that held him; and Maddie. Maddie with her pale face and straight brows, a hair escaping from her cap, a shadow under her mouth. She looks morose, as ever, and severely young. She stands in her white apron and cuffs, with one hand closed over the other, and her look says that she does not know why she has been asked to do this, why she has been summoned and made to stand in such a way, but that it is not an ordeal, and for that reason, she will do it. She is a strange girl, hardworking, it is true, but unfathomable. I look at those pale eyes of hers and I cannot tell whether or not she is speaking the truth.

In the picture Julia took of Charlotte, the child is seated beside her dolls' house, intent on her play, not looking at the camera at all. Her profile is as it was when she was a baby. What is it about an infant's face that captivates one so? An arrangement of curves and dips to stir the heart, to make one love it.

Yesterday the chaplain paid a visit. He is young and perhaps has ideas of reforming me. He reminds me a little of Harry, our eldest: his narrow frame; his eyes that are dark and serious, well intentioned; his hair that does not behave.

"God be with you," he said. God be with me indeed. God be with all of us. When he was leaving he stood up and put a book down on the mattress.

"I have no need for a missal," I said, but he simply nodded and left. When I opened it, the book was empty: pages of lined paper, and the stub of a pencil. Perhaps he thought I would make my confession. Perhaps I will. The warders do not know I have it, or if they do, they choose to ignore it. I have worked a hole in the mattress with the lead and pushed the book inside. When I lie down at night I feel the lump it makes under my head. The princess and the pea.

Maddie

15 SEPTEMBER 1968

There's odd things happens in this place, Anna. Mrs. Riley, who hasn't put her foot to the ground this two years or more, who needs a bedpan for her motions, and to be fed every drop of food that goes into her, Mrs. Riley walked past my door last night, and the nightdress near tripping her and her dead to the world. What can cause a person to do that? To think themselves incapable of walking when they're awake, and fit for anything when they're asleep! Isn't the mind a wonderful thing that can fool you?

I like your hair, Anna. Is that the style now? You've always had great hair. How do you get it to curl out like that at the ends? Oh, I couldn't sleep with rollers in my hair at night. Nurse Jenny does mine. She's very good. Not that there's much of it to do now. Like feathers on an oul' plucked turkey! But it was nice, at a time—at least that's what I was told. Mammy used to say that the fairies must have woven threads of their own into it while I was sleeping, for in among the brown that was the color of hers, there were strands the color of the copper kettle and others that were as yellow as a corn stook. It hung all the way down to my waist, for she said it'd be a sin to cut the light out of it.

My first day at the castle, Mammy helped me pin it all up tight under my cap and it was the oddest feeling walking along, like

I would overbalance if I wasn't careful, carrying all that weight about on top of my head. That and the strangeness of being shod: I never had shoes on my feet before I came to this house. Shoes change the way you walk, Anna. It took me a long time to get used to them.

I couldn't tell you what I had for my dinner last night, but other things, things from years ago, I can see like they're right in front of my face. June mornings, Daddy going out of our cottage in Bone Row with my brothers Sam and William, carrying the drift net. They'd haul the net at dawn, arrive back between five or six in the morning with the smell of bacon drifting out over the lane to meet them.

It was July, I remember, not far into the month, and not long after St. John's Day and the blessing of the boats. The fleet set off from the harbor just before midday, and headed for the mouth of the river trawling for turbot and sole. Three yawls, the *Ruby* among them, Sam and William and Daddy on board and a ton of stones in ballast for drawing the net astern. The wind fresh from the northwest, a bit of white water out by the Barmouth. The women, me and Mammy among them, standing on the slipway and the rocks, the way we always did, watching till they dropped anchor. About a mile out, a wave rose from the leeward, gathered itself up the height of the castle, moved steadily toward the *Ruby* weighed low in the water, and when it had passed, there was nothing left to be seen. The Logans, nearly at Downhill by then, saw that something was wrong, cut their net adrift and turned back. Jim Baker and Tam Molloy, in the third boat, bore down on the place where the *Ruby* had been, spotted William in the water, clinging to an oar. They shouted for him to hold on, and when Tam was within an arm's length of him he reached in to pull him on board. But William's hand slipped; he lost his hold and went under. Within an hour of them leaving the harbor and us waving to them, there wasn't a sign of boat nor man.

The Logans attached a buoy before they came ashore. It was two days before the steam tug came from Moville to overturn the boat and by that time, Mammy had spent so long praying that the net she'd been knitting before they went out had crushed a weave into her knees. The first day she said God wouldn't be so cruel as to take all three of them. The second day, she prayed they'd be found and we could bury them in a green grave. Sam was got in the net; Daddy inside the upturned yawl; William a way off. We stood on the quay, Mammy holding me tight by the hand, my other brother, Charlie, at her side, and me thinking it was more like a gala or a party of some kind, with all the people that were there. We waited for the *Eagle* to bring them in.

They took them into the ice house until the inquest was got ready in the hotel. Jim and Tam and Eddie Logan told the coroner what they had seen and then the coroner told us what we already knew. There was barely a mark on them: a scrape on Sam's chin, a bump on the side of William's head, and all of them whiter than the belly of a trout and bloated with seawater. By the time they were given back to us and put on the grocer's cart, every shop and hotel and house had its shutters down, and we had to walk home along the sweep of the long Parade, behind the cart, in the dark.

There was a wake and the neighbors came and told stories I'd never heard. Why do people wait till a person is dead to do that? Tam Molloy said he thought Daddy could never be drowned, for in the drought of September 1876 he had walked dry shod between the tides across the bed of the Bann at the Barmouth; from Portstewart to Castlerock and back, with me in his arms. I was hours old, there isn't any way I could remember that, but there are days now when I can feel the suck of the mud at his shoes, smell the sour smell of the seaweed drying in the riverbed, look up and see the white bellies of the barnacle geese as they fly in over the sea. Have you ever remembered something that you couldn't remember, Anna, a memory that belongs to someone else, that isn't yours at all? That's the way I feel about it. He's the only person who has ever stood there, before or since. Isn't that something to be proud of, something to tell your children?

Mrs. Graham organized a subscription list; Mammy made work for the Industrial Society, knitted caps for babies and embroidered napkins for the fancy stall to be sold at the sale of work. I helped her when I could but I wasn't a great hand at the sewing. Charlie ran errands for Mr. Faulkner, the grocer who paid him in flour and the odd bit of meat. Mammy said Faulkner was a crook and that his tea leaves were full of sand, but there wasn't a lot of work about and we didn't have much choice. What with that, and the bit of something the neighbors could spare us, and the money Mammy got for her eggs and butter, we got by. Then the spring after, the teacher, Miss Turner, put a word in for me at the castle, said I was obedient and just clever enough, that Mammy could use the money more than the help, and the mistress sent word for me to come. I was given seven yards of black merino with lining to make my uniform, and I was to have five shillings and two pounds of soap a month and every Sunday afternoon free.

One April morning in 1891, Peig met me at the yard door and led me into the kitchen. I couldn't believe the size of it; it would have housed the whole of our cottage twice over. Rows of gleaming white crockery on the dresser and racks of shining copper; a table spread with scrubbed wood chopping blocks and the fire blazing in the hearth. There were ovens to either side of the fire and a roasting jack and meat screen to the front, the sun slanting in the high arched windows and the smell of soda bread baking in the oven.

Peig sat me down and poured me a cup of tea and said, "I can tell to look at you there's no point in describing your duties 'cause you'll not take in a word of it. Never mind. You'll learn as you go along. I'll show you the house." She was right about that. I caught a glimpse of myself in a mirror going through the hall, and for a second I thought it was some other girl walking about in black and white with her back straight and her feet pinching and her hair pinned into a cap. It didn't look like me; I didn't feel like myself. Everything was strange. I thought about all the times me and Charlie had spent down on the rocks below the castle, collecting barnacles for Daddy to bait the lines, reaching in behind the brown kelp, twisting the shells off the rocks, all the times we'd raced each other home to see who had the most and who'd won a story. It hit me like a fist in the chest all those months later that we'd never do that again, that Daddy was gone. That this was my life now. And I walked about after Peig, winded.

Peig went easy on me that first day, giving me things to do that gave me a chance to find my way around. I got my first good look at the mistress when Peig sent me into the small sitting room for the tea tray. I'd thought the room was empty; Peig said the mistress had gone into the garden. But when I lifted the tray and turned round to leave, I caught a movement in the corner of the room. She was there with the master, her butterfly net resting against the divan. Neither of them noticed me, or if they did, they didn't show it. He had his hand on her elbow, looking down into her face. Her brow was straight, her features all at rest, her movements quiet, unhurried. She was holding a butterfly in the air on the point of a brass pin, holding it up to the light of the windows, showing how its wings changed from primrose to butter to cream. When she turned, the sleeve of her morning dress fell down and caught the April sun and then she was a halo of light, and for a second only, she looked like she might vanish into the full, thick, yellow air.

I heard her say: "It's important to get the pin through at just the right angle: you must be careful with the wings, not to brush off that delicate luster. The specimen would be useless then." And the master looking at her, like she was an angel come down from heaven to him.

Peig didn't stand on ceremony. As both housekeeper and

cook, she was entitled to eat in her own room but she chose to eat with the rest of us in the kitchen. That first meal was the first time I'd sat down with anyone but my family, and I barely managed to swallow a bite. Peig put me between Susan, the housemaid, and the parlor maid, Cait. The two of them talked over my head at each other and across the table to the lady's maid, Madge. Madge was a jittery type, full of energy and devilment. Most of her talk was directed at the two younger men who sat at the bottom end of the table: Feeley, who'd been introduced as the groom; Paudie, who Peig said was a footman. At the bottom end sat Mr. Hill, the butler, who hardly spoke, and oul' Peter, the gardener, who was half-deaf, I think. Mr. Hill, I found out later, was a bit overfond of the ether, but he never seemed the worse for it in the mornings.

"You'll never guess!" said Madge as soon as the prayers were said and the food on our plates. "I went up to empty the water from the basin in the moiselle's room . . ."

Susan leaned over. "Have you met the moiselle, Maddie?"

I looked at her, unsure. "Do you mean the mistress?"

Cait burst out laughing and sent a mouthful of cabbage over her plate. Madge looked at her in disgust and opened her mouth to protest but Peig silenced the both of them with one look.

"No," said Susan, "Mademoiselle Elise—she's the governess, French. You'll know her by her velvet tam-o'-shanter."

Cait snorted again but more quietly.

"Anyway," said Madge, "you'll never guess what was sitting on her dressing table."

Peig gave her a worried look. "No telling tales, Madge, not at the dinner table."

"Oh, Peig, you'll love this," said Madge. "You know what she's like, preening about the place, fixing at her hair, waxing her curls, getting me to pull her waist in till she can hardly stand, never mind run after the children."

"What was it?" Cait burst out. "Tell us, Madge."

"You'll not believe it," said Madge, "but I swear to God it's the truth."

"There'll be no swearing at this table," said Peig.

"Sorry, Peig," said Madge. "Cross my heart and hope to die, when I went up what did I see on her dressing table—only a brown hairpiece the exact color of her hair."

"I don't believe it!" said Susan.

"Jesus, Mary and Joseph!" said Cait.

"What did I just say," said Peig, "about swearing at the table?"

"Sorry, Peig," said Cait. "But a wig! I don't believe it!"

"I'm telling you it's the God's honest truth," said Madge. "What do you think of that, Feeley? What do you think of your French pussycat now?"

"God help us and bless us," said Peig. "What would she want with a thing like that?"

"Well," said Susan, stabbing a piece of bacon with her fork, "the fashion in France must be for the more hair the better. That would explain the mustache on her lip." And the whole table erupted then, Peig and all, into a fit of laughing. Only Mr. Hill and oul' Peter at the bottom showed their lack of interest by carrying on eating their dinner.

"She wants to let on she's twenty years younger," said Madge, "and her with a big bald patch at the back of her head. She must be thinking of marrying." And she shot a look again at Feeley.

"You needn't bother with your needling," said Feeley. "I have no interest in her and she has none in me. The whole thing's in your own daft head."

Peig stopped laughing and shook her head. "How could you expect a person with notions like that to be responsible for the education of children?" she said.

After a while I thought I'd better say something so I asked: "How many children are there?"

"Too many," said Madge, and got another look from Peig.

"There's eight altogether," said Susan, "but the three eldest boys are away at school. We don't have much to do with the children. The mistress sees to them most of the time."

"She sees to them, all right," said Madge, and got another look from Peig.

To me, Peig said, "You'll get on fine here, Maddie, if you keep your head down and your nose out of things that don't concern you. Your mother needs the bit of money you're bringing in. How the quality raises their children is no business of ours." Then she said there was a bit of apple cake left if anyone wanted it, and could we girls clear the table.

A few days after that, Peig sent me out to the yard to bring in a bit of turf for the fire. The yard had that look about it, just before the rain comes: the sky dark, hanging over the sun like the lid being lowered on the range and the last of the light catching on the sides of the stables. A sack with its belly full of turf lay where Peter had dropped it outside the coal-house door, and the mouth of it was lifting in the wind, like an old dog nosing the air. The master slammed the carriage door shut outside the house, and two white-bellied barnacle geese flew over toward the east, calling out in a low bark, the loneliest sound I ever heard. I was missing Mammy and Charlie something terrible. Then I heard another sound coming from the back of the coach house: children shouting. I went round and there was a little girl on the ground and two boys standing either side of her, their backs to me, singing and taunting. The taller of the boys, the fair-haired one, had a stick in one hand and was holding the bridle of a donkey in the other. It looked like the girl had fallen off, but the boys were doing nothing to help. The smaller red-haired boy was singing: "Sissy, sissy, Charlotte is a sissy. Crybaby, crybaby, cry cry cry!" She picked herself up and faced them, game girl that she was, but it wasn't till I stepped in between them that they stopped their chanting and the younger boy took a step back to let her pass. I'll never forget the look on his face: a half sneer at me, biding his time. My first meeting with Morris.

"You must be Charlotte," I said. "I'm Maddie. Come on into the house and I'll get you cleaned up." She reached for my hand, still biting back tears, and I led her inside. When I got into the kitchen, Madge and Feeley were at the table with cups of tea; Peig was kneading dough over a floured board. She opened her mouth to ask where the turf was and then spotted Charlotte, her dress dirty and torn.

"What happened you, darlin'?" she said.

"I fell off the donkey."

Peig gave me a sideways look. "Who else was there?" she said.

"Gabriel and Morris," said Charlotte.

"Here, Madge," Peig said, "bring her upstairs." And Madge put down her cup, took Charlotte by the hand and led her off.

"Those boys," said Peig, when they had left the kitchen. "They have the child tortured. It's a game of theirs to put her on the donkey and then whack it hard on the rump so it takes off at a gallop and throws her. They're devils incarnate, the pair of them."

"They're only youngsters," said Feeley, rising.

"They've neither manners nor breeding," said Peig.

"I'm away," said Feeley, winking at me, "before the keening starts."

"Get on out o' that wi' ye," said Peig. "You're only taking up room." But when he was left she said: "That Morris doesn't know what to be at. He was ruined when he was a baby and had the croup: wouldn't sleep anywhere but in the mistress's arms. The lengths that wean will go to, to get his mother's attention." Then she turned to me again: "Any word o' that turf?" she said.

It didn't fit with what I'd seen of the mistress, the idea of her cradling a baby in her arms through the night. But she was very particular about the children. She didn't like any of us to go near them. And there could have been something in what Peig said. I found Morris once, sitting on the floor of the stables, and when I asked him what he was doing he said, "Counting my bruises." He wore them like trophies: scores of affection. What kind of love is that, that leaves its mark on a child's body?

Peig was one of those people you could never imagine being young. She couldn't have been more than twenty-five at the time I started in the house, but she was so capable she seemed like a woman twice that age. She had a permanent wrinkle on her brow; I never saw her face clear of it, like she carried the worries of the world. Feeley said she was like one of those old women you used to see that went about at wakes with their shawls over their heads, crying for the dead.

She had a scald mark on her arm above her elbow, and when I knew her better I asked her what happened her. She told me she got it the time she was skying the copper, and the thing exploded and put her out through the scullery door. It never healed, for when she got annoyed or agitated about anything, she scratched at it like it was it that was annoying her and not the thing that was going on in her head.

I shared a room in the attic with Susan. There wasn't much to it: two beds and a strip of carpet between, that had traveled the length and breadth of the house before it'd ended up there. It must have held the dirt of every shoe that had ever walked over it but I was glad of it to have my bare feet to put on in the mornings. Before I came, Mrs. Quinn had given Mammy an old sample book from Brown and Thomas, and Mammy had cut them all up into wee triangles and then sewed them together in a basket pattern to make a quilt for my bed. She sewed all the scraps into the tops of the baskets so it looked like every one of them had something in it, and I would lie in bed at night and imagine what it was: mandarin oranges, eggs, turf and potatoes, chocolate, apples. There was great heat in the quilt, for the under part of it was an old coat of Daddy's with the buttonholes sewn up and when she was sewing up the pockets she put a handful of rosemary into one and a handful of lavender in the other, to help me remember home, she said (even though I was only yards away from my own front door), and to help me rest easy. I unpicked one of the pockets. I used to fall asleep with my hand where Daddy's hand used to be. I could smell the lavender and the rosemary, but underneath it smelled of turf, and the blackened skins of spuds that had been baked in the ashes, and the sea. Always the sea, salty and wild, under everything.

A while after I came to the castle, I was asleep one night, Susan in the bed to the other side of me, when I was wakened by a low crying and moaning. It sounded like it was coming from the room below and I was heart-scared it was a ghost or some otherworldly thing. After a while I took my courage in my hands and called out to Susan could she hear it too, and she must have been lying awake listening, for she answered me right away. She said: "It's one of the children, I don't know which."

"Should we not go down to them?" I said.

"No," said Susan, "there's no point."

"But whoever it is must be sick," I said. "Or they've hurt themselves, falling out of bed, maybe. Should we get Peig?"

"There's no point," Susan said again, "go back to sleep."

The crying carried on, a heartbreaking sobbing but with no words in it and no appeal for help. I got out of bed and reached for the candle.

"What are you doing?" Susan said, sitting up.

"I'm going down to the nursery, to see what's wrong."

"They're not in the nursery," she said. "Whoever it is they're in the wardrobe room, locked in. You'll not be able to do anything. There's nothing you can do."

I sat down on the bed. "Why?" I said. "Who would put a child in there? For doing what?"

"The mistress," said Susan, "and God knows what for. For

answering back, or for dropping a knife or for not saying their prayers or for sneezing; it could be anything and nothing at all. If you've any sense, Maddie, you'll get into bed and put the pillow over your head and go to sleep and pretend you can't hear it. That's all any of us can do if we want to stay here." She lay down again and pulled the cover up to her ears. "Some nights it's not that bad," she said.

I got back into bed. I must have fallen asleep. When I woke in the morning the house was quiet and Susan wouldn't look at me.

I went to look for the wardrobe room. I knew there was a door off the nursery and I went over when the children were at breakfast and I was emptying the chamber pots and I put my ear to the door and said: "Is there anybody there?"

A boy's voice called out and said was it time to come out, but the door was locked and there was no sign of a key. I went out through the nursery onto the landing and I nearly jumped the height of myself, for there was the mistress with a face on her like a week of wet weather.

She said, "What were you doing?"

"I heard crying," I said.

"Were you talking to Gabriel?"

"I don't know who it was."

She looked at me like I was something that had stuck to the sole of her boot and she said, "The servants are not permitted to speak to the children. See that you observe that rule."

I said, "Yes, madam," and after that I stayed out of her way as much as I could.

The mistress couldn't keep servants, and there weren't enough of us for all that was to be done. Susan took off a week or two after I arrived. She was such a hard woman, the mistress—Scottish originally, did you know that, from Inverness? She dealt out love the way she dealt the flour out of the store cupboard to Peig: as if there was only so much of it to go around;

as if you could only divide it up a certain number of times before it was all used up. As if love isn't like yeast, and rises where it's needed.

The hours were long: up at half five or six when the fires were lighting, and never in bed until twelve or after it. Lugging buckets and water jugs up and down three flights of stairs. My hands went from coal to spuds to soda and soap and then back again the livelong day. The job I hated most was sieving the salt: a big seven-pound block of it, and it would get in under your nails and in all the scratches and skelfs you'd got during the day and your hands would be raw at the end of it. And the coppers all had to be cleaned with sand and salt and vinegar. My feet were never warm from the day and hour I entered this house. The flagstones in the kitchen were like blocks of snow. Is it any wonder my joints are full of rheumatism?

The mistress was fond of a sea bath, and when she took a notion for it, the men would be sent down to the Big Strand with the copper cans on the cart to fill them with water. She had it in her head the salt and seaweed were good for the skin. And maybe there was something in that, for she had a lovely complexion, smooth and fine, hardly a line. Peig said it was smiling that gave people wrinkles and that's why the mistress didn't have any. "But," said Peig, "I'll take the wrinkles happily."

I wasn't long started at the house when one day Paudie and Feeley came back with the cans full of water, and Peig bid me boil it up in the laundry copper and then pour it back into the two-gallon cans to be brought upstairs. The men left the yard door open and a hen wandered in, and I was shooing it back out again and I made a swipe at it and hit the copper and over it went, and all the seawater, out over the floor of the laundry.

Peig heard the clatter and ran into me. "Jesus, girl," she shouted, "you could have been scalded." But I was more scared about what the mistress would say when she heard I was responsible for her bath flooding out the yard door and the hens picking through it.

When the two of us had gathered ourselves, Peig said, "Mop up that floor before somebody breaks their neck on it," and she went to the pump and filled the two coppers up again, and threw in a handful of salt. "When that's boiled," she said, "tip it back into the cans; there's still a bit of seaweed sticking to the bottom. She'll be none the wiser."

And neither she was, for she said nothing about it. I don't know why Peig saved my skin. Some of it was maybe to do with saving her own, but there was more to it than that. She was the kindest, the absolute kindest soul I ever met in my life.

Charlotte got it from all sides. Her brothers teased her something shocking. Morris was the worst of them: he was freckled and red haired with a temper to go with it, a sly look about him, like he was always plotting. He started a row in the dining room one morning, over whose turn it was to have the blue-patterned porridge bowl. He pulled the slip off the table and threw a spoon at Charlotte that caught her under the eye and near blinded her. We had to send for Dr. Creith; the cut left a scar. Even Gabriel, who was older and the mildest mannered of all of them, could be cruel. He and Morris hid her clothes and made her late getting dressed in the mornings. They rubbed horse dung into her new calf-kid boots that the mistress had brought her from Tyler's in Belfast; they emptied calomel into her milk and gave her the scour for a week. And she, the wee mite, hadn't the wit; she always went back to play with them again. As for the mistress, she never gave out to them for the way they treated Charlotte; over disobedience to her she beat the life out of them, but never for cruelty to each other.

"It's a hard station for a child that's shown no love by its mother," said Peig, "especially a girl-child that reminds her of what she used to be." I don't know if there was any truth in that, but I know I never heard the mistress give Charlotte a kind word.

For all her young years, there was a knowledge about the child that her mother couldn't stomach.

Last night, between watching and sleeping, the day at the Ladies' Bathing Place came back to me. You remember it, Anna. Me and your mother used to take you there when you were a wee slip. Just below the castle here, where the sea comes in gentle. I can see it from the windows on the east side. You used to love going down the chute into the water. There were still bathing boxes then for the modest, but there's none of that now: it's all bikinis and shorts these days. Nobody cares who sees what part of them. In my day, you'd have been scared to show your knee to a man, for fear of what it would do to him. Oh, the world's changed, that's for sure.

This day, anyway, down at the water, I'd maybe been started at the castle for a few months. No heat in the day, a white ball of a sun hanging low in the sky, and the mistress, already in the water up to her middle, bidding me bring the wean down, and her not more than three at the time. She was a bonny child, your cousin Charlotte. No, not your cousin. Your mother's older sister. She'd have been your aunt if she'd lived. That's a strange idea, to think of her as a grown woman with a niece like you, and maybe children of her own. "Winsome" is what people called her and winsome she was to all but the mistress. Hair the color of corn, and tight curls around her ears. She had a way of looking at you, like she understood every word you said to her.

The wean stood there, terrified, at the water's edge, refusing to go further, and I got down on my hunkers beside her, my head at the height of hers, and took her wee chin in my hand. "There's nothing to be feared of, Charlotte," I said. "It's just the sea—look!" And I turned with her and looked too, through her round gray eyes, and I saw mountains of ocean roll toward us roaring and curling, with no way of stopping them, and I put my arms around her and picked her up.

The mistress said, "Put her down, girl. She must learn not to be afraid!"

But Charlotte's two hands were locked around my neck, and I said (I can't believe now that I said it), "You want to see what she can see," and I carried her back to the blanket beside the bathing boxes.

Charlotte lay on her back and peered up at the clouds. She said, "I'm the judge, Maddie, and this is the game. You must not speak until you see a . . . giant's ladle!" I looked up at the sky and sure enough, there it was, and then a fairy bridge, and then a dragon's tooth. That was her way—she could draw you into a thing, whether you would or not. The mistress said nothing more, but I saw the tight set of her mouth, and I watched her open and close her hand, like I'd seen her do with the horses, and I knew I was in for it when we got back up to the castle.

She called me into the drawing room over there. She was standing with her back to the window, so I couldn't see her face clearly. She said, "At the beach, Maddie, what did I ask you to do?"

I said: "Put the child in the water."

"Did you understand the instruction?"

"Yes, madam."

"Then why did you not do as I said?"

"The water was cold," I said, "and the waves were so high. When I got down beside her and looked—"

"Did I ask you to test the temperature of the water?" she said. "Or comment upon the height of the waves?"

"No, madam, but the child was shaking—"

"Then I would instruct you in future to do as I say. An opinion is a luxury you cannot afford. It is simple: if you wish to retain your position here, you must learn not to concern yourself in the matters of those who know better. Follow me."

She walked out the front door and down the steps and I followed her. I thought she was going to put me out the gate. I was heart-scared she was sending me home to my mother, and what would I do then? What would I tell her? She pointed to the gravel in the drive. "Lie down there," she said, "facedown." I didn't really understand what she meant. I was in a bit of a daze, I think, still wondering if she was going to send me home, but I lay down with my face to the ground. "Stay there," she said, "until I send for you. Perhaps it will teach you to keep your nose out of the affairs of your betters, and in the dirt, where it belongs."

I don't know who saw me there and I don't know how long I stayed. I was so ashamed, but I didn't know what else to do. After a while I felt Peig's hand on my arm.

"Get up out o' that, girl," she said.

"I have to stay here till the mistress tells me to come in," I told her.

"Hell roast the mistress!" said Peig. "There'll not be a servant left standing in the place if you don't get up out o' that now and come in."

I don't know what it was about me that rubbed the mistress up the wrong way. She couldn't bear to have me near her after that. But she couldn't do without Peig and she knew then that the two of us were a package. Peig wouldn't have a bad word said about me. Poor Peig. She didn't deserve what I did to her, God forgive me. Though there's a big part of my heart that can't regret it, Anna. And you'll know why, soon enough.

Harriet

Grangegorman Prison, Dublin

Monday 18 April 1892

A child today, of not more than eight or nine years old, committed for larceny, along with her mother, who carries an infant still at nurse.

I cannot rid myself of the smell of tar, but still I have not picked enough rope to earn myself a letter. I know that the boys are all settled in their schools and with their charges, but I cannot help but worry about Edward.

There is a class system in prison, with privileges to be earned and lost for the most meaningless of tasks, the most minor of insurrections. I am on probation for the first month, after which, if I have gained sixty marks for good behavior, I will be promoted to class four. It is a game, except that the smallest of rewards take on an import that would be considered risible outside these walls. For having dutifully picked oakum for fifty hours and broken every nail on my hands and marked them, indelibly it would seem, with tar and blood, I am to have cabbage in my soup, and that there is to be cabbage now lifts even my sad heart. We are not permitted to speak to one another: no hardship for me, but the inmates here have found a means to communicate. We are required to attend religious service on Sunday and to raise our underused voices in song, to thank God, it would seem, for the situation in which we find ourselves. The first Sunday I was here, I became aware that the other prisoners were not correctly following the words to "*Adeste Fideles*," I assumed at the time because they were unfamiliar with the Latin, or that, as a minor act of rebellion, they had refused to learn them. Then I noticed that they seemed to dip in and out of the words, depending on how much attention was being accorded them by the warders who sat at the end of each pew. And last Friday, Good Friday, when we stood up in the church at benediction to sing "*Pange Lingua*," the prisoner next to me, without moving her head or in any way indicating a change in her demeanor, began to address me directly. "*Pange lingua gloriosi*," she sang, "*Corporis mysterium / Sanguinisque pretiosi* . . ." Then her tone lowered slightly and while the other voices continued with "*Quem in mundi pretium*," I distinctly heard her sing, "When is it your baby's due?" I almost choked on the next line. It was as shocking a thing as I'd ever heard, to be addressed thus, in the Gregorian chant.

I soon realized that messages are passed along and between the pews in this manner and that the warders are either unaware of it or, what is more likely, choose to tolerate it. Since the prisoners have become so adept, it would indeed be a difficult accusation to prove. I refuse to participate myself and this they have come to realize. I am the faulty link in the chain.

I do, however, hear things. Yesterday, Easter Sunday, at "*Surrexit Christus Hodie*" I learned that a prisoner has been put on bread and water for four days as a result of having been overheard to laugh in her cell. I cannot help but wonder what it was she found humorous about her situation, but it is a lesson to us all: if you must laugh, do it silently. There is no punishment for crying, as far as I am aware. We are quite safe from retribution on that account.

Today is Easter Monday. Perhaps Edward has ridden out to the races at the Livery Hills, with Mr. Casement or Mr. Walsh—that is, if there are any gentlemen who are still willing to be seen with him.

The night we arrived at the train station at Oranmore after our marriage, we were met by the Flute Band in full uniform: four of the younger men unyoked the horses and bore our carriage to the castle themselves. The air was alight with squibs and crackers, and all along the cliff top blazing tar barrels augured our arrival. I was not quite prepared for my first sight of the castle: the fanciful turrets that stood out against the night sky, the castellation. Perched on a cliff edge overlooking the Atlantic, it has the air, with its battlemented silhouette, of a feudal fortress. In actual fact it is less than sixty years old, built by Edward's grandfather in the 1830s because, it is said, his wife had tired of looking out over fields and cattle, and wished to look out over the sea instead. A modest enough house in its time, it was extended and modernized by Edward's father: a new seven-bay façade added to the south, with extra bedrooms and reception rooms to the east and north. There is a gargoyle on the west side, a jowly lion's head that yawns over the cliff walk, said to have been modeled on the face of Pope Gregory XVI. Edward's grandfather was a firm Episcopalian, as was his daughter, Edward's mother; as was Edward's father until twenty years ago, when he caused a furor by converting to Rome. If it was Edward's grandfather's intention to keep Rome at bay with the fierce papal gargoyle I am afraid it failed. He would be most disappointed with us if he had lived to see his house headed by two Catholic converts and eight little Catholic grandchildren besides. The lion's head looks out over the mountains of Donegal, and further north, to the island of Islay and the Paps of Jura.

"Look," said Edward, "you need never miss Scotland. You can see it every clear day." There were few enough clear days to test his assertion, but Edward need not have worried: I had no intention of missing Scotland.

Thought to be imposing generally, it can be seen from every point on the Parade, from as far along the strand as the Barmouth and, they say, from miles out at sea. Its back is set resolutely against the ocean. To me, it has always looked, and still looks, like a house playing at being a castle. The hall displays a number of paintings known to have come from the Earl of Bristol's gallery, dour depictions of sour-faced individuals, occasionally carrying a blunderbuss or leaning on a cannon but including, oddly enough, a portrait of the third earl's bigamous wife with both her husbands. Three-quarter-length oil portraits of long-dead relations in scarlet uniforms, one killed at the Battle of Ferrol, another at the siege of Badajoz, yet another at Madeira, where Edward's father had himself served. When Julia first saw the house, she declared it to be everything an Irish castle should be and immediately set off to look for a ghost; I thought her liable to swoon when she found the two spiral staircases. Personally, I find the whole place vaguely ridiculous: the neo-Gothic windows with their diamond panes; the eight staring *oculi* of the second story, like portholes in a man-of-war.

The place has one curiosity, though, in the small walled garden to the southwest, where old Peter grows rhubarb and red currant trees, gooseberries and marrows cheek by jowl with raspberries, artichokes and violets. A single apple tree has been trained to grow against the wall, its branches spread out in a perfect fan, its trunk flattened from the roots, as if it had been growing where a wall had accidentally taken root and been split in two by its ascent. As if, around the other side, one might find its other half. I went to look. There was nothing there but laurel trees, lush from years of growing out of the waste of the house, and a patch of nettles, full of caterpillars.

Even Edward seemed taken aback at our reception that first evening. There were speeches of welcome from the local hoteliers, an illuminated address from the tenants, many toasts drunk to our happiness and long lives, much praise for his grandfather. On reflection, it may have been relief that the tenantry was expressing: to be finally rid of Edward's father, Lord Ormond, as landlord and a hope that Edward, who they say resembles his grandfather in looks, would take after him in other ways.

Lord Ormond had assembled a cast of local dignitaries for our first dinner: Mr. Casement, Mr. Walsh, Mr. O'Hara, Mr. Shiels, Mr. Macky. I walked in with Lord Ormond, me in my wedding dress; Edward with Lady Bucknell. The cook had done us proud: artichoke soup and fillets of Bann salmon, plovers' eggs from White Park Bay, followed by lamb and new potatoes, wild duck, stewed celery, watercress. I was barely nineteen, Edward was twenty-two: we were the youngest couple seated at the table by a margin of a good ten years. It was an odd feeling, to sit there in a strange house for the first time, not as a guest but as its new mistress.

Although Edward's mother was long dead, her presence was everywhere I looked. Nothing can prepare one for the shock of the pattern of another woman's choice of plate, in this case Staffordshire chinoiserie, cobalt blue with red enameling. I could barely find my food, so busy was the design. Nothing looked familiar. The table was served by eighteen balloon-backed mahogany chairs, upholstered in crimson. Lady Ormond had had a brief flirtation with aniline dyes when they first appeared: there was experimental evidence on the dining room walls of fuchsine and Tyrian purple. She was, by all accounts, a timid and temperate woman and had evidently refrained from redecorating the entire room. She had retained the dusty old Turkey carpet and gargantuan curtain poles, each end of which finished in a kind of tortured hyacinth bulb and which allowed the oppressive crimson curtains to trail across the floor, no doubt to defy that old enemy, the draft. The overriding sensation was of dust and of weight. I resolved, as soon as I could, to embark on the redecoration of the rooms.

The meal was served *à la russe* and my neighbor Mr. O'Hara helped me to a slice of lamb. To his other side Mr. Walsh, an avid ornithologist, spent the evening discussing the coastal birds of Ireland. They seemed to occupy the poor man's head like characters in a novel. Happily, I was not required to speak so I nodded my head, raised an eyebrow occasionally (at "fulmar" or "kestrel" or "white-tailed sea eagle") and introduced forkfuls of food to my mouth. Edward's aunt Ormond sat to Edward's right, chewing on the celery, looking to all the world like a young horse getting used to the bit, though young she most certainly was not, even then, almost twelve years ago now. Beyond Lord Ormond sat Lady Bucknell, and beside her Mr. Shiels, Lord Bucknell's accomplished huntsman, who was being complimented on his skill at the hunt.

"I do not favor the lifting of the hounds," Lord Ormond said to me. "It may speed the hunt but I would rather take my ease and let them find the scent themselves."

"When the hounds threw up at Beardiville," said Lady Bucknell, "Mr. Shiels made a cast and had them off again in no time."

"The hunting is always good there," Lord Ormond told me. "They never meet before eleven until after the overnight drag is gone. It means the foxes run faster and the hunt has more speed."

"It is not for the fainthearted, Mrs. Ormond," added Mr. Shiels, "but it is an excellent hunt. The farmers on the estate refrain from culling and keep wire out of the fences."

"In exchange for lowered rents!" boomed Lord Ormond from beside me.

"I believe some landlords proffer the same inducement come election time," said Lady Bucknell sweetly, "though it is a different class of fox being hunted then." And the table resounded with laughter.

I remember that Mr. Macky—a farmer originally, whom Edward told me had made his money buying up land in the fifties, and whose house was filled with furniture from bankrupt landowners—Mr. Macky liked to pick the wax from his ear in a sort of corkscrew action, examine it briefly and flick it under the table.

"This used to be a country of landowners and peasants," muttered Edward's father at my side, "now it is run by shopkeepers and publicans." I was hoping they would keep up their banter and that I would not be required to contribute. It was clear from that first meal that politics in Ireland were never far from the dinner table.

"What do you say, Harriet?" demanded Lord Ormond. "What do you make of your newly adopted country?"

I looked down the table at Edward, who gave me an encouraging smile. "They say that Ireland, and the north in particular, has many similarities with Scotland," I replied.

"Indeed!" shouted Lord Ormond. "A strong tradition of dissenters, a fierce sense of independence, an aversion to being branded subsidiary to London."

"Bravo!" said Lady Bucknell. "There is, however, no sea between Scotland and England, and a sea is a powerful entity. It would take a long time to walk from Edinburgh to London, but the journey is practicable. The fact of being able to put your feet on the earth between the two places makes for a strong link, geographically, economically, intellectually. Ireland is a different country entirely and of all the things that make it different—that have always made it different—there is none greater than this: it is not, nor has it ever been, joined to England."

"Good God!" shouted Lord Ormond. "You sound like a Home Ruler, Lady Bucknell. Next you'll be telling us to vote for the Irish Parliamentary Party."

There was good-natured laughter around the table before Lady Bucknell sighed and said: "Ireland has been contrary always. The south and the west are busy plotting their independence from the crown while the north expends all its energy in asserting its allegiance, whether the crown wants it or not. The feeling everywhere is changing, however, and not just in Ireland, where nothing is ever the same as anywhere else in the country."

There was silence at the table, the mood a little altered. I was beginning to sense the complexity of Edward's, and now my, situation. Edward is a landowner but he is Catholic too, and rural to the bones. Not nationalist, certainly not in the traditional sense; but if one's nation is one's land, and one's attachment to it, and one's desire every day to stand on it, to have one's arms elbow-deep in it, to love it and work always to keep it, then yes, nationalist too, though there are few that would call him it, himself included. Where did he fit in, I wondered at that first dinner. He was as much an anomaly as was I.

Edward's tie to Oranmore is unshakable—to the land, to his mother's people, particularly to his maternal grandfather, with whom he is favorably compared. Not so Lord Ormond, who is generally disliked by the tenantry, a sentiment that appears to be reciprocated by him.

"It is true what Lord Dufferin says," he announced to Edward at dinner. "An Irish estate is like a sponge, and the sooner got rid of, the better. If it comes to it," he added, "if Ulster goes the way of Connacht and the others, if the government offers to buy the land and lease it to the tenantry, bite the hand off them. There is no other way out for us now."

"It will never happen here," said Edward. "The tenantry is entirely loyal. I will not sell."

Was that really only twelve years ago? Edward lived to rue his words. The tenantry have no loyalty to Edward, no more than if he were an unscrupulous rack-renter who made no improvements to the land and fully expected them to finance his extravagant way of life. The one time he stood his ground and refused to lower the rents, events took on a very threatening turn.

Mrs. Macky sat to Edward's left, unusually jowly for a slim woman. She was not much of a conversationalist. I heard her make some ill-informed remarks on the purity of Aberdonian English, as opposed to that of Inverness, but it was difficult to be angry with her, for her face, with her drowsy brown eyes, had the appearance of that of a Swiss St. Bernard. I heard later that she dosed every one of their children with Mother's Quietness, turning them into imbeciles with swollen stomachs and shrunken brains, in order to stop their crying. There are acceptable levels of abuse, it would seem, and it takes only a commercial patent to exempt one. I never gave the children more than a mustard spoon of calomel or syrup of poppies, and only as a last resort to shift a stubborn cough or settle an upset stomach.

There was a portrait hanging on the dining room wall of King William III crossing the Boyne. In Edward's grandfather's time, he told me, it had hung in the hall, but when his father converted to Catholicism, he had it removed to a dusky corner. Edward remembered the picture, he said, emblazoned with the square and compasses of a Masonic device, his grandfather's pride and joy. When Edward was born, his grandfather sent for water to be brought from the Boyne and had his first grandson baptized with it in the little Episcopalian church in the village, the one that had been moved stone by stone from the original site near Flowerfield. He often jokes that he is the only Catholic in Ireland to have been baptized in Boyne water, and in a church that had walked a country mile.

Delightfully, near the end of the dinner, during a particularly difficult speech by Mr. Walsh on the island breeding colonies of the gannet, the portrait fell off the wall and very nearly hit Mrs. Macky on the shoulder. I hid my amusement behind my napkin but I suspect Lady Bucknell caught me; I was sure she gave me a conspiratorial wink. There was a commotion, the lady attended to by Dr. Creith, the picture retrieved from the aspidistra where it had fallen, and when it was examined, the hanging wire was found to have corroded, in all likelihood, as a result of the fumes from the gas burners. The dinner disrupted, the ladies withdrew to the drawing room for restorative liqueurs (Mrs. Macky taking the opportunity to empty the bottle of Bénédictine) while the men remained, the picture now leaned against the wall. When the ladies had left the dining room, Edward later told me, and the bottle of claret been replaced by a bowl of whiskey punch, his father proposed a toast: that Gladstone choke on his breakfast porridge; that Edward and his new bride be blessed with a multitude of Catholic sons and that they all grow up in an Ireland with Home Rule. The toast was received with some variation, given the number of Episcopalians and Orange Lodge members assembled, but Lord Ormond did not seem to notice and drank heartily to his own joke. Edward, who is superstitious, did not like it that the picture had fallen.

Lord Ormond was not a fan of Mr. Gladstone. I understood this more clearly when I retired to my room later that night. In the nightstand the necessary article of china for nighttime use bore a portrait on the inside of the prime minister himself.

Edward's mother passed away when he was only seven. There is a painting of her on the landing, fringed and crinolined, pale faced, fair haired, still. The dress is a glossy intense blue of the ferocious color that was popular then in the fifties. I found it in her wardrobe and had it cut up for Charlotte. The seamstress, a clever, harelipped woman, made three dresses out of its voluminous cone. It was a good silk, and the color suited Charlotte: common blue. Edward loved to see her in it.

Edward clung to the paraphernalia of his mother's life like it were treasure. An appalling cup and saucer sat always on the oak server in the dining room, a pink and white creation commemorating the temperance movement and emblazoned with banner flags that sang out: SOBRIETY, DOMESTIC COMFORT, TEMPERANCE and FREEDOM. For me, the last of these seemed very much at odds with the other three, although I knew better than to say such a thing to Edward. An eight-pointed temperance star faced away from the drinker, and along the bottom of the cup, which depicted a young man and woman, was the biggest banner of all, which read: BE THOU FAITHFUL UNTO DEATH. Each time I looked at it I felt censured from the grave. Edward said that his mother drank tea from it every afternoon and that he could clearly remember her packing it up for dispatch to the basement, where she would personally supervise the removal of tea stains with bicarbonate of soda. I never once used it. The day Gabriel and Morris lassoed the dining room chandelier it was my only regret that they avoided breaking the cup.

It is a myth that men seek marriage partners who mimic their mothers' characters; she and I could not have been less alike. We have had but one trait in common: we have both been adored by Edward.

I was not unusual, I am sure, in wanting to put my mark on the place; every new wife who inherits a home must wish to do the same. I wanted the rooms full of light. Edward was loath to see furniture and coverings replaced. They were the pattern of his youth, he said. He murmured about the fading of the carpets and the chintzes but I had spent too long in a buttoned-up house behind heavy drapes and I craved air. I wanted as much of the outside in the house as possible. Even in February I insisted on the French windows being opened for at least part of the day. The drawing room curtains were a horror in pelmeted Byzantine gold, as if procured from a Persian harem. The Baroque plasterwork featured, of all things, a bunch of bananas. In one corner, Edward's grandfather's collection from his "grand tour" was carefully housed in mahogany and chinoiserie: an Indian dagger, an ostrich egg, a pair of Chinese slippers. Within a short time, I had replaced the garish reds and heavy greens with the palest of shades, colors that drew light to them, that made the most of the brief winter days. I had the decorators paint the gold-beaded walls in *café au lait* and the curtains replaced with wooden shutters, and after a little while, even Edward could see the benefit of the lighter shades. It was altogether more uplifting, he said, though he never changed a thing in his green leather study and I never intervened there.

I tried my best to let the house breathe so that I could breathe in it. There were some things Edward would not countenance my replacing: a portrait of a relative, a captain of the Thirty-fourth Regiment who had died at the storming of the Redan Fort in 1855; the volumes of divinity with which his mother had furnished the library; a Chinese gong in the hall she had bought at auction; a birdcage in the morning room. I have lost count of the number of guests who have asked me when the decorating will be finished. Clearly, my taste is out of kilter: there is too much on display, not enough drapery and mystery for the sensibilities of the eighties and nineties, not enough concealed.

The one exception to this meadow of color, the one necessarily dark room, is the small north-facing sitting room where the butterflies are kept, where I allowed the darkest of red curtains and crimson damask to remain and to which I moved the heaviest furniture that absorbed the light. I ordered a Morris wallpaper from the Maples catalog, an extraordinary design of white dove and gilt cage with a background so dark as to be almost black. Unexpectedly, when it arrived and was pasted on the sitting room wall and the light caught it near the window, the narrow bars of the cage all but disappeared, leaving only the gilt base and the bird apparently freed, about to take flight, while in the darker corners of the room the flickering firelight picked out the gilt and showed the bird to be exquisitely caged. Two opposing stories on the same wall, depending on how the light hit. Clever Mr. Morris.

On my first night at Oranmore, in a bedroom without drafts on a still night, I was woken by a rustle, a scratching, the sound of something small running across the floor. I considered my choices: get up, rise the servants and Edward, cause a stir that would leave the entire household sleepless and disgruntled for all of the following day and catch no mouse; or go back to sleep, resolve to employ more cats on the morrow. I chose the latter. Last night I woke suddenly with the sensation of something live having run beneath my head. It felt too big to be a mouse. Then, I had a choice; now I have none.

Maddie

7 OCTOBER 1968

It's good of you to come and see me in my room, Anna. I'm not feeling much like talking to the rest of them today. You get tired, you know, looking at the same faces, going over all the same oul' rigmarole: about the weather that none of us is fit to go out in, and about what's on the wireless or the TV. Wasn't it shocking about thon wrecking match in Derry? We saw the whole thing on Telefis Éireann: it was like something out of the dark ages, the police in steel helmets and riot shields batonning the life out of the civil rights marchers, and them all screaming and roaring and Gerry Fitt's face covered in blood. They say there was shocking trouble after it, bonfires and barricades and youngsters throwing stones, and half the shops with their glass broken and the stuff stolen out of the windows. But then there's always ones that will see an opportunity for trouble and take it: them uns that has nothing to do with the protest at all. The marchers shouldn't have been there, says Captain O'Neill, they were told not to go. They're one-half republican and one-half communist, he says. But haven't people a right to stand up against injustice when they see it? Giving houses out to single Protestant girls when there's whole families of Catholics living in one room. We were all sitting watching it and talking about it and saying how bad it was, and thon wee git John Roddy, who's as bitter as sloes, pipes up and says, "If they wouldn't go on breeding, they wouldn't need so much accommodation." Well, jeepers, Anna, if I was quicker on my feet, I'd have gone over and walloped him with my blackthorn stick. It's a good job *The Val Doonican Show* came on and distracted us. Isn't Val great? "Paddy McGinty's Goat," you couldn't beat it. Give me that over Nana Mouskouri any day.

You look well, Anna, pink cheeked, and getting rounder in the face. Do you like being back? You must worry when you see things like that on the TV, worry about bringing a child into the middle of it. I can understand that. But you'll be fit for it, you and Conor together. You're from good strong stock, the pair of you.

I want to tell you about Conor's grandfather Alphie—Alphie McGlinchy. Oh, Conor never knew him, he was gone long before he was born. He died when Conor's father, Owen, was only a baby. He was a very impressive-looking man was Alphie. The first time I saw him, he'd come to see the master about a job: rode up to the house one day on the most gorgeous bicycle any of us had ever laid eyes on. We all poured out of the kitchen, Peig with a patch of flour on her chin, and the men appeared from the stables and the fields, and we stood around him, looking at him and his bicycle. It was a remarkable contraption, all black and shiny like a beetle, and with a leather seat mounted on some kind of crisscrossed complicated metal spring. He explained that this was to take the bumps out of the road, to soften the ride, he said, and then he winked at Peig and the men laughed, and Peig blustered off into the kitchen, wiping her hands on her apron, the color rising in her cheeks.

It was an amazing thing to see him balanced upright on that two-wheeled beast of a machine, circling the yard from the coal house to the cellar and appearing back again like a magician, and of course Peig's head at the passage window because she couldn't *not* look at him; none of us could resist.

He had a white straw boater on his head with navy blue stripes in it and a matching striped cravat that hung down his starched shirt like a ribbon. A white handkerchief in his breast pocket and a watch chain that disappeared into the inside of his four-buttoned blazer. His mustache curled a bit at the edges and his eyes looked straight into you. He smelled of tobacco, not the sort the men put in their clay pipes, but the sort that you rolled: cigarette tobacco; exotic. He said I could sit on the bar if I liked, but then Peig called me in and said, had he nowhere to go, and gave off to the men for standing around gawking all day when they should have been working. Then she went back into the kitchen and tripped over the wood basket and nudged the dinner pot and sloshed water all over the fire and near put it out, and all the time pretending she wasn't a bit interested in him or had paid heed to a word he was saying. Peig knew him from before; they'd grown up together. Both their families were from Burnside; their fathers were on the boats. I don't know what went on between them before he'd gone away but you could tell there was a spark there still.

He had a dent in the side of his head the like of what you'd see in a pot that had been hit up against the range. You could have put your finger in it, it was that deep. Madge whispered to me that he got it when he fell in a ditch one time he was running from the peelers and the stump of a tree went into his head. Feeley said he was running from a girl's father who said he'd kill him if he got him. I don't know what was true, but every time I looked at him I had a wish that I could take the lid off him and hit that hollow out with a ladle. I know that doesn't make any sense, but there you go. I wanted to smooth out his brow; I had a yearning to fix him.

The only work there was going was in the fields and in the yard, but he didn't seem bothered about getting his hands dirty. Nobody knew how he'd made his money or if he really had any money behind him at all. Three years earlier he'd left for the Derry boat. Feeley said he'd made a fortune in America, Paudie that he'd gone no further than Liverpool, where he worked as a traveler for the tea and sugar business. Oul' Peter said he knew for a fact he'd been working at Bessbrook spinning mills and never left the country at all. Some or none of these may have been true. He himself threw around places and names without any real commitment to any of them. But it didn't seem to matter. When he was talking to you, you were the center of his universe and everything else flew out of your head.

He courted Peig with real gusto: the more she resisted the worse he got. He carried bluebells in to her in bunches. Peig said: "Aren't the flowers better off in the hedge where they belong?" He brought her a white pebble from the beach with a cross on it, said it was a sign that their marriage would be blessed. Peig said, "No priest can bless a marriage where there isn't one." But she put the bluebells in a jam jar on the kitchen window, slipped the pebble into her apron pocket. Peig said he wore her down in the end: she was the first woman he'd ever come across whose knees didn't buckle at the first sight of him, and he couldn't resist the challenge.

Alphie's parents were known throughout the parish for their bickering, but they had survived together for fifty-two years, when famously, old man McGlinchy fell into the harbor full of drink and never came out of it. The McGlinchys could agree about nothing. They were like two magnets, wanting to be together and pushing each other away. Peig finally agreed to marry the man we all knew as Alphie, and on their wedding day, when his birth certificate was produced, found she was to be Mrs. Alphabet McGlinchy. It turned out that his mother and father couldn't even agree on a name for their son and had settled on the one word that covered every letter. "Alphabet" was all the men would call him after that. I suppose that should have been a warning sign. No one should marry a man they believe to be named one thing and discover to be named something entirely different.

They were married in June. The master kept them both

on after the wedding. Peig carried on in the kitchen and Alphie carried on in the fields. They got old Sarah Meek's cottage after she died, and a good house it was, with a window and a cement floor, and a place outside for the pig. Peig had it looking lovely. She was a wild woman for the classes run by the board, always coming back with a new way of cooking this and a new way of knitting that. They were happy enough, I think, for a year or more, until baby Owen arrived. Poor Peig, she was the best friend I ever had in my whole life. Oh, I'd feel her tongue all right if I did something wrong. She wigged me for not putting the lid on the pot of spuds like I was bid, and when Feeley slammed the yard door a lump of soot fell down the chimney and into the open pot. She didn't waste breath on Feeley, mind you, for slamming the door. But that's the way it is always—you take your temper out on the one you can get away with wigging.

She lived a hard life, God bless her, and she had a hard end. Years ago, in the thirties, not long after you were born, Anna, I heard she wasn't well and I called to see her. She was in her bed and she lay and talked to me for a while, and I knew by the way she was going on that things weren't right with her. When I was about to go, she said, "Wait, wait, Maddie!" She climbed out of bed, pulled a pot out from underneath it, hitched up her nightdress and sat down and started to pee. When she'd finished and got off it, she held it up for me to see and said, "Is that enough, do you think?" I don't know what she was expecting me to do with it. I looked at her for a minute or two and then I got up and took it from her and said, "That'll do fine, Peig." I brought it down to the ash pit and emptied it. God love her. She died alone in her wee white house, with three wardrobes and seven chests of drawers, two to each bedroom and one in the hall. She could never turn away a piece of furniture.

At her funeral Owen asked me to come round, pick something out. "Mammy always had a good word for you, Nanny," he said.

(Everyone called me Nanny, even then.) "She told me to make sure and have you round when she'd gone. She wanted you to have something of hers." The truth was, Anna, she'd had something of mine all along, only neither he nor she knew a thing about it.

I went. Owen was there, and his wife, Greta, and Conor running about the floor. Conor was only about three or four at the time, and he was trying to help, packing up bags and boxes, some to keep and some to pass on, getting in everybody's way.

Owen pointed me to the smallest back bedroom. "She has drawers stuffed full of things in there, Nanny. Anything you want you can have," he said. Greta opened her mouth but he silenced her with a look. "You were always good to us."

It felt strange, going through Peig's things like that. She was a great hoarder. After the mistress died, Miss Julia left out a box of things that none of the family wanted, to be divided up among the servants. The drawers in Peig's room were full of jumble from forty years before: a handful of brown horn buttons; a calico petticoat, quilted and whaleboned; white lace-trimmed muslin underdrawers; a pair of long blue kid gloves to the elbow—things that Peig had never used or worn. "I'll keep that for good," she would have said, but she mustn't have come across any occasions good enough to unwrap and use them. It gave me a start to see them, those delicate garments I'd slaved over in the laundry, heart-scared of rubbing a hole in them. I was half expecting to feel a hand on my shoulder, a sharp word in my ear. I shook them out, and it was the oddest feeling seeing those long-forgotten but familiar items again, as if all the mistress's things had come billowing down through time, like clothes blown off a washing line forty years before, and settled in the drawers in Peig's wee house, with the mistress's shape still in them. I didn't take any of them, Greta needn't have worried. I had enough "good stuff" of my own.

In the last drawer, I came across a pair of pliers, an aged and water-stained prayer book, some objects that had been dug up out of the garden: a stoneless brooch, a bronze farthing bearing Queen Victoria's head, a sacred heart medal. She was a great one for putting a medal into the founds of a new house—to keep the occupants safe, she would say. And I saw her put a medal in her brother's coffin, for the journey. She'd shower you in holy water every time you stepped out over the threshold; that's the very least you could hope to leave with. And under a bundle of patterned head scarves, pots of talcum powder in lilac and green and a pile of embroidered antimacassars, I found the first of the stones. A handful in the corner of a white envelope, the edges folded neatly in, and written on the paper in careful angled capitals the words JACK'S, 3 MARCH 1932. In another paper parcel: GRANNY'S, 19 NOVEMBER 1922; in another, SALLY'S, 23 JANUARY 1935. The stones off graves, taken not on the day of the burial but some time after, on a visit: her brother, her grandmother, her friend. And in the corner of the drawer, wrapped up, not in an envelope this time, but in a delicate embroidered handkerchief that had never been used but had been unfolded at least once, CHARLOTTE'S, 3 MAY 1901.

I took nothing from the drawers, but when I was turning away, my eye caught on a tall, dark piece of furniture in the corner of the room. And would you believe it, Anna, it was none other than the butterfly cabinet. The master must have given it to Peig when the house was being cleared. All that time she'd had it and never mentioned it once. And by the looks of things, Peig had taken good care of it; it gleamed with polish. It took me right back, seeing it there, to the small sitting room in the castle. The mistress had the room all decorated in dark colors, what she called the "Moorish" style: mahogany and rosewood furniture, and the chairs stained dark with deep fringed red and black embroidered covers. There was a tall mirror over the fireplace, a torture to polish, and to the left of it the butterfly cabinet stood, just behind the door. I'd see her in there sometimes, when I was sent to put turf on the fire, or draw the curtains, or collect a tray. She liked to sew in there; a strange thing, that. She always mended her own clothes. She was at her most still in that room, with the light from the fire playing on the walls and her head bent over her work. You could see then what the master must have seen in her, what he must have loved. But it was all too rare for the rest of us, and for the children in particular. You can't rear children on morsels of love.

In Peig's cottage, I put my thumb and finger on one of the little wooden pulls and did what I had never dared to do the whole time I was in the house: I pulled open a drawer of the cabinet. I was standing there with the diary in my hands when Conor ran into the room. Isn't that a strange idea, Anna, that I knew your husband before you did? He was only a wee toot, and him up now the height of the spouting. He was a darling child, dark like his father and full of devilment, the two eyes shining like marbles in his head and that dimple that he still has, right in the middle of his chin. He had a wee truck in his hand, a red one, and he said to me, "Look out, Nanny, here comes Flash Gordon!" and he came straight at me with it, flying it like it was a rocket ship. I laughed and cried, "Help! Help!" and ducked out of his way. I slid the diary back into a drawer and Conor flew the truck over my head, the pair of us laughing, and then he came at me again and I took off with him on my heels, chasing me around the room. He made one big swoop with his arm, but his hand caught on the cabinet on the way past and a skelf came out of the wood and went right into the ball of his thumb, and his face changed, all of a sudden. Poor wee mite, he was trying to be brave but a tear came in his eye and I felt that bad; I should have had more sense, chasing round the room with him after me. I asked him to let me look and there was the piece of ebony, dark as a blackthorn, buried in his hand.

I said: "Will you let me try and take it out?" and he nodded and bit his lip. I slid my thumbnail under the skelf and caught it with my other nail and he screwed up his face but he stood steady, and I knew I had it—I could feel it between my fingers—and I caught it tight and pulled it right out.

He looked at it, at the small dagger of wood with the spot of red on the end of it, and at the blood seeping out of the cut on his hand, and he said, "Can I keep it, Nanny?" and I said, "Yes," and not a tear was shed. He still remembers that, I know, because he told me that day we were all on the beach.

I asked Owen for the cabinet and Greta said it was an ugly thing and I was welcome to it. Owen put it into Shivers's lorry and drove it round to the yellow house in Victoria Terrace himself, with the little black prison diary still tucked up inside. Look, Anna, in the corner there, can you see it, behind the door? I've used it as a kind of treasure chest: it houses all the things that matter to me, and all the things that I thought might matter to you and to Conor as well. It was the only thing I brought with me when I came back here. That's a strange journey when you think of it: from here, to Peig's, to your mother's house and back here again. You can see where Conor took the bit out of the side of it, Anna—can you see there? To the left-hand side? So there you are, it has history for both of you: it's only right that you should both have it.

Harriet

Derry Jail

Monday 9 May 1892

They have moved me north, like a parcel, on the mail train from Amiens Street. Second class; but only because there is no third. All dreadfully discreet; that strange Miss Callaghan accompanied me, looking every inch the traveling companion under her brown-feathered hat and not at all like a prison matron. The sergeant and constable from the Royal Irish traveled in a separate compartment, climbed out at every station to make sure I stayed in my seat but never once looked my way. No one would have guessed that the train was carrying such a dangerous criminal. They allowed me a newspaper and I read that the woman suffrage bill has been defeated by a majority of twenty-three. Julia will not be pleased.

Finally, after four weeks of oakum picking, I have warranted a letter from Edward. If I continue in this vein, the model prisoner, soon I will be permitted a visitor.

There has been some unpleasantness at his club. When he sat down to dinner, the dozen members present rose and left the room. Poor Edward. He is unused to cruelty. It is not in his nature to be vengeful or spiteful in any way and it baffles him when he sees it in others. He has resigned his position on the Board of

Guardians, and of course is no longer a justice of the peace. It hits him hard to be treated so. He has done nothing wrong, apart, it could be argued, from marrying me.

Not everyone has abandoned him. He has been to dine with Dr. Johnson. Dr. Johnson is a dreadful bore. He speaks always as if he is suppressing wind, as though the next sound to emit from his mouth may well be an involuntary one. It makes people anxious in his company, inclined to finish his sentences for him before he embarrasses himself. He fell in beside me once at the hunt in Dunseverick, in his tweeds and pot hat. He keeps his own harriers. What was my opinion, he wanted to know, of the long-haired fell hound as opposed to the Kerry beagle; would I concede to the superiority of the Brocklesby kennel; had I heard the story of how George IV's hounds had to be destroyed when they went mad like the king's father? I have a clear image of him, turning in his saddle to give me a better look and take note of the cut of my riding jacket: I was eight months confined, with Morris, at the time.

"You're not hunting today, surely, Mrs. Ormond?"

He seemed to be of Surtees' opinion that ladies should canter to the meet and home again to work up an appetite for luncheon. I fairly showed him my heels. Although, on reflection, it may have served me better to have acted with more decorum.

Dr. Johnson was the coroner at the inquest. Two days after Charlotte died, eighteen sober-faced men—known to us, every one—lined up on Edward's mother's crimson and mahogany chairs in the drawing room at Oranmore. District Inspector James wedged his considerable weight into the walnut armchair; Head Constable Wilson perched on the rosewood piano stool. The loo table was brought out from where it had been propped against the wall under a square of holland, and on it lay Charlotte, concealed by a white linen damask, bordered in white shamrocks. The resident magistrate, Captain Grange, opened the inquest; the jurors viewed the body one by one. I sat still beside Edward, my eyes on the carpet, imagined the bruises darkening at Charlotte's small throat.

Captain Grange asked me to tell them what had happened and I did. The whole time I spoke I kept my eyes on the marble-topped spider table to Dr. Johnson's side. The table was a vile thing, bought by Edward's mother at an auction; it always looked to me as if it might walk across the floor when no one was in the room.

The coroner showed inordinate interest in the manner in which I had bound Charlotte in the wardrobe room and asked me to demonstrate using Edward. It was a technique taught to me by Edward's groom, Feeley. He had showed me how to tie up the yearling by attaching the head collar to the tie ring in the stable by a piece of twine. That way, he said, if the youngster pulls back, it will only break the string and not the lead rope or the collar. Sergeant Shier produced the stocking with which I had tied Charlotte, and a length of twine was sent for to the kitchen. Edward stood up, miserable, and put his hands behind his back. I passed the stocking across his chest, bound his hands behind and attached a piece of twine to the stocking to show how it had been fastened to the ring on the wall. I described how, when I found Charlotte, her body was slumped forward, still attached by the twine to the wall, but that the stocking had slipped up and was around her throat, a spot of blood on her lip. I did not say what I was thinking: that a two-year-old horse is clearly stronger than a four-year-old child. The cord did not break. The difference between death and life: a matter of weight, or of inches, or of minutes. I avoided Edward's eyes as I undid the knots, but in the trembling of his white hands, I understood his anguish.

I did not know then that that would be my last opportunity to speak. The statement I made at the inquest was recorded and read on more than one occasion thereafter.

I must admit that when I heard it again in court, the words

I had uttered seemed cold, even to me. "I opened the door, and called her, but she did not answer. I did so again, and, on receiving no answer, went hurriedly into the room, and undid the string, when she fell down to the ground. I lifted her, and ran with her to my bedroom, and at once took off the stocking and her clothes." But those were, after all, the bald facts of the case. There seemed little point in mentioning the mislaid key. They asked me what I did with it and I said I put it in my pocket, which was the truth.

Dr. Creith was examined and described how he found us all on the Saturday evening; confirmed that he believed the cause of death to have been asphyxia: that the stocking must have slipped and caused pressure on the windpipe; said that the blood on the child's mouth could probably be explained by her having had a convulsive fit while in the room.

Julia too was examined, but since she had been absent for most of the time Charlotte had been in the wardrobe room, they did not overly trouble themselves with her. She was practically hysterical; we had to call the doctor back to give her something to calm her down. She and Charlotte had been close.

The inquest jury deliberated for an hour only, while I sat in the morning room with the sergeant. He looked decidedly uncomfortable in my floral chintz armchair, sipping tea out of one of Edward's mother's gilt-edged cups. We were called back to the drawing room, where the verdict was pronounced—that I did feloniously kill and slay my only daughter—and the case was returned for trial at the Derry assizes. The bail of £400 was accepted, later to become yet another cause for outrage among the newspaper editors of the country. The witnesses were bound over to attend.

Once, early in the year—January, I think, or February—I took Caesar down for a gallop through the surf. A seal pup, stranded high up in the dunes after the high tide of the previous night, was making its tortuous way back down to the water. It had dragged itself across the sand, and was lying exhausted, yards from the tide line, its mother's eager head appearing above the waves offshore. As we approached, the seal pup nosed the air, barked and snapped like a rabid dog, raised itself up by its flippers, its useless body anchored in the sand. I gave Caesar full rein, rode to the Barmouth and back, and when we had returned, it was gone, back into the sea, the only trace of it a trail in the sand like a slug might leave in gravel. In the drawing room, at the inquest, when the verdict was given and I raised my head, I looked across the room at Edward, and I thought of it again: weighted down; ridiculously ill equipped; desperate to escape.

A brittle day, the day they came for me, the air so bright and clear that dusk seemed impossible. A skylark in song, I remember, and the holly bush blackened to the north, by frost, or wet, or wind. Charlotte was dead a week, the inquest at Oranmore over, her body buried in the little cemetery at Bushmills. It was surprising. We had not been expecting any further proceedings before the assizes. But later we heard that there had been rumors of our planning a getaway: apparently they thought I might make a run for the continent. The order to commune a hearing had come, apparently, direct from Dublin Castle. The chief secretary was under pressure; questions regarding the inquest and my release on bail had been asked in the House. It was clear to me that the Unionists were point-scoring against Edward's father and his affiliations with the Home Rulers; the incident had not helped Lord Ormond's dwindling political reputation. I had no designs for escape. I was fully prepared to face the circus, brain-tired and gritty-eyed as I was.

Julia was alive to every noise in the house, her nerves a-jangle, Dr. Pepper's quinine and iron tonic never far from reach. I felt the opposite: removed from what was going on around me, strangely cocooned. The morning the sergeant came to escort me to the hearing, I pushed open the window sash in my bedroom, wanting the feel of the chill air on my face, and as I rested my hand on the sill, the wooden frame dropped straight down onto my fingers. Between the knowledge of what had happened and the register of the pain there was a gap that could have been a second, or a minute, or an hour, or a day. Except that when I heard my voice cry out, everything was still as it had been in the room a moment before, and Madge was still at the washbasin, tidying away. I was glad of the sensation of pain, grateful for the relief of feeling something.

The landscape here in February is as colorless as a Whistler, everything somber and muted. We left the house in the closed carriage under a wide sky, with just a little blue and green beginning to seep into the day. Blackthorns in the hedge; ivied tree trunks; mossy, rock-exposed ground; six fat-backed sheep. Edward held my hand in both of his, kneading life into my cold fingers. It hurt, but I did not tell him so: I felt the roughness of his fingertips, the ragged, worked skin, not a gentleman's hands—he spent too long on his turnips. The sergeant followed behind on an outside car. Julia stayed in the house. Edward was saying that there was no reason to fear, that everyone would see what a tragic accident it had been, no undue force used; that sense would prevail. I think that is what he was saying, but I was held by a family of starlings that rose from the trees at the bottom of the avenue and followed the carriage, swarming and re-forming like minnows above our heads, the whole way along the road. Edward leaned back and stretched up his neck in a nervous yawn and I smelled his stale morning breath, and I saw for the first time how he would look in years to come: elderly, ailing, disappointed.

My Edward. Up until a few weeks before, his only trouble had been the progress of his half-acre of mangelwurzel and the effects on it of the new artificial manures. Those days of waiting between the inquest and the hearing were torture. Peig, padding around the house like a tigress, sending up wordless meals. I do not suppose it was a shock to her; her kind anticipates tragedy. She has probably been expecting all her life to be part of a household with a dead child in it. She cannot be more than five-and-twenty but she carries the years of her entire race. Edward, dumbstruck, torn between grief and anxiety, making efforts to reassure me with the pall of death hanging over him. I avoided the other children. I heard them go about the house from time to time: Freddie's small feet on the stairs; George's infant burbling. Edward said the older boys had asked if they could ride out one afternoon. I did not see the harm in it. From the window, I watched Gabriel and Morris lead their horses back in, caught Morris raise his head and look up at me, his eyes even from that distance unmistakably grieving, though whether for Charlotte or for me I cannot say. I do not know if they asked for me.

On our approach to town, at the bottom of Ferryquay Street, the horses' hoofs began to slip on the icy road and it was soon clear that the pair were not going to be able to mount the hill with a full carriage. Early though it was, there were people in the streets. The sudden prospect of being made to walk to the police barracks in Meeting-House Street, through the Shambles, past the fishmonger and the butcher, the newspaper offices and the milliners, in the custody of Sergeant Quinn, was appalling to me. I jumped down, ran back to the sergeant to ask if I might travel in the outside car until the horses regained their footing. The poor man looked terrified. I believe for a moment he thought that I was going to make a dash for it, but when he understood me he readily gave up his seat and I was saved the ignominy of arriving on foot.

The whole way along the road I could smell the fumes from the distillery chimney in Killowen. Across the bridge at the Clothworkers' Arms, guests were descending from carriages like it was any other day. A nurse stood on the balcony at one of the windows in the cottage hospital; the fountain outside was still.

The magisterial inquiry was held not in the courthouse but

in a room on the second floor of the barracks, with the window blinds drawn against the street. Edward had insisted that Mr. Crankshaft be my solicitor; he had represented the Ormond family for years. We used to smile, Edward and I, over those notices in the local paper: Mr. Crankshaft contesting the ruling on the setting and lifting of salmon nets; his defense of applications for spirit licenses; his prosecution of the owners of goats that had allowed their animals to graze on the public highway. And now he was defending me.

The charge was read and Mr. Crankshaft politely objected to my being brought there, since it was his understanding, following the inquest, that there would be no further proceedings before the trial at the Derry assizes. He said he thought these actions to be most unusual, but the crown solicitor duly ignored him and carried on as if he had said nothing at all.

The sergeant made a statement in which dimensions featured gravely ("the room is six feet by eight feet"; "the ring was five feet eight inches off the ground"; "the stocking was thirty-seven inches long"; "the ring would carry the weight of the child").

Mr. Crankshaft objected to the reading of the statement I had made at the inquest, on the grounds that we appeared to be commencing the hearing as if no earlier evidence had been heard and that as such, I ought to be permitted to give a fresh account. Again, his objections were ignored, the whole inquiry appearing to treat him as one would a petulant child whose presence was to be tolerated but whose protestations were not to be seriously considered. "None of us seems to know why we are here today," he said, and if it had not been for the circumstances, which weighed heavily on all of us, I believe I would have laughed. Dr. Creith repeated his evidence and my testimony was read. I was not required to speak, and if I had been, what would I have said? That I had wanted to impress upon my daughter the value of self-government? That I had not intended that she be left alone in the wardrobe room for so long? That I had come so far down the road of believing myself to be entirely autonomous that I had forgotten what it was to need and to ask for and to acknowledge help? What good would it have done to have uttered such words?

I sat in silence and looked out from beneath the protection of my veil; the fine gauze made me feel a bit light-headed, like an invisible observer, as if I were present and absent at the same time. Outside the snow descended in short flurries. The press were lined up like vultures in the gallery; I saw that nasty little man from the *Watchman* whom Edward had admitted to the house the day after the funeral. Edward had thought it would help my case. Since neither he nor I was legally permitted to be examined in court, he thought it would go in my favor if he were to give the public our version of events. It did not help: the reporter did not libel Edward, of course—he was too clever for that—but he printed Edward's words entirely divorced from the sentiment with which they had been expressed. We are of the opinion, said Edward, that if a child's will is well broken in childhood, it will acquire habits of obedience that will serve it well in later life. "Mrs. Ormond was always watchful to combat anything like willfulness . . . ," the paper printed. "It is the tendencies that show themselves very early in some children that must be repressed . . . I do not consider this mode of punishment a hardship, as it is done for restraint." From infants we left them to cry: a child must learn self-control and the sooner it learns it, the happier it will be. Discipline goes in and out of fashion like waistlines and hats. Who is to say that in a hundred years' time parents will not be castigated for raising their voices to their children?

Edward did not tell and the reporter did not print the story of his grief. How he had lifted Charlotte's cold hand and held it to his cheek; how he had brushed the curls back from her forehead; how he had carried her up the stairs to Harry's vacant room and put her down on the bed and lit the lamp and sat at her feet the whole night, looking out into the dark. After some discussion, the magistrate admitted bail, and I was permitted to return home until the adjournment the following Thursday.

The public had not been admitted, the reasons for which were clear as soon as we stepped outside. A crowd of shawled women had gathered, wicker baskets at their feet, and a number of boys in cloth caps. When I emerged, they began to jeer and spit. Ashes and fish bones flew through the air; a rotten potato struck Edward on the side of the face. A far cry from our welcome less than twelve years ago when Edward and I arrived at the station at Oranmore. Much has changed since then, and it is not to do with Charlotte, at least not all of it. In the bitter breaths that hung misted in the February air, I smelled hatred: every drop of it reeked of rebellion.

In his letter, Edward tells me that the papers are full of letters of complaint at the leniency of my sentence: "twelve calendar months' imprisonment with labor suitable" for me, an overlong confinement, the equivalent of a pregnancy and a lying-in. "There is still one law for the rich and another for the poor," they say. God help us, there is even poetry, if you can call it that, with titles such as "Mothers of Britain" and "Babes in Arms." They will never forgive me because to the best of their knowledge I have remained dry-eyed throughout the whole business, and a female who keeps her emotions in check is, in their view, not to be trusted. I am not a popular cause, at least not among the sane, although I do have my supporters. According to the papers, there are hordes of ladies who have written to the home secretary in my defense, offered to take my place, even, to shoulder my punishment for me. They are the same people, however, who would free Mrs. Maybrick (whom they say did not poison her husband) and the perjurist Mrs. Osborne, who is also with child. With friends such as these . . .

In the early reports, before the trial, I was described as "handsome," but by the time the later columns were printed I had developed a remarkably determined cast of features: keen, cold eyes; a firm mouth; a powerful jaw; thin, tightly compressed lips. Whereas in my youth, I read, I had been "a young lady of considerable personal attractions," my countenance now betrays an unbending resolution, a calm and unmoved demeanor. I dare say, had I behaved in a suitably hysterical fashion, I would have occasioned more public sympathy, but sympathy is, in any case, not a particularly useful commodity in the circumstances in which I now find myself. I know how implausible I must appear. My behavior is not what would have been expected, but I am not inclined to deliver a performance in order to fulfill the expectations of newspaper editors. There would be no end to the deceit to which that would lead. They would not call it lenient if they saw me, I think, lying on my back at night, waiting for the dark to grow fingers.

I did not expect to sleep the first night she was dead. And then, when I did, I did not expect to wake. And yet, those two things continue to happen, in sequence, one after the other, and every time I am surprised. It is enormously difficult, I understand, to break the body's habit.

Did I kill her? I cannot think of what she endured; there would be no way back from there. I am responsible, without question. There is no escape from that day.

Maddie

21 OCTOBER 1968

You'll hardly go back to the teaching, Anna? Not for a long while, anyway. The baby will need you at home. Don't tell me now, I know the name of your subject. Biology, isn't that it? Plants and animals and all that kind of thing. Oh, it's lovely to have you both back again. And Conor teaching at the university, who would have thought it? There was a picture of the building in the paper; one million pounds it's costing. Not that I'm likely to see it finished. Look, Anna, look at my hand. The little bird is growing, its tail is all the way up my arm. Oh, don't look like that, I'm not sad about going; there's people I'm hoping to see. I have a bit of explaining to do, to them and to you. The truth is the hardest thing to tell. I know that look in your eye: "Get on with the story, Nanny"—that's what you're thinking. Oh, you needn't deny it, I've known you too long.

May morning, not long after I started at the castle, the mistress was in a fury because the fires were late being lit. Peig refused to light them till she saw the smoke go up from a neighbor's chimney. She was awful superstitious, Peig: she said the charm setters would steal the smoke from the first house that lit a fire on May morning, and spoil the butter and the milk.

The weans wanted a May bush and Paudie cut down a whitethorn from the far meadow. They'd kept all their dyed eggshells from Easter and some old ribbons Miss Julia had given them, and they put the day in out the back of the laundry decorating the bush, and the evening dancing round it like little heathens, flailing about with nettles to frighten the fairies. They begged Paudie to play the fiddle for them and Madge tied a ribbon round Charlotte's head and stuck it through with marigolds and buttercups. She looked for all the world like a fairy princess, like the pixies had left her behind. They were put to bed, exhausted, but it wasn't long till there were tears. I was going past on the landing outside the nursery when I heard Charlotte weeping. I knew the mistress was at dinner so I went in and found Charlotte, dripping wet, Morris standing in his nightshirt with the chamber pot in his hand, the look on his face changing when he saw me come into the room.

"Madge said we were to keep a lookout for fairies changing homes," he said, "and not let them steal one of us and leave a changeling in our place."

I grabbed a towel and wiped Charlotte down, the poor child crying sore, Gabriel giggling under the covers.

"Don't touch her, Maddie, she's a changeling!" Morris said. "Madge said we'd know by a mark. Look at her!"

"Look, Maddie," Charlotte said, and pointed to a place above her eye where the skin was reddened, risen up in white lumps where she'd been hit by a nettle. She looked at me, her eyes full of tears. "Is it true, Maddie? Have they stolen me? Am I not Charlotte?"

I scolded them sore for torturing her; I was raging with Madge for filling their heads full of tales. And I washed and dressed Charlotte but for a long time she couldn't be settled. In the end I got her a knob of butter and rubbed it into her head and told her the fairies couldn't take her now 'cause they had no power over the first butter made from the milk on May Day. And she was quiet for a while after that. But as I was leaving the room, Morris called me back.

"Maddie, will you tell Mother?" he asked. I said no, I wouldn't. I didn't add that I'd be in as much trouble as he would if the mistress found out I'd been in with them. But he gave me the oddest look, like he was disappointed. I could never work that child out.

After I went up to bed, I heard a footstep on the landing outside, and the door of my room creaked open, and there was Charlotte.

"Can I come in to you, Maddie?" she said. "The butter's rubbed off and I'm scared the bad fairies will come for me."

What could I do? I turned down my quilt and said, "Five minutes only," and in she bounced and fell fast asleep. I carried her back down the spiral stairs, past the lamp on the landing that cast our humped shadow on the nursery door, with my heart in my mouth for fear I'd meet the mistress. But she never caught us. All the times Charlotte crept in beside me she never knew a thing about it. And Charlotte never told. Young as she was, she knew how to keep a secret; she knew we'd both be in bother if her mother found out. You know, you look like her, Anna. Not the mouth—you get that from your father's side—but those same serious eyes, weighing things up, taking everything in.

Charlotte was everybody's favorite among the servants, maybe because we all saw what her mother and father failed to see: how tortured and aggravated she was. Her aunt Julia gave her a present of a dolls' house for her third birthday. It was a fine-looking thing with window frames and sills and a fanlight over the door. We were all taken with it. Peig knitted her a ceiling rose in white wool, exactly like the one in the drawing room. I crocheted a little rug for a bedroom and Peter, grumpy old Peter that would hardly more than give you the time of day, came in one afternoon with a tiny kitchen table and dresser he'd built for her out of scraps of wood. Him and his big old hands. She was so loved by us. When any of us had a spare minute, we'd be busy making something for the house, sewing covers for the beds, little curtains for the windows. In no time at all, the whole house was furnished from top to bottom. She loved playing with it. You could see her get lost in her own wee world, walking imaginary youngsters up and down stairs, tucking them in, washing their faces. One time she was playing, I had to call her down for her riding lesson, and you could see the wrench it was for her, the change that came in her eyes, how loath she was to leave her fairy world for the one outside.

There was something about it that the mistress couldn't bide, that play world of Charlotte's. She couldn't see what the wean saw. Charlotte picked up a handful of gravel and made an avenue for her dolls' house on the nursery floor. There was a moat and a drawbridge and a tiny maze, but all the mistress saw was a pile of mud and dirt. It was the thing that was sure to throw her into a rage, but it was all frustration, I think. Like she was locked out of something she didn't understand.

The thing that really riled the mistress was when one of the weans wet or dirtied themselves. You'd think they did it deliberately, the way she reacted. She'd beat the living daylights out of them, and it was into the wardrobe room with them, dirty clothes and all, where there was less ventilation than in a prison cell. That was the worst thing, I think. You can understand it when youngsters are punished for cheek or for lying, but a thing like that can't really be helped and putting them in the wardrobe room wasn't the way to cure it. It'd make you even more nervous, something like that.

Miss Julia and the mistress had a blazing row about it. They didn't even bother to keep their voices down: they stood in the nursery with the door wide open and yelled at each other for everyone to hear. It was after Miss Julia came to stay. Charlotte was only about two at the time and the mistress was trying to get her to use the chamber pot but she couldn't get the hang of it at all and she'd dirtied her underdrawers. The mistress was letting rip, shouting at her, and Julia came in and said it wasn't the wean's fault. Then the mistress told her to mind her own business and that she would rear her children the way she saw fit. Miss Julia said if she thought that was the way to rear them, shouting and roaring at them for making one little mistake, then God help them, and the mistress said that when Miss Julia had a child of her own she might be allowed to have an opinion on the matter but until then she could just keep her nose right out of it. Miss Julia said she was allowed to have an opinion about the way her own niece was treated, and the mistress said she could go write her opinions on a placard and parade up and down the street and see if that would get her anywhere, but that *she* wouldn't be taking any notice of her. Then Miss Julia said it wasn't right and the mistress said if she didn't like the way she ran her household she could go find herself some other house that would take her in rent-free, but that while she was there she could keep her mouth shut. And Miss Julia walked out and slammed the door, and that was that.

Miss Julia and the mistress were nothing alike; it was hard to believe they were sisters at all. Miss Julia had a way with the children: they would do anything for her. She spent hours with them painting and drawing, making up stories. I think it annoyed the mistress that her sister had so much patience. You'd have thought the way she went on that Miss Julia was doing it to annoy her. If the mistress put one of the children in the wardrobe room, Miss Julia crept up and spoke to them through the door. A couple of times, she must have got her hands on the key, slipped in with a glass of milk and a slice of bread. She found ways around the mistress's harshness, but after that row she did it carefully, without letting anyone know.

• • •

Hand me my stick, Anna, will you? Oh, my bones! I stand up and the whole house creaks. It's not easy getting your bearings. My bedroom now is on the third floor, not far, I think, from where my old room used to be. And we have a small sitting room of our own up there, with a TV in it, but I'm not sure what that room would have been. I think it must have been part of the governess's old room. There used to be two spiral staircases in the house, in two of the old turrets: one that went straight from outside the door of the governess's room beside mine down into the nursery on the floor below, and from there on down to the schoolroom on the ground floor. There was one on the north side, too, outside Madge's room, that led down into the hall outside Miss Julia's room and then on down again to the dining room. We weren't supposed to use them—we were meant to use the passage stairs—but they were handy, and many's the time I took the chance of getting caught to save my legs the longer walk. They're not there anymore: they put in lift shafts for us that can't make it up and down the main stairs.

The best view of the town was from the older boys' rooms on the north side of the house, so I never minded being sent in there to air the beds when the boys were away at school. I used to stand at the windows and watch the tram pootering up the Parade. You would see the funnel first, sticking up out of the front, and the steam flying out of it, and then the conductor in his official hat jumping from one car to the next, collecting fares. And the people all sitting out on top on a good day, with the quality underneath them in their upholstered seats. And up it would come to near the top of the Parade, past the bathhouses and stop outside the hotel. I was there the day the stranger came. I watched him from Master James's window, a small man in a tall hat, busy and important, stepping with his short legs out of the tram, walking up past the post office and the grocer's. And then he disappeared and I knew he must be on the Strand Road and taking the walk up to the gate in the rubble wall and up the drive to the front of the house to knock on the door. I'd never set eyes on him in my life, I'd no way of knowing who he was, but I knew as soon as he knocked on the door that it was me that had brought him there and that it would mean trouble for all of us.

Not long before this, it was evening time, between the lights. Peig sent me out to turn down the gas in the passageways before "the surge," as she called it, when the gas supply would flare up for the evening and blacken the walls if it wasn't regulated. I was standing in the main hallway when I heard a bump, bump, bump on the stairs going up from the schoolroom. When I went to the foot, I saw Gabriel's fair head bouncing off each step, and when I looked up, the mistress was above him, disappearing round the bend in the stairs, but with her hand holding him by the heels, not looking back. I couldn't stick any more of it, Anna. The boys were rascals, it's true, but no child deserves that treatment. You wouldn't treat a dog like that.

I went down into the scullery and I said to Peig, "Do you hear that?"

She was stripping the scales off a salmon, and she stood still with the knife in her hand, listening. "What is it?" she said.

"Gabriel's head," I said, "on the steps."

Peig looked at me with her face white.

"If we don't do something," I said, "if we don't tell somebody what's going on in this house, one of those children is going to be killed."

Peig put down the knife and wiped her hands on her apron. "Are you able to write a letter?" she said. I nodded. She went into the larder and came back. "Here, take this." And she handed me paper and a pen. She had the address of the Cruelty Society rolled up inside a napkin ring and she took it out and put it in front of me. "Write it all," she said, "write everything."

The day I watched the man stepping off the tram and coming up to the house, Madge must have seen him too. She put on her clean apron and went to answer the door. Then she went in and told the mistress that the inspector from the Cruelty Society was there and then she went back to the door and said the mistress was out. He said he'd be back at nine o'clock the next morning, and the next morning didn't the mistress up and breakfast an hour earlier than usual, her and the children, and away they went, I couldn't tell you where. They were gone for a full week. Twice the inspector came back in that time, and twice he was told the same thing by Madge: the mistress and the children were gone from the house. He got no satisfaction at all. The mistress came back in a black mood. She'd no way of knowing, of course, who'd informed on her, but the guilt must have been written on my face. She found fault in everything I did: the fire was too high or not high enough, the window ledge wasn't dusted, the carpets weren't beaten to her liking. But at least things calmed down for a while with the children. They were still put in the wardrobe room from time to time; she must have decided that was acceptable.

There's things that happens, Anna, where the fault lies with more than one person. Some people are more to blame than others, maybe, but still, it took all those things together to make this one terrible event come about. Charlotte never mastered toileting. When she was four she was put in the wardrobe room by the governess for dirtying herself. The mistress was in town, and when she came back she went up to the child, and tied her by her hands with a stocking and attached it by a piece of twine to a ring on the wall and locked the door and went away and ordered a bath, and by all accounts forgot she was there. I can well imagine what she said; she would have made it clear that this was an "apt punishment," said something in the way of "If you cannot be trusted to keep your hands clean they will be kept out of harm's way." Except they weren't out of harm's way. Charlotte must have twisted, struggled to get free, somehow got the stocking round her throat. She was never one for standing still. Maybe she called out, but no one came.

When the mistress found her, when she opened the wardrobe room door, the cry that came out of her went through the house and stopped everything. I ran up and she screamed at me to bring water, and when I got back with the basin, Charlotte was lying on the mistress's bed and the mistress was kneeling on the floor, her head flung back and her two hands rubbing, rubbing, up and down her dress. I couldn't get her to stop or get any sense out of her and when she finally did stop, the skin on her palms was as rough as from ten days of laundry. Charlotte was on the bed, undressed, lying strangely, her lips black, a tiny red mark on her throat. And the mistress was screaming, "She's gone, she's gone, she's gone."

I could tell then that she was dead. Everyone who looked at her knew it. But still, we had to help the mistress slip her into the hip bath filled with warm water, separate her lips, pour brandy down her throat and over her chest, and still not a breath from Charlotte.

When Charlotte died, that feeling, the feeling from the time our boat went down, came rushing back to me. I can remember standing there on the rocks as the *Ruby* was swallowed up by the sea, expecting to see it bob back up again, not able to believe it was gone in one instant. Not able to believe I could be witness to something so black and so terrible, and not able to do anything about it. I remember Mammy stretching out her hand, out over the water toward the boat, as if by some will of her own she might reach it, pick it up, right it again. If wishing and hoping and praying had been enough it would have been done. It all came back to me then: that impulse to reach out, to stop the thing that was happening, to go back and make it unhappen, by whatever means.

The mistress was a study in the days after, kept to her room the whole time between the inquest and the hearing; there were whispers even then that she was carrying again. Madge said that in itself would keep her out of prison: she'd never heard of a child of the quality being born behind bars. Peig said that nothing would happen to the mistress, that nothing ever did; there was one law for them and another for us, and that's the way it'd always be. But Paudie said the times were changing, and wait and see. "There'll come a knock to the door one day," he said, "and after that, things won't ever be the same."

For days and weeks afterward, I woke at the creak of the door, a draft, and I knew that it was Charlotte's fairy footfall I was waiting for, her shape in the doorway, the whispered request to come in to the heat of me. It was the lack of a thing that woke me, like when the rain suddenly stops at night. She has taken a long time to leave this place, each day faded a little more, grown less here than she was before. But I'm not convinced she's gone yet, Anna. Even now, I think she may still be here.

Harriet

Derry Jail

Friday 20 May 1892

The procession I witnessed this morning has imposed something upon me of the seriousness of the fate that I have escaped. A few minutes before light, before the prison bell sounded and the gas flared up and the first cry of "All out!" I rose and looked out the window to catch the first lightening in the sky. Two warders walked into the yard carrying lighted tapers, a prisoner between them with his hands bound. Two clergymen followed, also bearing lights. They walked a few paces, from what I now know to be the condemned cell across to the scaffolding room. Midway, the procession halted and the warder to the right produced a white cap that he slipped over the prisoner's head. After that there was silence, and an hour later, a black flag hoisted on the tower. They say he killed his wife, the condemned man, in a fit of jealous rage.

I had woken from a strange dream. My mother, a red admiral, darkly velveted and crinolined, bordered in red satin, white fur at her throat and cuffs, was roosting on the edge of the divan in the sitting room at Oranmore, where she had never visited. She was talking earnestly to me, telling me something important, and I was a brimstone, pale green with thickly veined wings, fruitlessly trying to mimic an ivy leaf, hopelessly conspicuous on the red and gold divan. I could smell the cod liver oil she took for her joints, slightly fishlike, a little distasteful. What was it she was trying to say? I cannot remember. It glides from me as I reach out to catch it.

The strongest sensation that is left from a dream is the feel of it, that other body that one has inhabited. The detail fades over time, color, texture, even smell, but that sense of being oneself and at the same time being someone or something else—that is what lingers. It is only when one awakes that one sees the absurdity of it, but while one remains asleep, inside the dream, one does not question the sense of it. I was about Charlotte's age when Julia was born. I can remember Father in a jacquard silk waistcoat, smelling as always of leather, leading me by the hand into Mother's room, where Mother was arranged, as if for a photograph, on several white pillows on the four-poster bed. The heavy green drapes cast a shadow on her pale face. On her cheeks were two round spots of color. She looked, in her lace cap and cambric nightgown, like a porcelain doll. Father said, "Come and meet your new sister, Harriet," and I walked to the nurse, who was holding a bundle of muslin, and looked at the baby's tiny head and hands, the pale down at her temples, smelled the milky breath of her. "This is Julia," said Father, and her name was a jingle of silver. The room was as it had always been, ordered and still. The pier glass gleamed in the candlelight; two crisp white towels hung from a rail on the birch-wood washstand; the hip bath was polished and dry, angled into the corner. The stage was set, but there was something different: a pulse, a sensation as if some calamitous event had taken place and had been hurriedly tidied up, swept away, all made to look normal. I do not know why, but I felt that the success of this domestic scene rested on me, so I smiled, said, "She is very small," which seemed to be exactly the right thing to say, for they all smiled back, Father and the nurse, even

Mother, and there was a kind of sigh in the room, like we had all performed our parts as required.

It was clear to me that I had not been expected to love Julia, and though I made an attempt to appear as though I did, I fooled no one. The gap between us was too great. We had nothing in common, she and I. I yearned for the outdoors, open spaces; she asked for nothing more than to sit by Mother's side and sew.

Mother's health deteriorated after Julia was born. Eventually the doctors told her that her only hope of improvement was to travel, live abroad, in Egypt, they suggested, or Africa. I could barely contain my excitement. Those stories I had read in the *Quarterly Review:* Isabel, Lady Burton, riding through the deserts of Syria, a bowie knife in her belt, a rifle strapped to her back, her silken headdress flowing in the wind. I could see myself, scandalously astride a silver-gray Arabian steed in Palmyra or Luxor, where one could see for miles on end, breathe air that had traveled for centuries and had not once paused to scale an orchard wall or a clipped hedge. I would pick about among ruins, making sketches, deciphering hieroglyphs, my only companion a trusted native guide. And at night I would lie down under the stars, and there would be no limit to the thinking I could do. Childish aspirations, and short-lived. It was soon clear that separation from my father was not an option. Mother chose to linger at home on the sofa, while her joints slowly fused into immovable knots, reminding us all of how ill she was. She chose a half-lit life with him and to shun the sunshine completely in a blinded room. Years later, I learned that Lady Burton was born in 1831, the year before my mother. How different can two lives be?

There was a picture among the things that Julia brought from our London house when she came to us: a cutting from the *Illustrated London News*. It was of Blondin, from an engraving made at the Great Exhibition in the Crystal Palace the year of my parents' marriage. The acrobat is sitting on a chair, at a small table with a glass of wine raised in his hand, and for the first few seconds of looking, he seems an unremarkable, somewhat overtheatrical, but relatively ordinary sort of man. Until one allows one's eyes to travel down to his feet and one sees that he is shoeless; that with the toes of his right foot he is gripping a tightrope; that forward of this, his left foot is poised on the bottom rung of the table and that it in turn is steadied on the rope; that with the weight of his whole body he is balancing the chair on which he sits on its cross-rungs; that with his entire concentration he is keeping himself upright, preventing himself from plummeting to a depth of twenty feet or more. Remarkable balancing act: a triumph of coordination of mind and body; how totally in tune he must have been, how completely aware of his utmost capability. What made my mother keep it, I wonder. Her own sense of imbalance, perhaps; her growing failure to find purchase on solid ground? A difficult trick to master, the skill of staying erect, which might explain my mother giving it up entirely. These days, it is a skill I have to work at myself.

Julia uses it to explain herself, of course, the fear of ending one's days as an invalid. Hence her compulsion to be constantly on the move, grappling with the newest fad. Our parents permitted her a visit with me at Oranmore during my first confinement. While she was there, Edward presented me with the Italian dresser, a gift for our first wedding anniversary. I say Italian—it was clearly Flemish in origin, an odd, delicate, unsteady-looking piece with a dozen useless drawers and barley-twist legs and stretchers, which it must have acquired on its dubious journey through Italy. Bizarrely, also in Italy, some semitalented romantic had painted "scenes" on the drawer fronts: there was the Duomo and Baptistery from Florence; the Venetian Santa Maria della Salute; St. Peter's Square; the open-air amphitheater at Verona where Rossini's music had drifted out over the poplars. I understood Edward: he was sending me a belated postcard from our honeymoon, a souvenir from those first months alone together, when he could not bring himself to let go of my hand. Julia thought it the sweetest gesture; I actually think I saw tears in her eyes. And it must go in my bedroom, of course. There was no other place it could possibly reside. Julia cooed over the artistry of it, vowed to go to Italy as soon as she could manage it and filled the dresser full of brushes and hair ornaments. It has a dark marble top that is much too heavy for the piece itself, but with one redeeming feature. It was placed under the window, to the left of the brass half-tester bed, and when Madge came in the morning to open the curtains and I lay in bed waiting for the house to rise and the day to begin, a little piece of sky appeared, mirrored on the still pool of its surface, a living transfer, complete with the passage of gulls and clouds.

We were always at odds, Julia and I. Sometimes we tried to get on, often we did not, but it made no difference; it always ended in one of us feeling aggrieved. As a child, I had a treasure, a vulcanite hair comb brought back from London for me by Father. It was not a particularly expensive object, it was of a crude chain design with a nonprecious stone and it was much too big. Father did not have much of a sense of proportion. Still, I treasured it: a gift from him was unusual and I practiced putting up my hair, looking forward to the day when I might wear it. I was playing with it one day when Mother called me away and when I came back to where I was sure I had left it on the dressing table, it had disappeared. I suspected Julia, of course, and went looking for her, found her in Mother's room. She said she did not take it, she did not know where it had gone, and Mother said nothing, but all through the room was the unmistakable smell of singed hair, and the next day, in the ashes of Mother's fire, a little blackened paste stone.

Mother insisted on brushing my hair, every night one hundred strokes, her one maternal act toward me. I sat beside her at the dressing-table mirror and as every pass of the silver-backed brush dragged at my tangled curls, I watched and felt the skin at the nape of my neck pull out like a bat's webbed wing. I used to catch the flesh of the inside of my mouth between my back teeth and bite back tears until she had finished. If I sniffled at all, betrayed the pain, she grew agitated, brushed harder, insisted she was not hurting me, that I cried to irritate her, ungrateful, unruly-haired child that I was. It was as if she concentrated all her maternal duties into that one exhausting act between us, and having dispensed with it, she could rest easy. Julia never cried, of course. Julia had our mother's sleek, shiny flaxen mane that fell into place without the slightest coercion.

It will be some time before I require hair combs or brushes again. On my arrival here, a warder laid the blades of a pair of scissors cold and flat against my scalp and cut all my hair away. For the first time, I can see the shape of my skull, how it dips at the temples, how my ears protrude, the widow's peak of my hairline. I look like a lunatic, head shorn, mad eyed, pregnant. Still, I wish I had the Italian dresser here. In a whimsical moment I imagine that the scrap of sky over Oranmore is trapped on its enchanted surface the way the sky is sometimes captured on the glassy strand at low tide, that I could pass some time lying on my mattress gazing on it, watching the clouds glide in and out of vision, waiting for the gulls to suddenly appear, and just as suddenly vanish.

It is strange how we remember things. Edward's pretty dresser is as far removed from my memory of our honeymoon as is a pansy to a heather. I find it hard to believe that this is how he recalls our first days together, these pasteled landscapes and misted views. We postponed our honeymoon until the spring. From Italy we journeyed north into Switzerland and France. Edward wanted to walk the lower slopes, feel the Alpine air in his lungs, he said. I walked with him some days, and filled my pocket box with butterflies, and spent the evenings with the striking hand-colored plates from Berge's *Schmetterlingsbuch*, identifying and setting my finds: the zebra-striped scarce swallowtail, with its sapphire-jeweled train; the sooty Camberwell beauty—rare sights at home.

What I remember best is a June night near Menton when I drew back the bed cover and found a Spanish moon moth on my pillow. My heart seized. Impossibly far north, against the white linen its pale green body moved translucent. Rusty-veined, swallow-tailed, the markings on its wings like lidded eyes, its skeletal frame suggestive of the hair and bones of something dead. I gated it between my hands and my breast, moved to the window, where the curtains twitched in the breeze, and stood there, feeling the appalling thrum of it against my skin, the life of it battle between my fingers. Then I leaned out, released my hands and freed it into the night. Edward walked in and stood by me at the window, his fingers resting on my shoulders. "It *is* a lovely night," he said.

He had been a patient husband with me, allowing me time to slip out of my whalebone armor, undress and slide between the covers before he entered the room in darkness. Those early nights he had treated me like a nervous yearling, never once touched me without speaking to me first, had pushed the hair gently back from my forehead and kissed me there before we both fell into the relief of sleep. Slowly, we found our way around each other's bodies in the dark, grew bolder with each passing day, mapping new territories of skin with our fingers and our tongues, until we had discovered every surveyed inch of each other. On that night in Menton, I pulled the window shut and turned toward him, heard the moon moth beat its wings against the glass outside, and I reached up and kissed his lovely throat. Against my waist as I pushed toward him, I felt a movement and I reached down then, between his legs, and felt the swell of what was there beneath my fingers, and at my ear his intake of breath sucked the air from around me. I pushed my body further into his in search of the beat of his heart, the pulse of him, to feel again that appalling desire for life battling within.

I ought not to write such things, I suppose, nothing intimate or self-incriminating. I should have learned that much from the inquest: my one opportunity to speak; my words preserved and recorded, repeated over and over again at every new hearing until even I began to believe them all true. It is company, this little journal; undemanding; a good listener; it waits patiently for me to write my way through to the truth.

Sometimes at night, I think I hear the sea. It is the drone under the bagpipes when Mr. Campbell used to play for us at home in Priorwood, a wind that does not gust or pass, unwatery, steady beneath every other sound. Here, time is not measured by the hands of the clock, the circling of cogs that turn and lock into place. It is fluid, capricious, unmeasurable. Some days, I feel like I have spent it all. On other days, and they seem no different on the surface from the ones that have gone before, I find myself with an hour to spare between the sewing room and the putting out of the gas, bewildered as to how this surplus came about, paralyzed by choice. To write, to sew, to pray, to put away, to sleep.

Charlotte was as soft and as round a bundle of girlhood as ever was produced. She never tired of embraces, begged constantly to be allowed into a lap, the opposite, in fact, to the child that I was. When she was a baby, and put to bed at night, she would clutch her woolen doll under one arm and with the other, reach up for a lock of my hair, curl it around her finger until sleep overcame her. I leaned over her cot while she curled and curled, ringleting me at the temple. When her own hair grew long enough she curled that in its stead, twisting and twisting until she slept.

I am in among thieves and rogues and madwomen. Deliberately, they have put me beside a prisoner who mistook her own child for a dog and trampled it underfoot. Along the stretch of hall with which I have become familiar are housed a drunkard and a prostitute; a suicide; a woman accused of poisoning her unborn child and driven to madness by her insistence on her innocence; a blasphemer; a Fenian sympathizer and me. Between us, we make up several circles of Dante's hell, and nowhere is this more apparent than in the radial exercise yard where we trudge, one behind the other, in three concentric circles, never permitted to speak or sign to each other in any way. They mean to make an example of me so that no one can say I was treated better than a common thief, but they err on the side of caution and treat me worse than anyone else. I polish the floor, keep up the luster of the brass basin, roll up my mattress and bedclothes, mimic the model prisoner. It is excruciating to have to perform these menial tasks in front of warders and other prisoners, to watch them jeer and smirk at me, while all the time I am doing my best to disappear. I make no sudden movements here; I deflect attention; I have learned to become small. I am camouflaged to the best of my ability.

Maddie

23 OCTOBER 1968

You'd think the way people go on that if they stand too close to old age and loneliness they'll catch it themselves. I suppose that's true in a way, because you do catch it, if you stay around long enough. But you don't get it from other people; you don't get it from anybody but yourself.

There's to be no putting the clock back this year, did you know that, Anna? By rights, it should be changing in a week's time, but we're staying in British Summer Time, the papers say, for the whole year. Wouldn't that be great, if it turned out that way? Sunny and bright in December and January. It makes you realize what a farce the whole thing is: how we put numbers on the hours passing as if that gives us any say over it, when the hours will pass all the same, regardless of what time we call it.

I dreamed a dream again last night, one I dreamed a lifetime ago. I dreamed that Charlotte was dead again. There were people, men, two or three of them, their backs to me, carrying her coffin into the house, and there was going to be another wake because the first one had been conducted all wrong. All those stiff-dressed men in the drawing room looking at her for bruises, and none of us allowed in to see her, to twine a rosary through her fingers or make the sign of the cross on her brow or say an *Ave* over her before she was coffined. Peig's keening was for real then, all right. She couldn't lift her eyes for days. And when she stopped keening, she lashed out with her tongue. You couldn't have looked at her sideways. When she opened her mouth it was to spit out some new venom at the mistress: "A child is not a horse to be tied to a wall," she said, "and have the spirit beaten and starved out of it."

In the dream, though, when the men brought Charlotte in, there was a smell of incense burning, and kelp, wet and salty, fresh from the sea. They lifted her out of the coffin and put her in her little bed, where she lay, eyes closed, her arms straight down by her sides, the fist of her left hand clenched tight. The men turned round and then they were Daddy and Sam and William, and they all smiled at me, and Daddy put his finger up to his lips to shush me and they all walked out. I knew it was important for me to sit down on the chair by her bed so I did. Then Charlotte opened her eyes and winked at me and stretched out her arm and began to open her hand. She was wearing a nightdress that wasn't a nightdress but was the linen damask tablecloth from the dining room. I could see that whatever she was holding was bloody and slippery and I didn't want to touch it but she kept motioning for me to hurry up and take it, and how could I refuse her? How do you refuse a dead child? I got up and leaned over and looked closer, sure that what she was trying to give me was some part of her, a heart, maybe, or a liver, however foolish that must sound. What I could see of it put me in mind of the innards that used to lie on newspapers in the scullery when Peig was gutting a rabbit or a hare, red and black, sinew and slime. But I had no choice but to reach out and take it, and when I looked down to see what it was, it was a key, white and spotted with rust, and then it was gone, the way things vanish in dreams, and a white and brown speckled butterfly was knocking its wings against the glass of the window.

Mammy used to say, "Dreaming of the dead is news from the living," and here you are, Anna. Here you are, the both of you.

I never saw the mistress with a cloth in her hand but the one time, the day after Charlotte died. She went round every mirror in the house before they were covered or turned to the wall and she polished them till they sparkled. As if that would make a difference to what she had seen. But she never set foot in the wardrobe room, not after the day she found Charlotte.

Sometimes I think I hear Charlotte, her light foot on the stairs, feel the breath of her passing my ear. I think she might want something from me. I think she might want what all ghosts want: to hear the truth about what happened told.

After the funeral was over, me and Madge were sent up to clean the wardrobe room. Peig said the wardrobe was French, all in mahogany with two big mirrored doors. We had to empty it of the old clothes that were kept there and scrub it out. The wooden pegs were still where they'd always been, on a picture rail that ran around the room; but the ring had been taken away. We were to wet the wallpaper with carbolic acid and strip it off the walls and take it down to the laurel trees and burn it. Pretty wallpaper it was, white with red flowers, hardly a mark on it. I didn't like to be in there. I knew that Charlotte had been buried in the grave in the churchyard in Bushmills. But the whole time we were working, I couldn't shake off the feeling that she was still there, that she was trapped in the mirror in the wardrobe. When we had it emptied, me and Madge pulled the wardrobe out, turned it toward the other wall. And when I went to tear the paper off behind where it had been, I found a little spoon, wedged in tight at one of the joins. One of the children must have hid it there, I suppose, but for what purpose I don't know. I don't think it had been there all that long. It was sticky with some kind of medicine, calomel maybe, or syrup of ipecac. The mistress was a great believer in purgatives for anything that ailed you, cough or cold. I slipped it in my apron pocket, washed it and put it away that night. We heaped brimstone in an iron dish over a bucket of water, shoveled live coals out of the nursery fire over it and sealed up the door from the outside. The next day all the clothes from the room were washed with carbolic and boiled. Then the door was opened again and Paudie was sent in to lime-wash the walls.

One Wednesday morning, a few days before the trial in Dublin, there was a fluster in the house. All the younger men were in the big meadow harrowing the ground for the potatoes, and me and old Peter were called to the library. Mr. Carter, the carpenter from town, had been to the house every day for a week, for what purpose we hadn't been told. "I need help with this," he said. "It's to go into the carriage and onto the Dublin train." He pointed to what looked, in the dark room, like Charlotte's dolls' house on the library table. I couldn't work it out: why would the magistrates want to see her toys? But it wasn't Charlotte's dolls' house on the table; it was a model of the castle itself: the battlements and windows, the big porticoed entrance, the chimneys and part of the basalt wall. I didn't like it, not one bit, and I could see that Peter didn't either. Mr. Carter took the roof off so we could get it out the door and then he slid the attic rooms out like a drawer and I could see the wardrobe room, plain as day, the door off the nursery; the master and mistress's rooms; the hall outside. He had made models of the staircases and all the bedroom furniture, exactly where they were in the rooms; the very windows were glazed. When we got it in the carriage, he slid the top floor back in and put the roof back on, like the lid of a pot. It gave me the strangest feeling to see it leave the castle, as if we were all going with it, our little tiny selves, all in our rightful places, inside the model house, all going on the train to Dublin.

By that time I'd had my summons: I knew I was going to have to give evidence at the trial. I couldn't stop thinking of a story my father had told. He was coming back one morning early from a laying-out near Ballyleese. It was June, the time of the year when the sky darkens no deeper than navy blue and the birds sing all through the night. I woke up when I heard his step at the door. Mammy had been sleeping in the chair by the fire, waiting for him coming home, and the door of the room was open a crack. He said he'd seen a strange thing. Coming down over the rocks above the Warren he looked down and saw a black circle on the low ground and something at its middle, and when he got closer he could see that it was a flock of crows gathered round three more birds. He said it was like a meeting of some kind, with the three middle birds all cawing at one another and the rest all looking on. And then, as he was watching, two of the crows left the center of the circle and walked out to the edge and joined the rest of them and just as they did, the whole circle closed in on the one bird. Daddy said when they'd done with it, there wasn't a feather of it left.

"I don't like that," Mammy said, "I don't like that one bit. What do you think it means, John?"

Daddy said he'd heard tell of them doing that before, maybe when the one had stole a nest or had broken a wing or something, but he'd never seen it with his own eyes, and it was chilling, he said, the way the whole group of birds behaved, like they were letting the accused have its say, before they tore it to pieces.

Me and Peig went to Dublin to give our evidence on the Friday, April Fool's Day, my first time ever on the train. Everywhere you looked in Dublin there were people rushing around: butchers' boys in their smocks and aprons with trays of meat on their shoulders; shoe-blacks and the cockles-and-mussels men; boys shoveling up dung from the horses passing in the street, selling it from door to door for garden manure.

"It's true enough, then," said Peig, "in Dublin they could sell shite and people would buy it."

It seemed like everyone had a job to do and in a hurry: I

saw a man in Sackville Street with a pole carrying half a dozen rabbit skins. And the noise of them: the lavender girls crying, "All a-growin'"; the old-clothes men chiming their bells; gypsies shouting, "Chairs to mend"; the knife grinder with his rickety oul' wheelbarrow. Outside a pub, there was a man balancing a ladder on his chin! The streets were full of tuggers: women in shawls with prams stuffed full of scrap and rags. And the stalls! I've never seen such a variety of things being sold: stewed eels and sheep's trotters; oysters and apples and oranges. It made me think of my quilt that Mammy had sewed for me, and that all the things in all the baskets had sprung to life in Dublin. And then I started to wonder what other magic could happen there; what other dreams could you live out in such a place? It made my head swim, the noise and the color of it. Me and Peig stayed in a boardinghouse in St. Michan's Street in Smithfield, with no quilts on the bed to speak of.

We had to register at the Four Courts and then we were free to do what we wanted until Monday, when we had to go back to give our evidence. We went for a walk down Sackville Street, past the Gresham, where the mistress and the master were staying. It was very grand, with hackney cabs all waiting outside. I've never seen a street as wide as that in my life; it made you feel like you were no size at all. But you hadn't far to go to see the other side of Dublin: a glimpse down Gardiner Street to ragged, barefoot weans in houses that looked like they were about to crumble. It hadn't occurred to me that you could be poor in Dublin, yards away from the likes of Clerys department store; poorer even than in a cabin, where at least you'd have a chance of a fish or a potato. There's nothing there to grow, nowhere to grow it. It's the nearest thing I've seen to an open sheugh, with the water running down the middle of the street and the weans stepping over it, and the smell in the air of sulfur from the coal fires, but above it all, strange enough, hanging on poles out of the upper windows, clean sheets strung out like flags the whole way down the street. I saw a big red-brick building with white pillars and a grand door with glass in it, and I thought that must be the courthouse, and when I got closer it was the fruit and vegetable market. And the courthouse, when I did see it, good God, as if I wasn't scared enough! White like an iced wedding cake, and with a green hat on it reflecting in the Liffey. I've never seen anything so impressive.

"You've no need to worry," said Peig, "none of us has. Just answer the questions truthfully and you'll be grand." And that's what I did. But I had a dread of the place, standing on the stone flags in the Round Hall, with its big cream pillars and the dome like a chrysanthemum opening up above us, petaled black and white, and all those figures looking down: judges and lawyers from the olden days, statues of Moses, Justice, Mercy, Authority, Wisdom. The more you looked up at them the dizzier you got. The place was packed with pressmen and lawyers and clerks, and people pushing and shoving and trying to get in to hear the proceedings. We were shepherded in by Mr. Crankshaft and put in long wooden seats like church pews, not far from where the mistress came to sit.

When my time came, they put me up on the stand and that solicitor Morell, with his big long legs and his huge bushy eyebrows and his nose like the beak on a hen, and the big blue flowery cravat at this throat, he took off his glasses and he looked at me. He asked me if I'd ever witnessed harsh treatment of the children and I told him about the crying I sometimes heard from the wardrobe room, and about the time Freddie picked up the mistress's riding boots with his buttery hands when Feeley had just that minute finished boning them. The mistress hit him a clout with her riding crop that nearly sent him into next week. I told them about the time she hit Morris with the umbrella and he asked me if I knew what that was for and I told him she'd found out he was keeping crabs in his chamber pot, and everybody in the courtroom laughed. He asked me did I know anything about a letter that was written to the Cruelty Society and I told him yes, that it was me that wrote it. And that was all true. It was strange to be standing up there, to be looking at the mistress in front of us, to be answering questions and speaking out, knowing that she was never going to get a chance to speak. I thought about that time at the front of the house, when she made me lie facedown in the gravel, when she told me to keep my nose out of her affairs. I told the solicitor nothing but the truth; I answered every question he asked me. But I didn't give him the answers to the questions he didn't ask.

If he'd asked me did I see a key lying on the spiral staircase I'd have told him "Yes." If he'd asked me did I pick it up and hide it in my hair I'd have told him "Yes." If he'd asked me did I leave it back, after a while, in the same place where I found it I'd have told him "Yes." But he didn't ask me any of those questions. He only asked questions that didn't matter, one way or the other, and when he said, "You may go," I got down from there as quick as my legs would carry me.

Harriet

Grangegorman Prison, Dublin

Tuesday 7 June 1892

It is feared, apparently, by the members of the House, that I am being given special privileges, that upon my infant's birth, my supporters will win my release on the grounds of ill health. Alas, my health looks likely to thwart me in this, as it continues robust as ever. They move me around like a checker on a board: from Grangegorman to Derry and back again. They do not seem able to determine what to do with me. And still the House has not tired of my case. "A monster of cruelty" is what one Unionist member has labeled me, and demands to know why the separate charges of cruelty have not been pursued. Meanwhile, the Nationalists harp on, counting on their fingers the number of Catholic jurors instructed to stand down at the trial. Edward writes this to me in a letter, not wishing me to hear it from any other source, and to say that his memorial for my release has been rejected. I am to give birth in Dublin, it would seem.

It is not so surprising, I suppose, to hear that my name is mentioned in the House, given my association with Lord Ormond. One editor famously wrote of him, "Neither side of the House listens to him with patience, much less respect, and even the Home Rule party look with disfavor on their Anglo-national ally." He locked horns with Mr. Gladstone years before I came to Ireland, over the question of papal infallibility, but we continue to hear of it on a regular basis. He is a most contrary man. Whether it be the price of corn or the fixing of rents that riles him, he can be relied upon always to take the opposite view of whomsoever he happens to find himself in the room with at the time. He is master of the one-liner. Once, on his way to the hunt, he stopped off in the morning room to ask Edward the date of the next meeting of the Poor Law Guardians. They entered into a discussion over the nomination for chairman, which ended, as ever, with one of his enigmatic quips. "You do not know a horse's character till you place a saddle on its back," he said, and off he went, leaving us at a loss as to whether his mind was on the hunt or on the nominations.

Edward must appear loyal to his father, of course, no easy task as it transpires, since Lord Ormond, like the good sailor he is, appears to change tack with every shift in the political breeze. He has converted from Episcopalian to Roman Catholic; from high conservative to Home Ruler; from a sound seat in Huntingdonshire to a rocky one in Westmeath to no seat at all; from loyal hound of Disraeli to a lapdog for the newspaper editors to kick. Loyalty to a father is to be admired in a son, but it is difficult in Lord Ormond's case to see to what one is being loyal. Edward pulls from the ruins of his father's disastrous choices what he can. I dare say my connection with his family has hammered the nail in the coffin lid of Lord Ormond's political career.

Edward is a good son, and an indulgent landlord to his tenants, and they abuse his good nature, take advantage of his affection for his grandfather's estate. The election results of 1885 caused a stir throughout the nation: eighty-six seats for the Irish Parliamentary Party, undoubtedly a Nationalist victory; the prince and princess of Wales pelted with onions on their visit to Cork.

Since then the tenants, with the National League behind them, have consistently demanded rent reductions, at times of up to 30 percent. Edward has had no option but to sell part of his land. The only thing that has saved us is that the Catholic Church is the mortgagee and has brought its own considerable weight to bear on its congregation. It angers me to see Edward so blinkered by his love of the place. The tenants line up to speak to him each morning after breakfast, carrying their grievances and tales of woe about the fall in the tillage prices or the price of butter. They do nothing but murmur and grumble. The rents on the estate are set far below the Poor Law valuations, and if there is a bad year for potatoes or grain they come memorializing in their droves, the *Freeman's Journal* tucked under their armpits, claiming that the fixed-rent system is unfair where the quality of land is so variable. Edward sympathizes with them, accepts a cartload of turf or a day's plowing in lieu of payment. Left to his own devices he would have us all destitute.

"Did they come," I said to him, "last year, when they were getting over seven shillings for a hundredweight of potatoes, and say, 'We have over and above what we need this year, your honor, and would gladly put something down against a bad harvest'?"

"Of course not," said Edward, "nor would I, if I were they."

In my opinion, therefore, they have no argument. If weather or disease or the market is an excuse in times of want, why is it not a reason in times of plenty? Let them put something by for when they need it. They make no provision against a worse time, and so long as it is not required of them, they will never learn industry or foresight. Charity lessens self-respect as well as self-reliance. The potato blight hit just as hard in Scotland as it did in Ireland and not one of my grandfather's tenants died of starvation. And he could never have been accused of having a soft hand. He knew how to manage an estate: how to be fair and yet firm; how to encourage industry in his tenantry, to administer relief where it was due.

Edward's grandfather knew the skill of it, but Edward . . . I do believe Edward would be content to be a tenant on his own land, if he could be left alone to try out the best methods for turning the soil, and never be troubled with matters of landlordism. In these days of tenant rights and rates tribunals and fixity of tenure, Edward, it would seem, has no say in the matter of who may tenant his land nor what they may pay.

I have just now remembered my checkered skipper experiment: the little green-and-white-lined larvae I collected from Mountsandel Wood in October, safely encased inside their grass-blade tunnels and housed in a hat box on top of my wardrobe. There was nothing much to observe over the winter months: soon after I collected them they stopped feeding on the false brome and began to pupate. They must be ready to emerge now, if they have not done so already. What excitement: to lift the lid and peer inside and see not pupae but fully emerged butterflies, beating their powdery brown wings. If they have emerged early, they may already be spoilt. I will ask Edward to release them. He is not capable of setting them. It requires just the right amount of pressure on the thorax to still the wings, the correct angle for the pin to pierce and hold the abdomen in place. He would not know to secure the front wing behind a vein. He would not be up to the task. I am sad to have missed it, my first rearing. Had I been there, they would have been perfect.

Today, the strangest kind of rain, hardly rain at all, a damp flurry blown about by every draft and breeze, the sun shining throughout. Not wet enough to mark the ground or dampen the air, an undirected, ineffectual falling. There is a face in the grain of the wood of my platter, a downturned countenance with one closed eye and a wrinkled cheek and chins that become scarves that stretch all the way to the edge of the plate. Beside it, there is another face, a long curved nose, a mouth that could be a smile or the hope of one, an eye that looks askance, away from the other. I cannot escape the impression that they are the faces of old children, too long in the womb, emerging misshapen from lack of space, born knowing too much. I dread this birth in this place. What kind of legacy will this child carry, born behind bars to a mother convicted of killing its sister?

Something has broken in me, something irreplaceable. I cannot get back to where I was before; there is no way back from here. I try not to dwell on the things I miss: the salty waft of kelp when it catches one unawares on the Parade, the sensation of cool cotton when one slips one's naked legs between the covers at night; the sound of the longcase clock striking in the hall. Would that I could go back there, open the casing, wind back the hands, shorten my life by a critical three hours.

At Oranmore, Gabriel rose one morning complaining of itching and when his arms and legs were examined, his pale skin was found to be covered in bites. We had to call for Mr. Carter to come and dismantle all the beds in the nursery and have the children moved to the guest rooms. The beds were taken outside to be washed, Keating's powder sprinkled everywhere. For days the smell of sulfur hung about the nursery. I have become so used now to prison fleas that if I were to have a night without them I think I would not sleep at all.

In the yard today the liquid pain sloshed about my head like milk in a gourd. Then, before me, a young woman with the most serious face, her eyes gray, her hair pale and parted, exposing a perfect line of bone-white scalp, a tiny scar the shape of a crescent under her right eye. She neither smiled nor frowned but, wordlessly, reached out her hand and put the palm flat on my brow, where it rested as cool and smooth as a pebble from the brook at Cappaghbeg. I felt the pain from behind my eyes pool beneath it. After a moment, she drew the flat of her hand away from me, until only the pad of her index finger rested on my brow, pointing straight at me. I felt the pain move again, line up behind the point where her finger touched my head, and then slowly, like a seamstress winding a thread onto a spool, the finger began to circle and turn and she pulled the pain straight out of me. She sighed once, betrayed only a slight weariness, then she crooked her finger into her hand and slipped it into her pocket. She said some words that my ear did not catch: foreign, I think, from some other place or time, a melodious lilt and fall, not a language I could understand. I had not seen her before and I have not seen her since. No warder approached us the whole time we were there.

It is exactly seventeen weeks since the high sheriff's Grand Ball. All that has happened between then and now is time. Some movement has occurred, nothing sudden, but everything surprising. It is a good thing we cannot see what is ahead of us.

It is hard to believe now that only ten days previous to my appearance before the magistrate in Coleraine, I was at the county courthouse, guest of our friend Mr. Potts, JP of Lismore House, high sheriff of the city and county of Londonderry. It occurs to me now that had my case not been transferred to the Four Courts (abominable interference from the fool parish priest, who accused the all-Protestant jury of bigotry) it would have been heard in that very same building in which I had so recently been a guest. The Misses Grange were there, poor things, in last year's colors; they never seem to tire of their cousins' castoffs. Miss Dawson was resplendent in Limerick lace; I thought at first she was wearing a bustle, despite its having been out of favor these last three years, but I soon realized her rear was her own. I cannot look at her without thinking of a cello; she has an unnaturally long neck and no breasts to speak of. And Mrs. Hardy was in the most extraordinary creation: a kind of pink and white confection of a dress; it cheered me to see it, though I doubt that

that was her intention in wearing it. It was a variety of striped tulle marshmallow, but with something of the admiralty about it.

She sidled up to me, attracted by my mesmerized look, and from behind a marabou fan whispered: "'*Directoire*,' Mrs. Ormond, absolutely *de rigueur* this season. You heard it first from me." She attempted to engage me in conversation for some minutes but I could not hear a word she was saying above that dress. It was not until I was rescued by Captain Grange that I found myself able to concentrate.

"May I help you to some *baba au rhum*, Mrs. Ormond?" he inquired at my elbow, and I gratefully accepted. We were surrounded on all sides by sheriffs and regimentals in ceremonial dress. I was not to know then that the next time I saw him it would be in the drawing room at Oranmore, he in his capacity as resident magistrate, I in my new role as the accused.

I knew then that I was carrying again. With every new birth I am diminished: for each one more of them there grows less of me. There is a type of wasp that lays its eggs in the body of a caterpillar. As the eggs hatch, the wasp larvae eat the host, devouring it from within. If one is unfortunate enough to collect such a caterpillar and keep it for weeks in the dark as it forms a cocoon, hoping that one's patience will be rewarded with a flowering of orange or purple or green, there will be disappointment. On the lifting of the lid one will uncover not a butterfly but a vicious swarm, and nothing left of the grub. For each little birth, a little more death. Will it work like this, now in reverse? Now that Charlotte is gone, will there grow more of me? There certainly seems to be more of me lately, for I am everywhere. In every newspaper, on every tongue, even on the billboards outside the courthouse. But I am spread very thinly.

When the older boys were young—Harry, Thomas and James—they tried my patience sorely. Their incessant taunting drove me to distraction; when I crossed them they eyed me as a pack of wild dogs might eye a wounded lioness. I could not pierce their conspiracy. The idea that I could be both enemy and prey to my children was a shock to me. I beat them and it stopped them at the time but it had no effect, it seemed, on their behavior thereafter. They made no association between the punishment and the transgression. The harder I hit them, the sooner they forgot. And they never understood the disproportionate amount of time they occupied; they never knew their place. Once, I remember, I caught Thomas whipping Caesar, on a whim, it seemed, for no good reason other than that he could. He looked at me with those insolent green eyes of his when I questioned him and I chased him around the house with the riding crop. Afterward Edward came to me, concerned at the blood he had witnessed on Thomas's shirt.

"There is a time to whip a horse," I said, "and that time is not when it is housed in the stable."

"The boy must learn," said Edward, "but it seems most severe to treat him as he treated the animal."

"He had the advantage of being able to run," I said, but I could see that Edward was not smiling. "He will not forget the punishment. The association will be strong in his mind."

"All the same," said Edward, "perhaps we should adopt a different policy, one that does not result in a bloodied shirt."

"What do you suggest?"

"Isolation? Allow him to cool his heels for a while? Think over what he has done?"

So we agreed: the wardrobe room, windowless and without a fire, would serve as punishment from then on.

There was an evening in the nursery, trying to put the three of them to bed. I must have been carrying Gabriel at the time: three boys under the age of five and another on the way. They thought it was a game to kick off the covers as soon as I had them settled. I scolded and threatened but nothing I said could curb their spirits: they must have sensed that I had not the energy to lift my hand to them. I turned from them, walked to the fireplace, dug my nails into the wallpaper and dragged them down the wall and screeched. I can still feel the sensation of the paper and plaster gathering under my breaking, bleeding fingernails.

So much is in question here. I do well not to think too long, better to allow my limbs to operate according to habit. A second's hesitation and I am lost. How does one go about the business of buttoning a dress, tying on an apron, washing one's hands? I am a child again, relearning the simplest of tasks. Luckily for me, it seems, the body has a memory; one's limbs know what is required of them.

The walls close in. There is a new kind of seeing, each dimension in sharp contrast, every object more vital than before, angles sharper, colors more vivid. One finds oneself asking if that window bar came down in quite that same way yesterday. It seems impossible not to have noticed it before. That face in the wooden platter, that crease, just so, in the mattress.

There is a kind of trick employed by the snout butterfly when it pupates. It attaches itself by means of a silken thread to the underside of a twig, hangs upside-down by its feet and begins the process of divesting itself of its skin. When it has shed all but the covering on its legs—the legs that are still attached to the twig, preventing it from dropping to disaster on the ground—it performs an acrobatic twist, shakes off the last shreds of its molt and reattaches itself, by means of a silken hook, to safety. How hard the smallest of creatures will try for life. Constantly under threat, they devise new methods for survival. Everything they do is for the continuation of the species: to mature, to reproduce, to die. One aim, one goal in mind, so beautifully simple. I wonder, have I succeeded or failed? I am better than what I have done, than the one act for which I have been reviled, will be remembered.

To follow orders is not so much of an ordeal, so long as one understands the rules and knows how to avoid punishment, but to be constantly watched is an unbearable incursion. They have taken great pains to impress this upon me. The spy hole in the door of my cell is a work of anatomical perfection. It has been carved and painted to resemble a human eye, with pupil, iris, eyelashes and eyebrow, always open, always on the watch. There is no escaping it, there is nowhere one can go.

These are the things I know. That the last occupant of this cell was a clever woman. She knew that the bracket for the gas jet was set too low for her to hang herself, and that eating soap produced horrifying agonies of the stomach. She had witnessed fellow inmates sew copper wire into a leg wound in order to make it fester and gain a week or two's respite in the sick ward. She had eyed the netting that hung newly suspended between the galleries around the upper stories of the prison to prevent "accidental falls." She saw all this and still she knew that she could not bide another morning of waking up cold to the rancid smell of gruel and creosote and the burned chloride of lime that had failed to obliterate the stench of the waste of a hundred other miserable individuals. Another day of headache and nausea at the whiteness of the walls and the threat of the canvas dress for insubordination. She had calculated that if she tied the sheet from her bed in a loose knot between the bed frame and the gas jet on the wall that she could lever the heavy bed off the ground. With practice, she learned that the knot would hold for a given length of time until she pulled it in a certain way. She understood that it would be possible to lie down on the cold floor, directly underneath the place where the bed leg had rested, and to pull one end of the knot so as to untie it. If this were done suddenly, then the bed would fall and the leg would come down with enough force to go through her head and kill her outright. She was an excellent theoretician, and then, like the best kind, she proved it to be true. This I know because I have been whispered it in relayed messages, by the prostitute, or the thief, or the madwoman. And now that I know it, there is a mark under the bed that will not scrub away.

They think I will be afraid of her ghost, but what can her ghost do to me? They do not know the meaning of "horror." It is a silence in a dark room where there should have been an answer; it is a spot of blood on a lip; it is a small slumped body; it is a doctor shaking his head; it is eighteen dark-dressed men in the drawing room with a dead child between them; it is the bile that rises in the throat each time one opens one's mouth to speak; it is the sound of words at an inquest that make no sense. "I tied her hands and attached the stocking to the ring to prevent her running around the room and picking the paper off the walls." I tied her to prevent her from making a mess, and look at the mess I have created. I have my own ghost; I brought it with me. There is no warder's search that will locate it. Charlotte is with me like a song without the music. I carry the melody of her; she wraps herself around my every thought.

She never lost the smell of being birthed, the smell of blood, and sweat and vomit and soiled linen. It was strong on her skin for days, a kind of metallic undertone, impossible to miss, the smell of the inside of me. No one should have to smell that every day. Lighter and smaller by far than any of the boys, she was the most difficult birth of all. She seemed happy where she was, reluctant to emerge into the blinking light. In the days before her birth, I experienced a sensation like a claw being dragged along the inside of my womb. She was born with nails grown beyond her fingertips; two tiny teeth, chips of bone extruding from her gums, like she was ready for the world, whatever it threw at her, like a thing hatched rather than born. She rarely cried, a serious child, often frowning. She knew her own mind; that much is certain.

Edward doted on her, of course. He could not help himself. Those serious gray eyes, those waxy curls. She was afraid of the dark and he arranged for a lighted oil lamp to be left on the landing table. He told her he would engage a fairy to guard her and that if she woke in the night, she might just see the light from its wings flicker underneath the door. She was not to come out, he said, because fairies do not like to be seen by humans, and if she did, it might go away and never come back. He used to balance her on his feet: her right on his left; her left on his right. She'd throw her arms around his legs and he would stumble forward, walk her backward, his arms outstretched, calling, "Charlotte? Charlotte? Has anyone seen Charlotte?" until she collapsed into laughter and sang: "Here, Dadda, I'm here," when Edward would feign surprise and discover her, suddenly, right under his nose.

Then he would pick her up and hold her tight and say, "There you are! I thought you were lost. Where have you been?"

And the answer was always the same: "In your shadow, Dadda. You could not see me for looking!"

She called him her magician, said he could make any bump or bruise or scratch disappear. She would run screeching to him, leap into his arms, and he would hold her, pass a hand over the hurt, whisper an incantation in her ear, and all was quiet. Except for the last day. He could not fix his little porcelain doll in the end.

Some would call her precocious, I suppose. She began to talk at around twelve months, much sooner than any of the boys, and surprised us all by speaking in sentences. The boys accumulated language, word on word, a process one could track from one week to the next. They confused sounds, dropped whole syllables, said "pook" for "book," talked about "elphant" and "graffe," but Charlotte took to language like it had always been in her and the learning was the learning to uncover it, a patch at a time. Whole sentences emerged intact; the delivery imbued her words with a sense of meaning that was far beyond her years. Questions, all the time, none of them easily answered: Does Caesar *like* to run? How do we know when it is morning? Where does the moon sleep? What do we do when she has gone to bed? Her engagement with life was exhausting.

Her advancement led me to believe that she would do other things ahead of her brothers, but there was one thing she could not or would not grasp, that flouted me at every turn. She would not learn to use the chamber pot. She seemed terrified of it, of the sensation of air around her, the loss of the comfort of her binder and underclothes. Julia suggested that we leave off some of her undergarments in the warmer months, allow her to go about in her chemise without drawers or stockings, to get used to the sensation, and with the added benefit of speed when the time came to toilet her. Against my better judgment, I eventually agreed to try it. Incredible will in a child of two years. She held back: I could see her do it, gripping her nails into her hands, her face growing redder by the minute, until she could not control herself any longer and suddenly there was mess, like sheep droppings, all over the nursery floor. She made herself constipated; we dosed her with calomel; she screeched in pain when the purgative took effect. Dr. Creith came and explained that her bowel had become impacted, that most likely the violent evacuation had caused a small tear in the back passage that only time would heal. He advised that we abandon our efforts to have her use the chamber pot and return to it later when perhaps the memory of the incident had faded. He prescribed sieved fruit and jellied soup, boiled water to drink. I felt utterly defeated. The battle over the chamber pot was no less exhausting or messy with the boys but it was straightforward: they understood what was required of them and they succumbed, after time, to habit and discipline. Not so with Charlotte. The behavior was inexplicable to me. I was thwarted at every turn and it did not help to have my failure witnessed by Julia. Her interference made me more determined to win the battle with Charlotte.

Like Charlotte, I too have questions that are not easily answered. What happens when I leave here? What is it that I am hoping for? I tell myself that all I have to do is endure this year.

That part is not so difficult, not when I consider what lies ahead. Where will I go when I leave? Where will I not be known? I would like to drift, I think, like the sycamore seeds the children used to collect and pick open, a dry husk, boneless, clean, light enough to be lifted by a breeze.

24 October 1968

Dear Nanny Madd,

I'm sorry. I can't come today. I have to see the doctor. Don't worry. Everything's fine. Just the anxieties of a first-time mother, I'm sure. I'll see you as soon as I can. Conor will bring this.

Anna

Harriet

Grangegorman Prison, Dublin

Friday 24 June 1892

Eighteen seventy-seven: a clouded yellow year, the sky in June a fall of sunshine flakes. One of Mother's better days, Father drove us to Nairn, where the butterflies arrived in their hundreds and settled in a field of clover near the beach. At rest, with its wings folded, it might have been mistaken for a brimstone, but in full flight no such mistake was possible. Father pointed out to me how it had camouflaged itself, its wing spots mimicking leaf mold, its leg a stem of clover; how it had uglified itself for a better chance at survival. I fell in love with it then, that hardy little ghost of a butterfly, pale and camouflaged. My first specimen.

Father allowed me his cabinet. He said he had done with gathering rocks and birds' eggs, a young man's pursuit, and I could have it for my interest. Mother had always disliked it. She called it an ugly piece, "unforgiving," but it was perfect for my purposes. A disused dental cabinet he had come by at auction, it had over a dozen swing-out trays that were snug and dark and preserved the butterflies in their original state. He showed me how to feel for the thorax through the net while the butterfly's wings were folded, how to squeeze gently with my thumb and finger. It was surprising how soon the little movements stopped. We rinsed out a marmalade jar in the stream, dried it on the picnic cloth, folded our napkins into triangles and wrapped the tiny specimens inside. Father explained to me how the wings would have to be relaxed in order to set them. Apart from the chest that contained my clothes and linen, the cabinet was the only item of furniture I brought with me to Ireland.

When I grew more practiced, I used the thorax-pinch to stun the butterfly only, to prevent it from beating the scales off its wings, so I could drop it into the killing jar. On the bottom was a piece of muslin soaked in chloroform, courtesy of Dr. Creith. It had an odd effect. Each time I dropped in a new specimen and that overpowering smell escaped, I was reminded of giving birth. Once home, the specimens were transferred to the relaxing jar, so the wings would become pliant enough to set them: a jar partly filled with sand and water and left on a windowsill for the sun to create a little tropic to humidify and relax the wings. Mold is the real enemy. I once had to remove a whole drawerful of *Cupido minimus* because one had become stained.

Butterflies are cold-blooded creatures: they need sunlight to power their wings, and given the climate in this country there is not much opportunity to net them. I know lepidopterists who use bleached linen sheets to attract them. I myself have been known to wander around with a jar of honey, smearing it on tree trunks in order to capture a specimen, but I feel foolish enough carrying a butterfly net. The end result is magnificent; I wish the catching of them could be more dignified.

Mine is not a large collection; I have never seen the point of buying samples from other people's sets. Each butterfly is personal to me: when I look at them, they take me back to the day I netted each and every one of them. The comma, a rare treasure, an impossible paper cutout, all curves and flourishes, a true amber and brown baroque, netted near some woods in Huntingdonshire.

The large white, easily caught among the cabbages in the vegetable garden at Priorwood, not white at all but the palest of green undersides, veined like a leaf, the most edible-looking of butterflies. The orange-tip, increasingly rare at home, found among some cuckooflower near the brook at Knockancor. The green hairstreak, a reminder from Gallows, caught in a bilberry bush on an outing to Dearna Woods. The rare heath fritillary roosting on some foxglove near Inverness. They take me back to places and times, and then to the people I have known. The small pearl-bordered fritillary: Grandmamma McIntyre before she went into mourning, draped sleeves and voluminous skirts, pearl strung and amber jeweled. The grayling, a shaving of bark, old Peter at the woodshed. Edward: ink-smudged, oak wood dweller, distinguished, graceful, the silver-washed fritillary. Julia: the wood white, insubstantial, only barely there. And Charlotte . . . Charlotte is easy. The black-veined white: a scrap of charcoal-etched parchment; a bank of snow through a leaded window, a creature of sharp contrasts.

When one holds a butterfly up to the light, one is an alchemist changing matter, transforming solid to vapor with one movement of the hand, from tangible into breathable, from wing into air. Edward did not share my fascination, but the fascination itself seemed, at least at first, to intrigue him. We were introduced at our neighbors the Campbells', a house I had no reluctance in visiting since Mr. Campbell had his own obsession: a passion for all things African. Their drawing room was filled with exotica, objects collected by Mr. Campbell himself, who had spent time there as a colonial administrator near the Niger. In the right frame of mind, he could be persuaded to play his African thumb piano, a crude instrument, which produced an even cruder sound from cane "tongues" that resonated over a makeshift box. Edward had come down from Oxford with the Campbells' younger son, Victor, the young man my mother had in mind when she had tried to dress me that evening, but whose self-absorption and greasy eyelids and incessant talk of cricket left me cold. Mother and I had argued before I had left. I came down in my ruched olive-green silk, a fabric she insisted was impossible for me to wear, and the color of which she declared to be poisonous. I said that nothing could have pleased me more since I had dressed according to my mood and had not made my mind up to be bartered off just yet. She was insisting I go back up and change when Father entered, said we were already fashionably late, that any later would be insulting, that the marrying could wait for another night, and steered me out by the elbow.

On the night of Edward's visit, Mr. Campbell was in ebullient mood, in his clan tartan, and was entertaining the company with his rendition of "The Gypsy Laddie" on the thumb piano. The merriment was infectious, and as I sought Father across the room, my eyes fell instead on Edward's face, as he leaned gracefully against the back of a settee, his gray eyes looking directly at me. I turned to cover my confusion, but not before I noted his long lean limbs, the smile that played around his lips beneath a well-trimmed mustache. I lifted a strange little figure of black-painted wood from the mantelpiece and began to examine it minutely. Its eyes were chalked white and its bald head and body bristled with tiny pieces of hammered metal from its head to its knees. The song was ending. A voice at my elbow asked if I had an interest in African art, and I turned to find Edward, alarmingly close and not at all injured by my arsenic-green dress. His light hair was parted to the right, cut well above his ears, but when he bent to look at the object I held in my hand, I saw how it kinked and curled at the back of his neck, against his starched collar. I'd never before felt the urge to touch a man's throat, smooth an eyebrow with my thumb, breathe into the whorl of an ear.

"Ah, Miss McIntyre, you have found out my *nkisi,*" bellowed Mr. Campbell from across the room. "A fine specimen." He was coming toward us with that startled expression he always bore, as if he had only just discovered himself to be alive and was amazed at the concept. "The natives believe that the metal tokens will bring harm to those who wish harm upon them. It is a kind of primitive attempt at natural justice, you see. Rather crude, but fascinating, do not you think?"

I was trying to replace the figure. Every head in the room was turned toward us.

"Look closely, Mr. Ormond," he went on to Edward, taking the figure from my hand. "See the decoration on the feet and the eyebrows. Really quite detailed. An interesting piece. Of course, the natives believe it has other powers. It is used for swearing oaths, for example, and for ensuring that promises are kept." His old eyes twinkled; I am almost certain he winked. He leaned in: "Will we need it for that purpose here, do you think?" And off he went with a guffaw, leaving the two of us stranded.

Edward asked if he might call upon us when we were next in London, perhaps accompany us on a tour of the British Museum, where he believed there was an interesting collection of Egyptian and Assyrian artifacts. He may have mistaken my sudden excitement for something else. In 1880, the natural history room at the British Museum housed some of the oldest butterfly sets in the world: Sir Hans Sloane's famed collection, now almost two hundred years old; the rare Glanville fritillary; and at that time, it had just acquired a number of Bates's famed Amazonian specimens. Sixty-six species of butterfly are native to the British Isles, three hundred and twenty-one to Europe; within an hour's walk of the small Brazilian village where Bates spent eleven years of his life, he found seven hundred different species of butterfly.

It was on that visit that I decided to marry Edward. It is a day that will stay with me for the rest of my life.

When the fated morning arrived, Father (prompted, no doubt, by Mother) claimed pressing business matters and allowed

Edward and me to go unaccompanied. We walked through valleys of mahogany-doored cabinets, each one standing taller than Edward, each one holding dozens of drawered specimens, each one a box of unimagined treasures. For someone who has never excelled at French, or at drawing, or at piano or at needlework, to find an interest that helps one to feel talented, knowledgeable, informed, is to create an obsession. We stopped at Wallace's milkweeds, jewels of color, toxic and nontoxic females and males, greens and browns.

"What an astonishing color," Edward said.

"It is a message," I told him, "designed for potential predators. By choosing it, she means to say that she is unpalatable to taste."

"Is she? Unpalatable to taste?"

"I cannot tell; I am not an experienced collector. Some are and some are not. Bates has written about it. The butterfly may be mimicking a bad-tasting species of similar coloring in the hope that a predatory bird will know to avoid her."

He looked at me, clearly impressed. Then he said, "I do not think she tastes bad. I think she is bluffing."

"You can think what you like. It would take a brave jay to test the theory."

"I believe I would be willing to risk it," he said, and he wandered off down the row of cabinets, with a smile playing around his lips.

Julia never understood my interest. For all her proletarian rant she one day declared herself surprised that I should be so preoccupied with what was primarily a middle-class pursuit. "All that chasing and pinning and labeling," she said. "What is the point of it? I find them as pretty as does the next person, I like to see them flutter past, skit from flower to flower, yes, it lifts the heart even, but close up, gathering dust in a cabinet, with all their ugliness on show—I do not see the point of it."

I remember that I did not humor her with an answer.

What one sees of a butterfly in the meadow is a pretty blur, incomparable to what one sees in the cabinet. The colors, the markings, the scales on the wing, each one different, each one unique: the wonder of nature transfixed. To really appreciate the mastery of patterning and shading, the triumph of camouflaged loveliness that it is, that can only be done up close, when the wings are displayed open, when it has stopped altogether. It is a piece of earth made heaven-bound. To look at a butterfly is to remind us of what we are and of what we will be again. To some, the relation between the two seems impossible: the hard-headed grub and the delicate airborne beauty; that such random glamour should emerge from a creature that crawls on its belly seems ludicrous. They are honest insects, butterflies. They may get one's attention with spots and swirls, great flourishes of color, displays of dazzling brilliance. One does not have to look all that closely, however, to see how fragile that beauty is, how it is held together by the worm that it once was, and will be again.

There are collectors who claim that butterflies can taste with their feet, smell with their antennae, have ears on their wings, see using their reproductive parts. It is entertaining to talk this way, to describe the differences in behavior of insects or animals in human terms, to translate it using the only language we have. None of this makes any difference to a butterfly. It simply carries on doing what it has been doing for centuries, unobserved, unrecorded, uninterpreted. They are not apologists for themselves.

That day at the museum, I offered Edward my hand on parting. He took it in his, raised it to his mouth, brushed it with his lips. I prepared to draw away, say something fitting, thank him for his company. My mouth had already begun to form the words, but a small pressure, his thumb above my fingernail, made me hesitate, and then I felt it, a tooth on the knuckle of my ring finger. A shiver went up my spine. He bowed, let go of my hand and took his leave as if nothing had happened, and I stood there, gazing after him, in no doubt as to the covert messages he was sending out.

I began to see that marriage might not be a bind, but in fact a way to be free. Mother was more shocked than appeased by the proposal, but I remembered something she used to say: that there is a time for a girl to marry, and if she misses it, through indolence, or idleness, or inattention (Mother's words), then the chance is gone forever. I knew that Edward was my chance and that I might not get another. I had been counting time. Perhaps if I had seen him on another night, he would have made no impact; perhaps the change was all in me. I think I thought myself ready to marry. I had some vague idea of children: that they would come, one or two perhaps, that Edward would be pleased, that I would love them, naturally, that I would hand them over to a nurse, that they would thrive. I was not in any way prepared for the impact of them, for the exhaustion, the impingement on liberty, their number, their variety, their demands. I have been publicly declared to be an unfit mother and perhaps they are right; it would be easy if it were as simple as that. It would be a relief, in fact.

Have I been a good wife to him? Who can tell? I have produced heirs in abundance, far more than were required; I have managed the house and staff competently enough, if without enthusiasm, for I am not a homemaker. My interest does not lie in handiwork, in arranging ferns in fireplaces or scrapbook keeping, or, God spare me, devising means whereby drafts are to be kept from under doors. The indoors gives me headaches. I would far rather be off, galloping over the whins at Dunseverick, than sit over a piece of beading. Does that make me a bad wife? I think if I had been forced to stay indoors I would have been a worse one. Confinement does not suit me. Edward never wished to be troubled with domestic worries and I never brought any to him that I could resolve myself. I dare say other women in other homes deal differently with these matters. I can only do what I can do.

What I know now is that I have lost him, and it is not because of Charlotte, although her loss has made his irretrievable. I lost him years ago.

What was it Peig said to me that day when she came in the room and found me sewing, my back to the lamp? "You're in your own light, madam." I asked her to explain the strange expression. "You're in the way of yourself," she said, "working in your own shadow." My whole life spent in the way of myself: working in my own shade, not able to crawl out from underneath it, obliterating with my own being what I have been striving so hard to try to achieve.

Maddie

31 OCTOBER 1968

Anna, is everything all right? Are you sure, daughter? You'd tell me if there was anything amiss with the baby? Who was it you saw? Oh, Dr. Shaw is a saint. I'd trust him with my life. And he said it was all fine? Sit down now and rest yourself. Can I? Are you sure? But my hands are cold. Look at you, your belly as round and ripe as a plum and my old hand on it like a diseased branch. Oh, Anna, I can feel it, a little bursting bubble of life moving around inside you. God willing, I'll be spared to see your baby, lay my eyes and my hand on it for real. God bless you, Anna, and Conor and your child, and keep you safe always.

I saw Conor, when he brought the letter. Oh, he's a fine-looking fella, Anna, he is. And getting on great at the university, he tells me. Lecturer in education, isn't it wonderful? Owen would be that proud if he was here. And Peig. She'd be strutting about like a peacock at news the like of that. Sure, he'll be a professor in no time. Oh, he was always clever. And interested in all sorts of things. I remember him as a wee lad gathering seaweed on the big strand and able to tell me all the different kinds and their Latin names, and what was the word he said to me one day, and him only a young pup? "Algae." That was it. "Algae," if you don't mind!

Oh, sharp as a billhook, he was, like his father and his grandfather before him.

I was told by a fortune-teller I'd have a long life. Me and Bella went to her one day on the Parade for a joke. She had a wee wooden hut near the rocks, down by the Carrig-na-Cule, and a beaded curtain in the doorway. I always remember the sound of it when you walked through, the way the beads all knocked together, the way you felt like you were passing through a solid waterfall from one kind of living into another. It was dark inside; you could barely see her face under the old black shawl she wore. Dark lines ran from her ears to the corners of her mouth and she'd a voice like the whisper of a wave breaking. The whole place smelled salty and high from the seaweed that washed in and got trapped under the hut. Her hands were cold, I remember, and her nails were as thick and tough as horn. She told me I would never marry, for there was a lie in my life. Imagine telling that to a person, Anna. Not a mistake, or a regret, mind, but a lie. Is a lie always something you've said that's not the truth, or can it be something you've never said? Can a lie be a truth you've never told, not to anyone? Not in the confessional, and not in the witness box? Is it any defense to say you were never asked? I don't know, but I think there's a time for telling it all the same, and that time's not far off.

Well, she was right about the marrying, and the long life. Hallows' Eve today, Anna, the eve of All Saints. My first Hallows' Eve away from home, Peig baked charms into the apple cake and the barnbrack, and Madge got the ring and I got the thimble. I pretended not to care but I was annoyed. Peig teased me and said there was no danger of me being a spinster, not the way the boys looked at me, but I would never take the barnbrack on Hallows' Eve after that and it was right enough in the end, for Madge married a couple of years after, and I never did.

The mummers came, I remember that. The master and

mistress were out somewhere, and the mummers appeared and Madge let them in the yard door and on into the kitchen. Peig wasn't happy, but she said that since they were in, they might as well get the children down to watch the proceedings, and their eyes were like saucers. First came Rim Rhyme, with his hat all covered in ribbons and a sash and a sword, and then Prince George. The two of them fell to a sword fight that took them all round the table, with the weans squealing and Peig shouting at them not to knock down the coppers. Then the prince got an injury, so in came the doctor, in his tail coat and top hat, to sort him out, and he was a cheeky rascal and had made up some rhyme of his own that went, "I have in the waistband of my breeches a cure for anything that itches." Paudie gave a big snort out of him and gave Feeley a dig in the ribs, and Feeley was raging, so we can only guess what that was about. Then in came Slick Slack with the fiddle and the griddle, and Beelzebub with his face all blackened with ashes, and Joe the Butcher with a carving knife, and the Wren with his clothes all stuck over with turkey feathers, and last of all poor old Tom Fool with bells on his cap and a bladder on a stick that he gave all the other mummers a good whack with. Then up struck Slick Slack on the fiddle, and such a bit of leppin' and jumpin' as there was round the kitchen, legs and arms flying, weans and all, and up on top of the table Paudie put Charlotte and she laughed and danced the whole length of it till the music stopped and the porter came out and they all got supped. What a bit of entertainment we had that night. I didn't recognize any of their faces, the way they were all got up, but when the doctor started rhyming I knew his voice. I'd have known it anywhere: Peig's man, Alphie McGlinchy. And Charlotte knew him too, for he was her favorite among the men. She begged to stay up and hear the music. And when Slick Slack started up the fiddle, Alphie took my two hands in his and whirled me round the kitchen, round and round till the whole room swam.

We all gathered round the fire after that, when the children were put to bed, the men telling stories of meeting the dead, trying to scare the wits out of us. And Peig started to tell the story of oul' Molly that walked the roads. Everybody knew Molly. In the winter, when the sea got rough and the water came scooting up out of the blowhole at the harbor, and the gulls flew inshore laughing and wheeling about above the Parade, the people would take pity on her and take her in to save her from a cold bath in the workhouse. She had a great hand for spinning flax and wool and she got enough that way to keep her going. When oul' Molly was a girl, Peig said, she was full of spirits and up to all the rascalment of the day. She was courting a young fella, Seanie Hogan, and everyone said they'd be married, but an oul' widow man, a neighbor of her father's, had taken a wild notion of her, for she was a lovely girl, with a plait of yellow hair down her back, and he asked her father for a match. Of course, the widow man had a bit of land, and the father had his eye on it, and he tried to talk Molly into taking him, but Molly was having none of the shriveled oul' goat, as she called him, and she wouldn't humor them. Well, at the heel of the hunt, the oul' widow man died—James Thinaker was his name—and that looked like the end of it. The father was sore and said, "Didn't I tell you! You wouldn't have had to put up with him for more than one winter and there he is away and you could have been a rich widda and married who you liked!" But sure there was no point in talking any more about it then.

Anyway, Hallows' Eve came round, and all the young ones were up to their usual tricks and the girls went up to the standing stone and got up a game of the building of the house. They tied pairs of holly twigs together with pieces of hemp until they had twelve pairs around in a circle, and after a lot of giggling and getting on, they named the pairings after themselves and their sweethearts. Then Molly put down in the middle of the circle a glowing turf she'd taken from the fire, the idea being that whichever of the holly "couples" caught fire first, they would be the first to be married. And when that happened, the girl had to call out in the name of the devil for her future husband to come and put out the flames. So when it came to Molly's turn, she called out, believing, I suppose, that Seanie would appear. But who was it came out of the dark, only James Thinaker himself, still wrapped in his funeral shroud, and took Molly by the hand and led her away. The rest of the girls stood stock still, rooted to the ground in fear, and when they did manage to stir themselves, shrieking and crying, and went to look for her, they found her wandering around talking gibberish, not able to say where she'd been or what had happened to her but only that she was Molly Bradley no more. There's them that says that one of the boys followed them up to the stone to play a trick on them, that it was Phonsie Clarke dressed like a dead man that led her away by the hand and did what he did to her. But if it was, he never owned up to it, and it was no joke for Molly. The fright of it nearly killed her. A bit of fun is all right, said Peig, but you don't mess about with the devil or the dead; stay well away from games of that ilk on Hallows' Eve night. Then she went out to the pump and filled a bowl of spring water and set it down on the table for the thirsty souls and said, "Away to bed with you all now and get your sleep."

Who's to say whether that really happened or not? There was always a point behind those stories we were told. Dark warnings as to what could happen to a girl who didn't guard herself; keep your coat buttoned up tight; stay out of the dark of the hedges; don't talk to the tinkers, they'll turn your head; be wary of men. Staying warm tied in with staying safe without anyone ever saying anything outright. A kind of sorcery surrounded the business of what happened between men and women, a business that seemed very one-sided, that was all about what women must defend and men would steal given half a chance. It was meant to warn us off. It just made us more curious to know what it was all about.

Look at these hands now, Anna: parcels of skin and vein and bone. You can see where my life's mapped out on them. They're the oldest living things I know. But at twenty, at twenty they were soft and round. How can a person look at your hand when you're a slip of a girl and say that your life is already known? How can that be, Anna? Have our hands been here before?

How many of them have I outlived? The mistress, of course, and Charlotte. The master remarried after she died, moved to his father's old estate in England, but he was never right. I felt a pity of him. One day, you're Mr. Ormond, master of a household, justice of the peace; the next, you're the father of a dead child, husband to a killer. Everything around you is different and there's nothing anyone can do to turn it back.

He never took much to do with Florence, left her in Miss Julia's care. I think he was afraid of the damage she might do to his heart but it gave way in the end, all the same, about 1916 I think it was. Poor Harry was lost in the South African war, always the honorable one, like his father in that way. He can't have been more than twenty at the time. Thomas and James were both killed in the Great War. Gabriel died in the twenties, a stupid accident. He fell off the roof of a house at a party one night, down in Sligo or Mayo. He was always gadding about, that boy. Morris survived well into his sixties and died of TB, the same as your mother. He'd always had a weakness in his chest. Do you know, it's an odd thing to say, but I think of all of them Morris missed his mother the most. I think his mischief was a way of calling her to him, and it never failed, for she struck out at him more than at any of them. Freddie died of some childhood disease—he was buried in Scotland; George disappeared swimming one night at a beach in Italy and was never heard tell of again. Miss Julia moved back to Scotland when Florence married. I think she lasted the longest: she must have been in her seventies when she passed away. You were only a child at the time.

A morbid list, that one. Your mother never really knew her brothers, wasn't close to any of them; she was brought up separately, almost a different family. I looked after her till she was grown and when she married, she asked me to come with her and nanny her children. For a long time we thought there weren't going to be any. By the time you were born, I was nearly past minding weans, but Florence wanted me to stay with her. None of them but Florence had any offspring that I know of. That just leaves you, Anna, with a heavy burden of family to carry.

You used to love stories, do you remember? You used to beg me to tell them to you at bedtime. "Another one, Maddie," that's what you'd say. "Tell me the one about the swans." That was your favorite: "The Children of Lir." Do you remember? The terrible spell that Aoife put on her stepchildren, that turned the four of them into swans. I think you liked the sad stories best of all, but you'd hear anything to put off the dark. You'll need those stories now; you'll be telling them yourself to the wee one. That's what we do: tell made-up stories to fend off the night, to put off telling the truth.

Harriet

Grangegorman Prison, Dublin

Monday 11 July 1892

My child is born. A girl, again. She came easy into the world, did not utter a cry until the midwife slapped her hard on the behind. She is a placid infant with dark wiry curls and a sweet bow for a mouth. She does not seem to object to her surroundings, is no more perturbed by the iron bedstead and grilled windows than are the other infants here. In any case, she will not have the opportunity to accustom herself to these sights. She has brought a visit from Edward.

He is thinner. Little wonder at that. We stood several feet apart, separated on my side by iron railings, on his by a square of wire gauze, and with a warder in the corridor between us. The pauses between our attempts at communication were filled by the shouts of other prisoners and their visitors. Nothing less intimate could be imagined.

"How are you, Harriet?" he tried.

"I am well, Edward. We have a daughter."

His eyes, at that distance, were black, his face pale and strangely blurred behind the wire netting. He nodded across at me.

"Good news," he said, with a catch in his voice. "She is healthy?"

"Over nine pounds in weight."

He managed a smile, and then a thought occurred. "Has she been christened?"

"Almost immediately she was born. The chaplain happened to be visiting."

"What name have you given her?" As soon as he said it, I saw him brace himself against the uttering of the one name neither of us could bear to hear.

"Florence," I told him, and he smiled again, relieved.

"Like the city," he said, and I nodded.

"Like the city."

There was a pause while we both considered this. Then Edward shouted, "I have found a wet nurse, a quiet girl, from the Salvationists here in Dublin. We will travel back together."

I tried a smile. "Look after her," I said.

"Yes," he said, and the warder shouted, "All back," and Edward raised a hand in farewell.

What will she remember of me? Can the body carry memory before the mind? Will she know by this touch and this smell that she is mine? Will she know how to mother, not having been taught?

When Charlotte was born, Dr. Creith suggested that I should try nursing her myself. He hinted that nursing was widely believed to reduce family size. Perhaps he thought we had been holding out for a girl. I declined to follow his gentle advice; I had no wish to be further confined by the demands of a feeding infant. Yet when this little scrap was born, quiet and gentle, in a chloroform haze, and they laid her on my breast in the bare prison hospital ward, and she turned her tiny mouth toward me, I did nothing to stop the nurse who unbuttoned my nightgown and put her to my breast. Love is like water, it gets through regardless, and a bricked-up heart is no defense against it. There is a nursery here where prisoners are permitted to keep their babies, up to the age of two. Florence is three days old and they are taking her away from me. Night and day, I hear babies crying.

The wall is dark today: "the black stone wall" in which there is not a single black stone to be seen. Gray like the sea from Harbor Hill; rusty brown; pale mortar; bird droppings. The stones are arranged in strata, layer upon layer, one above the other, and the more I look at it, the less it seems like a recent structure built up out of the ground, and the more it looks like something ancient that has been unearthed, laid down centuries before and only now brought back to light by the archaeologist's brush. I can picture him, the serious explorer, safari clad, brushing gently at the soil; his excitement as a ridge of wall emerges, a chimney, roof tiles, eaves, then guttering, lintels, casements and sills all revealed intact. A delight: a dolls' house, for his entertainment. How excited he must be when he finds it peopled! I feel like I have been here for decades, and only now am dug up, exposed to the light.

The wall is the height of five men. There is a jagged crack that runs like the path of a thunderbolt down its height and disappears, all energy dissipated, before it reaches the ground. My square of view is cloud soiled, the palest of grays, moving across, or rather away from, the window. It feels like the sky is receding, and I traveling away from it, like a passenger on the last train carriage, looking back down the railway line at a scene that is disappearing.

The occupant of the cell next to mine is the woman accused of being a Fenian. I hear the priest go in to her. I hear her voice, steady, and then his, low and quiet; I think he is hearing her confession, which is, of course, forbidden, if she is still a member of a secret society. I have watched her trudge the circle in the yard, eyes down, lips moving, fingers keeping count, and she could be one of Edward's poorer tenants walking round the wellhead, counting off the decades of the rosary. For her, prayer is a ladder that leads up and out and away from here. She is here and not here, brought back to herself only by the jangle of the warder's keys. Escape is entirely within her means.

I wonder is there a special place in hell for the killers of children? I am shocked to know suddenly that I do not believe in the hereafter. I suppose I must have believed in it at a time, and I cannot point to the moment when that belief abandoned me, but there is the truth of it now. I have no faith. How can there exist a heaven or a hell when life is as chance as two bodies that fit together in the dark, when death is as arbitrary as a mislaid key? We all go to nothing.

There was a January morning on the point above the Herring Pond, looking back toward the village, the rainbow gone, the sun above the castle deadened by mist, blackened battlements daguerreotyped against a white sky. The strand beyond, and the hills and dunes devoid of color, shades of black, and white, and gray: a charcoal drawing. The sea glittered, a heaving expanse of flint and spray. Where I sat, mounted on Caesar above the harbor, the color bled back into things, the grass, green, swaying, bending away from me. Ahead of me, on the path, the sky puddled in a little sea. When the rain finally came in, in fine glittering drops, it was as if the sun had shaken itself out. And the sea was a blanket over a sleeping child, all that energy dormant: the power to jump and shriek and cry and throw and pick paper off the walls and overturn bowls and spill and soil and emit life and elicit love, asleep.

We are, at any given time, only a heartbeat away from chaos, a horde of outcasts ruled over by a handful of senseless warders. What makes us behave as we do? What forces us to get up and dress and eat and walk about and nod to one another as if anything has any meaning? I am a stranger here, an interloper. I have learned the language; I know the new names for things. I alter my markings in order to blend in. The others seem prepared to accept the artifice and now that I have played this part for so long (how long is it now? Weeks? It feels like years) I have to remind myself that it *is* a part. It takes a certain energy to do this. I am in danger of forgetting who I am. I am free only inside my own head, and in this little book.

The arrogance of the living and the free is near palpable. They saunter around, behave as if they are immune to pain and weakness, forget it as soon as it is passed. That is what it is like with childbirth. It is more than one ever thought one could bear, and yet the memory of it fades, until the next time the pains grab at the stomach and it all comes flooding back, too late.

I was a clumsy child, bony and angular, embarrassed by the space I took up. I recall my mother wincing at my overtight, elbowed efforts to show affection. I did not persevere for long. That pained attempt of hers at a half-smile was discouragement enough. Once I saw her rub her upper arm as though I had bruised her. Around her, I felt obscenely well. I felt my robust health to be an affront to her every time she looked at me. Yet she was always glad of Julia's light step. I never seemed able to make myself silent enough. I knocked into furniture; objects put themselves in my way. One day when she had one of her headaches, I sat for hours in her darkened room reading under a low lamp while she slept, not once uttering a word. At last, Julia glided in, placed her hand on Mother's brow, and without opening her eyes Mother sighed and said, "Ah, Julia, you have the touch of an angel." I sat still, holding my breath, not moving. Mother turned her head the slightest fraction toward me, the sleeve of her day dress draped over the back of the divan, linen lawn, blue and white, trimmed at the wrist in satin and lace. I can still see her small hand, encased in a satin glove that failed to disguise the swollen knuckles, the witch deformities. She said: "Harriet, ask Lily to bring up some tea." For hours I had sat there, listening to the house move around me, believing I had made myself disappear, and all the time she had been aware of me. One touch from Julia and she was well again.

"Only criminals and lunatics and women are without the vote," says Julia. I begin to fear that I fall into all three categories. I look around me now, at the disenfranchised. The Fenian woman has begun a hunger strike. Not much of a hardship, considering the fare on offer. That's one way to end, I suppose—in a protest. It would not be my choice.

We drink from tin cups that we do not keep in our cells. They are taken away each evening and returned the following morning containing a slick of what passes for cocoa, along with a crust of stale bread. If one looks inside when they are emptied, it is sometimes possible to make out a message that has been crudely scratched on the base, using a nail or a piece of copper wire. Since the writer can have no control over the direction of her message, these missives are unspecific. Once I thought I made out "Take heart," another time, "All pain ends." Today I read, "She is quiet now." When the warder came to collect my utensils, she looked inside and left without uttering a word. There is a sound in me that is stuck in my throat, that will never be heard.

Maddie

13 NOVEMBER 1968

They don't do it anymore—name a newborn child after a child that's been lost. Anna Charlotte. Do you ever use your second name? Your mother, Florence, was born in Grangegorman Prison, five months after Charlotte died. They sent her home to the castle when she was just a few days old with Bella, the wet nurse the master had found for her in Dublin. By then all the other youngsters had gone, Freddie and George, the two youngest boys, to a convent in Bognar, the older boys back to the Jesuits at Stonyhurst, Gabriel and Morris along with them, sent early to school. They went straight from Dublin, after the trial. The governess, Mademoiselle High-and-Mighty, hightailed it back to France, and Miss Julia went back to the castle to manage the house and help look after Florence.

Bella was a quiet girl, a Salvationist, with a story of her own. I asked her what it meant to be a Salvationist and she said it meant they had been good to her when she hadn't a friend in the world. They'd taken her in when all others turned their backs on her and she would never turn her back on them, not till her dying day. She used to sing hymns to Florence, airs I'd never heard before with strange names, "Calvary's Fountain" and "Sins of Years," and when she sang, her voice was like a place where you would want to go and live. Lucky Florence, growing up with that sound in her ears, and not the ring of the mistress's voice.

Your mother was a bonny baby, placid and content. After she was weaned, I had the care of her for most of the day, me and Miss Julia. Every little thing I hadn't been able to do for Charlotte I did for her. She was like my own. We weren't allowed to talk about the mistress, or about what had happened. To hear the family, you'd have thought she'd gone to the continent for a few months to take the air. But you can't make a thing vanish just by not talking about it. The mistress came back once—Florence was about a year old at the time—and when I saw her again she looked almost the same. Her hair was as black as boot polish, short under her cap; the same broad forehead and pointed chin. She was thinner, I think. You could see her cheekbones sharp against her face. If anything, she was more handsome than she was before. She must have been about thirty-two or -three then, I suppose. Peig used to say she had the mouth of a tyrant, the eyes of an angel. But after she came back, her eyes were different, pools as dark as the water round the Black Rock. The first thing she did, she ordered Feeley to get her horse ready, and rode out by herself, across the gardens and down toward the Big Strand. And the baby waiting in the nursery to see her mother.

She didn't stay long. I remember her fussing about the butterfly cabinet, giving instructions that it wasn't to be touched. She had it covered in a dust sheet and none of us ever went near it. It must have been that time she put the book there, for she never set foot in the house again. She and the master went to Switzerland, and some time after, the word came back that she was dead. A fall from her horse was what we heard. Her skirt caught in the saddle and the horse dragged her for miles. She never spoke again. She was buried in Scotland with her own people. But since we're in the business of telling the truth, Anna,

I'll tell you this. Feeley said she was the best horsewoman in the country, and no horse that he knew of would dare to throw her off if she didn't want to be thrown. I suppose it's something to have a choice of death; it's not everyone has that. Charlotte didn't.

Do you know, Anna, my mother could untangle any thread or rope, no matter how knotted it was? People used to bring them to her and she'd sit, picking away at it, looking as if it was getting more and more tangled by the minute, until there'd be a sudden loosening, and you could see how it would all begin to come apart. Every Sunday I left her to go back to the castle, the same thing: a dead cinder from the hearth in one pocket, a slip of mountain ash in the other. Until the night she gave me something else.

Reach out there, Anna, will you, and open that drawer in the butterfly cabinet. Do you see something glittering there? This night when I was preparing to go, she looked at me strangely and then she unpinned this from her throat, the turquoise brooch Daddy had given her, and she fixed it onto my apron. She said, "You'll be a woman before you know it, Maddie. That pin is real steel, it'll keep you from harm. Keep that color on you always." And I walked back up the hill, with the air so close and still you could hear the train rattle and whistle on the far side of the river and follow it in your mind, echoing through the tunnel at Downhill, on its way to Derry, with Mussenden trembling on the cliff above it. I thought about what she'd said, and about Peig's stories of warning, and about what Mammy used to say to me when I was a child. She used to say I was got in a jenny wren's nest. Then one day when she said it, and I said I wasn't, she said, "Where did you come from, then?" and I realized—I was only seven or eight at the time—that I didn't know, I hadn't thought about it. It hadn't occurred to me there'd been a time when I wasn't in the world. But I wouldn't give in, and I said, "The same place as everyone else," and she laughed and laughed. But it set me wondering. We never had that conversation, Mammy and me:

the one where you find out about where babies come from. I sort of pieced it all together myself, from stories the other youngsters whispered at school, and from one time I watched the sow pig, and from the odd fumble with the boys up at the ferns on the Green Hill, where we went after school some days when the weather was good. And the rest I learned from Madge and Cait up at the castle. I knew enough to know better, that's the point. That's what Mammy must have seen. Here, Anna, I want you to have this, it's for you, and the baby. To keep you both safe. I must seem like a rambling old woman to you, with nothing to say worth hearing. But I'm getting to it. I can't come at it cold. I'm warming my hands over old stories.

I was fifteen; Charlotte was four years old, Peig and Alphie only about six months married. This particular morning, there was no drying. I knew by the way the fire was burning high, there was frost. The milk, frozen in the larder, an odd watery color, not like milk at all. I had to break it with the ice pick and heat it in big chunks on the range, stir it till the lumps melted into creamy white. By then the frost had lifted, but the mist had left everything damp to the touch. The sun, a day-moon, high in the sky, strange to look on, and the fog boiling up over the dunes at Castlerock, wiping out the sea curve, rolling past the house faster than the tram.

Laundry day: I was heart-scared of washing the mistress's things in case I would do something wrong. There was so much to learn: soda in the water to stop mauves and violets from running; vinegar for dark green; salt for blue; pepper to protect cambric; ivy leaves for rinsing prints. There's none of that bother now: everything gets thrown into the machine together and comes out as good as new. But in those days the dyes weren't fixed; you had to be very careful. The mistress was awful fussy and she'd a shocking sharp tongue in her head, and I'd no desire to hear it.

Peig insisted on the sheets going out, frost or no frost. They'd come in, stiff as boards that evening, and steam in the laundry all through the night. "At least they'll have had a breath of air on them," said Peig, and sent me out with the basket. I was at the line, half-frozen, arms stretched up to drape the wet linen, a cobweb in my face, and I heard a footfall behind me. I didn't turn, didn't lower my arms; I knew it was Alphie. A misted breath came over my shoulder, carrying the sweet smell of his tobacco. A finger touched the nape of my neck and began, slowly, to trace the line of my spine, through my shawl and my dress, the whole way down my back. I stood completely still, hardly daring to breathe, with the pain of the cold in my wet hands, still holding the sheet. Then another footstep, and he was gone, and I was left. I was still there when the mist lifted, and there was Castlerock again, the little white houses, the church, unharmed, as if nothing had happened.

Another day I was standing under the archway to the yard. I'd come out with the ashes and, because it was winter, and early, there were still stars in the sky, and I'd stopped on my way to the dump under the wet laurels. I was looking up at the North Star, which I know from its brightness, when Alphie's voice beside me said, "Old light." I turned and looked at him and he said that the light I could see was not the star shining that morning but what it looked like when it shone hundreds of years before and that that star might already be dead. He raised his arm and his sleeve crept up and there was a tiny heart tattooed in Indian ink on the inside of his wrist. He said that the starlight I could see could be as old as Dunluce Castle. I looked at him and I told him he talked the biggest load of nonsense I'd ever heard, and he smiled at me and my heart turned over. Then he walked away, up the yard, swinging the oil lamp in the dark, with the light trailing behind him, like the tail of a comet.

Christmas Eve, I'd washed my hair as always because Mammy said if you washed your hair on Christmas Eve you'd never take a headache in the year, and it was hanging loose, drying on my shoulders. We were all doing the Black Fast and our bellies were rumbling the whole way through our work. I was helping Peig to clean the kitchen before the prayers, and the men were nearly all out in the yard and stables, doing a bit of tidying up for the holy day. My hair's not much to look at now, Anna, but it was a different matter then. I don't know if that's what Alphie saw when he stepped in the door, straw and hay sticking out of his *geansaí*. But whatever it was, it stopped him in his tracks and he looked at me like he was seeing me for the first time.

I don't blame anyone, Anna. I wasn't much more than a child, that's true. I didn't know what would happen, but I was curious to find out, and I couldn't, no matter what I tried, stay out of Alphie's way. Collecting eggs in the barn, he was in the doorway. He stepped aside to let me pass but it was me who stopped beside him, the warm eggs wrapped in my apron, he who leaned across and kissed me gently on the lips, me who walked on, shivering, into the kitchen.

Madge teased me and said I must have a boy on the go, for I couldn't carry the milk in without spilling it and the spuds were only half-scraped when I dropped them in the pot. Paudie told her to whisht and not judge everyone the same as herself. But I couldn't stop thinking about him: the way he looked at me, the things he said. It was harmless enough, I told myself; I hadn't done anything wrong. There was no harm in smiling back at him, no harm in imagining his fingers on my spine, no harm in remembering his lips brushing against mine. No harm at all. But at night, in my little bed in the attic, I dreamed of stretching out beside him, skin against skin, his hands in my hair, my legs wrapped around him, and I didn't want to wake up from that. I wanted that to happen.

Harriet

Grangegorman Prison, Dublin

Wednesday 17 August 1892

Edward writes to say that the *Buddleia davidii* I planted next to the wall is in full bloom and is already doing its astonishing work. "Yesterday," he writes, "I spotted a small tortoiseshell, a peacock and a red admiral. I wish you were here to see it." My darling Edward, how he makes my heart ache. He cannot tell one butterfly from another but he has found out their names to lift my heart. He tells me the outcome of the election: Gladstone is back in, but only just, and only with the help of the Irish Parliamentary Party. And, he adds, Mr. Morell, staunch anti–Home Ruler, my erstwhile prosecutor, queen's counsel at the Four Courts on the day of my trial, Mr. Morell has won a seat for the Unionists and Dublin University.

I was thinking today of the day Morris ran away, three-quarters of a ragged moon hanging over the castle from noon. We searched for him for hours, calling through the house and the gardens until our throats were raw, and every minute that passed, the moon climbed higher and the sun sank lower in the sky. At four o'clock, the milk cart came with him, a sorry sight, his cap perched on the side of his unruly red hair. They had picked him up on the road to Coleraine and, not knowing to whom he belonged, took him into the village, where he was recognized by Dan Faulkner. That was another black mark against me, of course. And Grocer Faulkner was only too glad to testify, at the readjournment in the courthouse in Coleraine, to the boy's alleged mistreatment and neglect. Faulkner with his hooded eyes and the neck hair that bristles up over his collar. He puts me in mind of an oversized moth, the gray dagger, in tailored clothes. He was still smarting from the dispute over his right of way that he imagined ran across the bottom of Edward's field of turnips but that, actually, ran nowhere at all, except in his imagination. If I had been permitted to speak, in the place of my buffoon of a lawyer, I would have asked the jury this. Was there *ever* a boy who has been reprimanded by his mother or father, and has said that the punishment was just? Insufferable interference.

At the readjournment Mr. Crankshaft made a valiant last-minute attempt to have me acquitted. "Scandalous rumors have been put in print," he said. Everything had been done in the power of the press to hold me up to contumely and odium. My case, he attested, had been "seriously prejudiced in the eyes of the public." He proclaimed me to be a person of the utmost candor who had done nothing to conceal the happenings of that fatal day. I thought I traced a note of regret in his voice; I almost felt that he wished for a more amenable client, one whose statement had been less concise and detailed, one whose recorded words had betrayed more confusion and distress. I am not sure that the public would have thought differently about me had the press championed my cause. Mr. Crankshaft might as well have saved his breath. The bench took no time at all to return the case for trial to the assizes with two of Edward's fellow justices of the peace (one of whom, Mr. Gregory, had sat on the jury at the inquest) acting as bailsmen for me. As it happens, there was worse to come. The crown had brought a further charge against me under the Act for the Prevention of Cruelty to Children, about which Mr. Crankshaft appeared to have no previous knowledge, and off we went again, Mr. Crankshaft appealing to the bench not to proceed, on the grounds that a hearing would prejudice the case that had already been returned to trial. Mr. Crankshaft was once again duly ignored and the case was heard.

Faulkner was not alone among my detractors. There was no shortage of disgruntled former servants, only too delighted to have their fares paid back from Dublin or Liverpool, or indeed Kidderminster, for their moment of celebrity, to testify to my unmotherliness. Interesting that, how they assembled them all so quickly. It would seem that the Cruelty Society was already preparing a case against me, before Charlotte's death.

It took me weeks to negotiate the warren of passages and entrances in the servants' quarters at Oranmore. Down there, there was a palpable sense of machinery. It was all winches and wheels, as if we above were the figures one sees on those strange German clocks: automatons kept moving by the machinations from below—hidden revolutions underfoot. As I listened to them in the courthouse in Coleraine, powerless to defend myself, I began to feel the noose tighten about my neck. The list of witnesses for the crown I could have drawn up myself: Susan Barry, who, when she was dismissed for stealing five shillings, swore she would make money out of me yet. Madge Adams, insipid lazy child, whom I suspect of philandering with the footman. Cait Jones, who spoke to the crown about the children's swollen hands and feet, and pieces out of their toes "as if they had been cut." One would think the girl had never seen chilblains. I warned the children not to put their cold feet directly onto the hot water bottles, but of course I was ignored in this as in other things. At least Maddie, insolent as she is, and Peig and Elise, the governess, stood firm. If not exactly glowing in their terms, they spoke no lies. And Mr. Walsh, the ornithologist (he of the gannet tales), sat on the bench and dissented from his fellow justices. He hinted at prejudice on the part of the witnesses and objected to the charge of cruelty on the excellent grounds that if everyone's discharged servants were to be called to give evidence, "if all the little details of our own households" were to be brought to light, we might none of us come out of it well. Indeed we might not. Fortunately for them, and unfortunately for me, my household was the only one under scrutiny.

There is one incident that stays in my mind. I had been out in the yard with Feeley, breaking in the two-year-old. She was softening up nicely. I entered the house through the front. A tinkle of crystal, a silvery sound, coming from the dining room as I passed through the hall in my riding habit. I dropped the lunge whip into the umbrella stand, imagined a breeze passing through the opened windows. Then the sound again, louder, more savage, and another sound, a whoop, a stifled shout. I turned at the bottom of the stairs, put my hand on the doorknob and walked in. Gabriel and Morris, dressed in the naval costumes they had worn for the Christmas party, with a rope each and a loop on the end, were taking it in turns to lasso the Venetian chandelier, which was swinging wildly across the room from window to door, plaster dust falling gently from the ceiling rose as the great screws in the floor above loosened with every movement. It had taken me months to find it, almost a year of correspondence with Sibthorpe's before they secured exactly what I wanted, and now it looked as if I might have to watch it shatter to the floor, all twelve arms of it, over a hundred pieces of delicate Italian crystal. They both stopped, red faced, sweating, one blond, one redhead, arms raised, frozen to the spot. I yelled for Feeley, who ran into the room and then stopped, eyes fixed on the swinging chandelier.

"Get help!" I shouted. "Bring something! A quilt or—anything!"

He came back with two of the stable boys and the winter

cover for the carriage. Together they dragged away the dining table, stretched out the canvas between them and positioned themselves under the chandelier. All of us stood, mesmerized, watching as the great flower of crystal slowly came to a stop and hung glittering in the room above all our heads. The carpets and floorboards in the room above had to be lifted in order to tighten the great bolts back into place, the work of the stables and yard halted for half a day over the act of two thoughtless little boys.

It must have been that day Maddie was describing when she told the court how she had witnessed me drag Gabriel up the stairs by his heels. I looked across at her in the courtroom, at her white face and her shaking hands: she looked like she was the one under sentence; she would not meet my eye. It turns out I was right to suspect her: she told Morell it was she who had written to the Cruelty Society and brought that nasty little man to the door. I do not remember the incident with Gabriel all that clearly. I know that when the chandelier finally completed its terrifying arc, I commanded the two boys out of the room. I know I lifted my riding crop out of the umbrella stand. I know I put Morris in the library and told him not to move until I returned. I know I got Gabriel up the stairs somehow, that he resisted because he knew what was to come, that I threatened him with the crop and put him in the wardrobe room, from which I could hear him crying, "I am sorry, Mama," over and over again. I know that I went away and left him then and that I had no energy for Morris, so I had Feeley take him outside and tie him to the horse chestnut (not securely, as it turned out), so that everyone who passed would know of his misbehavior. Why did he run away? What did he hope to gain from that? I almost think he wishes to provoke my anger. He allows me to catch him at misbehavior he knows will attract punishment. Why does he bait me so? I caught his look as I left him in the library to drag Gabriel up the stairs and it was not a look of repentance or even of fear at what was to come. He appeared upset at being abandoned, envious of the attention that I was about to bestow on his brother.

How are they ever to learn the effects of their thoughtlessness, if not by punishment? They value nothing—not their clothes or their toys or their warm beds or their freedom. They are robbers of time, demanding and unthankful. They must be taught to appreciate what they have. God only knows if any of this will have any beneficial effect. It is just as likely that they will go from being careless children to being careless adults, imprudent with their time and with that of those around them.

I wonder if Edward has stopped loving me. There are aspects of the management of the children over which we do not agree, but since he does not wish to be troubled with domestic matters, he acquiesces, for the most part, to leave them to me. After Morris freed himself, however, was lost and then found again, Edward came in to me in the morning room, where I was bent over the sateen lining of my riding jacket, trying to mend a tear in the seam where I had raised my arm too high. It was not something I could leave to the servants: their work was acceptable when it came to joining the sheets or mending a hole in the linen, but this was from Redfern's, mohair trimmed, and a clumsy hand could have made the injury worse. Edward sat down opposite, picked up a copy of the *Contemporary Review*. The low winter sun stretched a finger in through the window, killing the fire in the grate.

"I have been speaking with Morris," he said from behind his magazine.

"Then you know what he was doing to the chandelier," I answered, without lifting my head from my sewing.

"You had him tied to a tree?"

"Indeed. I could have done more but by the time I had finished with Gabriel I had no energy left."

"Do not you think you have been a little harsh, Harriet? I know they can be trying, but it is high spirits for the most part; it is not done to torment you. When they are absorbed in a game it is as if they are in another world; they do not see the consequences."

"Exactly," I replied. "They do not think. They never think. They show no appreciation for the time and trouble of other people. They have no respect for what others hold dear to them. They are pests and nuisances; every one."

I heard the paper rustle as he lowered it. "Don't you remember what it was like to be a child, Harriet? To lose yourself in an imaginary world? A princess fleeing from a dragon, a—"

"No, Edward," I said. "I never forgot for a moment who I was, what my duties were, where my responsibilities lay. And that is the difficulty with them. You fill their heads full of nonsense about battles and wars and monsters until they believe the entire world is a circus, that the adults around them are characters in the drama and that every object they come across has been placed there to be used by them as a plaything. They must learn that life is not a playground." I looked up at him. "It is our duty to raise them with sense, not to produce savages."

He was quiet, looking straight at me with a strange expression on his face. Not affection, certainly, and not interest, but I think, possibly, pity.

"I did not raise my hand to either of them," I said. He got up, closed the magazine, dropped it on the console and walked out of the room without another word. I do not think things were ever the same between us again.

It is a kindness to teach them as soon as is possible that they cannot always do as they would, without regard for others. It is for their own safety and their own self-preservation. There is too much talk these days of leniency and compassion. Had I not learned as a child to armor myself against the world, I would never have found the strength to endure this place, now. I do not know what my parents saw in me to distrust. I used to think it was a hardness that repelled them, but now I think that what they felt toward me was fear. I was not the child they had expected; Julia must have been that for them. She was perfectly happy to be preened and paraded in ribbons and bows, to sit for hours learning a piece at the piano, to sketch hills and fields and cottages, to while away hours in an imaginary world with her dolls. I could not be held by such activities; I preferred the world at firsthand. I wanted always to be out, galloping over the hedges, rolling down dunes. I craved air, always. But that was unseemly, more so as I grew older. It was impressed upon me that I must learn to behave as a young lady.

I remember clearly being fitted for my first corset. Elsa, the maid, stood behind me, my mother in front. Elsa slipped the straps over my shoulders, wrapped the boned casing round my middle and drew the stays tight according to Mother's instructions. I was seven years old. I knew it was an important moment. The stays were uncomfortable; my breathing grew more shallow as Elsa pulled them tighter. I found it hard to believe that I was expected to wear this garment every day from that day forward. After we were married, and I grew large with Harry, I left the instrument of torture aside and never wore one again.

Raising children demands a certain kind of mental energy. Not the energy that is needed to cross a field at a gallop or scale a hedge. I would far rather break a yearling than go head-to-head with Morris or Gabriel when either one of them throws back his head. One needs to be on top of everything: brush your teeth; wash your hands; say your prayers; do your lessons; comb your hair; button your shirt. I am sick at the sound of my own voice repeating the same instruction over and over. "A gentle tap about the hocks is usually sufficient," Lord Ormond would say, "that will help them toward the correct way of going." If only it were that simple.

I have been dutiful, I believe, taken most of my meals with the children, not left them to the care of servants. In this respect,

I am unusual among my peers, but I have wanted, always, to be available to the children and to do what was correct. I brought them into the world; they are my responsibility. If their behavior is not what it should be, I have no one else to blame. There were days, though, when the burden of what that entailed weighed on me like a blanket, and I felt like I would never get through. I will never, I thought, have them all bathed and dressed and down to breakfast by eight, and in the schoolroom by nine; I will never see that they have had their walk by luncheon; I will never manage to round them up again for tea at four; I will never have them ready for bed and their prayers said by six. I was always underneath, looking up, straining under the weight of it. My days were gated and barred, like the shadows the stair railings make on the wall when the sunlight pushes its way through the glass at the front entrance. Through it all I must make it look easy, as if no effort were required, and speak to Peig about what can be salvaged from dinner for luncheon and see that the housemaids have seen to the fires and the beds and not bother Edward with trifles. Then it takes only one interruption to upset the most fragile routine: the butcher has not come, or the milk has turned, or Morris has a cough, or fleas have been discovered, and there is no way to recover from any setback because no contingency has been allowed. I watched with relief as Harry and then Thomas and James were sent off to school, regretted only that the others were too young to go.

They have never been required to tend to me. I have asked nothing of them. The balance has been exactly as it should have been. Julia is free to be the indulgent aunt if she so wishes—except in the matter of discipline, in which she has no business to interfere. She doted on Charlotte, of course, invested wholesale in the frills and curls, insisted on quilling a lace bonnet for her herself, bought her that ridiculous dolls' house. I have never understood this fashion for the miniature—why must a thing be declared "delightful" by virtue of its having been made smaller? A ewer, a chair, a tablecloth, ordinarily they attract little interest, but produce one that has been shrunken, and it will have ladies and maids alike in salons and kitchens throughout the country swooning over its detailed execution. I see no point in it. A doll cannot mount a horse, pour tea, arrange flowers—why pretend otherwise? Why bother to surround it in tiny pieces of china, equipment for grooming "so like the real thing," when it is all for show and no function at all?

I expressed my sentiments on the matter to Julia. "Your failure, Harriet, is a failure of the imagination," she said to me. "You see only what is before your eyes and not what is behind the eyes of others." I take it she meant it as an insult, but no offense was taken on my part. She reminded me of Maddie, that day on the beach when Charlotte refused to enter the water. "You want to see what she can see," she said. As if I could not. What is it that makes them believe that their vision is superior to mine?

Julia's nonsensical pursuits include tile painting, sewing unusable pincushions for every new birth that is announced and, surely most inane, flower pot drapery that she contributes to charity bazaars. She is always engaged in a project. For a while, the summer after Charlotte was born she and her friends took to sketching. I could often see them from the castle, perched on Harbor Hill among the whins, taking in the long curve of the Parade, the Drontheims in the harbor below them; the laundry drying on the rocks; St. John the Baptist's church spire at the other end; the tram toiling along, past the cast-iron railings and balconies of the shops and houses and the hotel in between. She would come back with an armful of oxeye daisies and wander the house, thrusting them behind pictures and over doorjambs, where they would fill the rooms with flies and then wilt and droop until eventually the servants yanked them out. She salvaged the neglected wardian case from the hall, emptied it of its sad-looking ferns and orchestrated a dyed seaweed display. If that is evidence of the imagination being employed then I will do well without one. Although it had the advantage of keeping her out from under my feet.

She and Charlotte would spend hours with their heads together, drawing and decorating. Julia taught her how to draw around her hand, in and out around her small fingers, and then to decorate the sketch with sennaed and sequined tattoos: robins and hearts and roses. They plundered the sewing box for bright scraps of fabric and colored thread, discarded ribbons, lace collars, buttons and bows. They are everywhere in the nursery, those elaborate appliquéd drawings, rings on every finger, jeweled bracelets dangling from disembodied wrists, the imprint of Charlotte's small hand.

After the day of the chandelier, I perfected a kind of self-willed absence: a distracted attendance that allows me to be both present and unavailable at the same time. The children, with their sixth sense, have come to recognize it quickly, have walked straight past me to ask Elise for a book or a slate that was right by my hand. Soon, I think, they will be able to walk through me. I will not exist for any of them. I will be the ghost of their mother, recognizable in outline but not in substance, the insubstantial remnant of something that once was.

I will not see Charlotte grown. What kind of woman would she have made, I wonder.

Maddie

29 NOVEMBER 1968

Did you pass the fishermen at the harbor, Anna? Did you come that way? I love a bit of fish on a Friday. I can see them from here, the boats pulled in, jostling against each other and the seagulls wheeling about above their heads, swooping for anything they can get, and the stalls all laid out with the catch. The master was particular about his salmon: he didn't like to wait until the cart came, when the whole catch, he said, had been picked over. He used to send Peig down as soon as the boats came in to get the pick of them.

This particular day, when Peig had gone down to the harbor, the mistress sent down word that she wanted a seawater bath. The copper cans were kept just inside the cellar door, off a dark passageway to the other side of the lamp room. They weren't heavy when they were empty, but they were awkward to maneuver in that tight space and it took two people to carry them out, one at either handle. I was in the scullery, scrubbing the earth off the spuds, when Alphie came in.

"Can you help me with the cans?" he said, and his voice was the same deep lilt that it always was, and no one that heard or saw him would have raised an eyebrow at him asking that, but I knew as I dried my hands on my apron and walked through the kitchen and out down the passageway, I knew what I was going to and I couldn't have been stopped.

The passage was well enough lit as far as the lamp room, for there the windows on the right looked out onto the yard, but there was only one window in the cellar itself and it looked onto the passageway, so it was dim in there, even on the brightest of days. I turned the handle of the cellar door and walked in, and then I turned round to face him. We stood there looking at one another in the dim light. I could hear the water gurgling in the pipes and the sound of oul' Peter's ax outside cutting wood, and I could smell the wine from the bottles in the cellar and a whiff of paraffin from the lamp room, and then the smell of Alphie: tobacco and grass and earth. That smell was like something you had a craving to eat and couldn't stop yourself from having. I stepped toward him, and put my two hands down, and God forgive me, I lifted my skirts.

I was sure that feeling must be love; maybe it was. It's too long ago now, and too much has happened, too much to go back on. There's no undoing that knot, except maybe by telling it.

That was the one time between me and Alphie, and not long after, I started to gag and retch in the outside drain. The smell of the bog deal splinter I used to start up the fire, a sweet smell I'd always loved, was enough to set me off. The rest of the servants were usually too busy to notice, and I pretended to be going out to break up clods of turf. One morning Peig found me, the bile hacking at my throat, but I blamed it on a bit of bacon I'd eaten that I thought had gone off and she had me taking ginger for the stomach, and extract of beef, none of which made any difference to what was wrong with me. Peig had no faith in any remedy that came out of a bottle. She said Godfrey's Cordial and Dalby's Carminative were full of opiates and would bring on convulsions, and she would take nothing to do with them. Luckily for me, the sickness didn't last; Peig thought she'd cured me, and I didn't grow too big. I bound up my stomach as tightly as I dared. Peig said that I was growing into a woman, blossoming almost overnight. To this day, I don't believe she suspected me. She had a blind spot where I was concerned, but in those days after Charlotte's death, there was a blindness about all of us. There wasn't a day passed when we didn't think of her and say a prayer for her soul. I never missed a day from my work. Peig said I was the only one could put the slack on the range at night and not kill the fire. In the morning the ashes could be raked out, the grate blackleaded and the whole thing cleaned. Then it would only take a nudge through the black crust with the poker to bring it back to life again. "I don't know what you do," Peig used to say, "but you do it well, girl, God bless you."

I pulled off a patch of the blanket that Mammy had made for me and I went to the prayer tree, barnacled with wishes, and got down on my two knees and prayed hard to St. Jude and St. Patrick that I wouldn't be punished with a baby for what I had done and I rubbed the cloth on the tree. But that was a bad prayer, Anna, and the saints must have known it. You can't undo what's been done and for that I'm thankful now, though it was a hard road I took then. When it was clear to me that the baby was growing in my stomach, I put the cloth under my pillow and said a prayer for an easy birth.

It was November. Duffy's Circus was camped in the fields outside the town and most of the house had cleared out to it. As I slid into bed, I could hear the music and the shouts of the crowds through the open window. I was in the attic room on my own. The pain started in my back in the middle of the night. I thought I'd hurt myself, lifting the big pot over the fire maybe, but it was an odd thing for a hurt like that to wake you up out of your sleep. It was a kind of ache to begin with, and then I knew that it must be the baby coming, because it began to come in waves, like the tide breaking on the strand, bigger and deeper each time, and then closer and closer together, until I started to feel like I was rolling inside the highest, greenest wave there'd ever been and that it would never break. I remembered the cloth from the prayer tree and reached under my pillow for it, and started to pray. I got scared that it was going to kill me, that the wet glassy wave would carry me away, and after a while, I thought that maybe that would be a blessing, and that at least if that happened, I wouldn't have to go through with the next part, the thing I'd decided on. I started to think about the servant girl I'd heard about way down the country in Enniscorthy, who was found bled to death in her bed, and the blue baby found after it, under the mattress.

I must have pushed, trying to push out the pain, because then the worst was over, and there was my baby, wet and slippery as a pat of butter. I cut the cord with a kitchen knife I'd hidden in my room, and I wrapped him tight in an old flour bag. There was another shudder of pain—for a moment I thought another baby was coming—but then there was the afterbirth, lying on the sheet like a heart, and I buried my face in the pillow until the sobbing stopped. I hardly dared look at him: I don't remember him crying, but when I did look, I don't know how long after, he was asleep. I dipped the prayer cloth in my basin and wrung it out and wiped his head and his little curled fists and his feet the size of acorns. I was afraid to touch the stump that stuck out of his belly button. Then I gathered myself up, slipped out to the turnip field and set him down, cradled between two furrows. I clawed at the earth with my hands and dug a hole and set him in and pulled the bag down over his head. Then I reached down for another handful of earth and my nails sank into a rotten turnip and the smell of it filled my nose and I tried, Anna, I tried my best to bury him. I thought of what I'd heard the priest say from the altar, and I thought of Mammy and the broken look in her eyes, and I thought of what I'd heard the men say about the women at the docks in Derry, and I thought about what it would feel like to tramp the roads like oul' Molly, not knowing where your next bite was coming from. Then I thought of the mistress and what she'd done to Charlotte, and I couldn't put the earth over his head. And then I thought about Peig. It was a terrible sin what I had done to her, but it was nowhere near as bad as the one I was trying to commit, and I lifted him up, and I walked to her house and I set him down outside her door.

I sat down for a while behind the turf stack, but there was no sign of life from the house and in the end I couldn't stick it any longer, sitting there on my hunkers in the cold, bleeding into the ground, and I said to myself, "It's in God's hands now," and I walked back to the castle.

Peig said he was like a gift from God. I hadn't seen it in her, how much she wanted a child. I was ashamed of how happy he made her. And she called him Owen, for he would keep her young, she said. Yes, Anna: Conor's father; my son, Owen. I'm sorry. It's a shock to you. I'm sorry to tell you this way. I've been so long carrying it around, not telling it, coming at it from this side and that, I don't know how to do it right. I have no practice, for who else could I tell it to? Who would understand but you? You're the only family I have, Anna, you and Conor, and your baby.

No, no one ever suspected me. Everyone was sure it was one of the circus people that had left the baby. And it suited people to believe that, so they didn't have to look around among their own for a girl who had abandoned the product of her shame and sin.

Peig asked Miss Julia if Bella could wet-nurse Owen. Your mother, Florence, was only about four or five months old at the time, but Bella said she had plenty of milk for both of them and Miss Julia agreed. Peig carried on with her work in the kitchen, though there was little enough done those first few days, so anxious was she about the child. "Will he do?" she kept asking Bella. "Do you think, Bella, will he do?" Bella said he had a good chance and with the help of God he would do, only would Peig leave her to it.

I felt like everyone who looked at me, at my pale face and dragging feet, must know that the baby was mine, but no one guessed, no one except for her that had her own story to tell. He was hard to settle. He wasn't more than a couple of days old when Bella brought him in, looking for Peig. He was hot and crabbed, had been crying for hours. Peig had gone down to the meat safe under the horse chestnut tree and Bella handed me the baby and said, "Mind him for a minute, Maddie, will you? My arms is broke holding him." She went to get Peig and I stood with my back to the table, cradling him in my arms, and the breasts that had ached and leaked for hours, and that I'd wrapped in cabbage leaves, began to swell and sting under my clothes until I thought I would burst.

Peig came back in and took him and caught sight of the damp patch on my apron and burst out laughing at the expression on my face and said, "Jesus, Maddie, you'd think you'd been stung. It's only a bit of boke. You'll have to get used to that, and worse, if you're going to have weans of your own someday." Then off she went, out into the yard, cooing and swinging him and telling him stories, and left me with Bella.

Bella put her hand down flat on the table and looked at me. Then she pulled out a chair and sat down and she told me her story—how the Salvationists took her into the rescue home in Dublin when she was eight months gone, gave her good references and got her a place in the lying-in hospital when her time came, and took her back into the home afterward. At the time the master came looking for a wet nurse, her own child was almost a year old and ready to be weaned. She knew her time there was at an end, that she'd have to find work outside, and the Salvationists said they'd keep her little girl and look after her until she was able to come for her, and she sent them what she could from her wages.

She'd known nothing about what to expect, she said, the pains and the pushing and how much blood there was. And at the end of it she said, "It would be hard to hide something like that. If I knew anyone that needed help I'd do what I could for them," and that was all she said. I told her I had the washing to do and I'd need to go and get on with it.

I fainted in the laundry. I remember standing there, over the tub with the sheets in soda, ladling the hot water out of the copper, beating the linen with the dolly, and then I remember seeing the ceiling, and the way the lime was starting to flake off with the damp, and the way the spiders had built their webs in the corners, and I remember not being able to make my eyes stop moving, and everything going around and around and the two legs going from under me and then falling down further than the flagstone floor. Peig wasn't there; she'd walked down the road toward the strand with Bella to settle the baby. But the men must have heard the clatter from the yard and when I came round, it was Madge looking down at me, and me lying on my bed.

"Jesus, Maddie," she said, "you're like death warmed up. Feeley had to carry you up the stairs."

"I'm grand," I said, and I tried to get up.

"There's nothing grand about you," she said, "I'm sending for the doctor." But I wouldn't hear tell of it for I was heart-scared that he would work it all out, so I said, "No, Madge, please don't send for the doctor."

She looked at me and said, "What's wrong with you, Maddie?" and I thought as hard as I could.

Then I said, "Paudie slipped me a drop of poteen last night and there must have been some other thing in it for my head's been spinning the whole day."

Madge said, "Ye hallion, Maddie, it's drunk you are! Who would have thought it?" And she said she'd bring me up a cup of tea and cover for me as long as she could but that I'd better be up by evening to help with the dinner. I think she was glad to hear I'd been up to some devilment, for she used to say butter wouldn't melt in my mouth. I was as weak as water for days but Peig was too much taken with the wean to notice or even look the road I was on, and for all my legs were shaking I never missed another day of work.

It's often the way that people don't see what's right under their noses until it's pointed out to them. And the people who could have done that were never going to, having the most to lose by it. I stayed out of Alphie's way and he stayed out of mine. I was that ashamed afterward, I couldn't look him in the face. He would have known that the story of the circus girl wasn't true but he seemed happy enough to go along with it, for Peig's sake. Then one Sunday, I was passing their cottage on my way down to Bone Row and I heard singing in a man's low voice, a song I knew well, for Mammy used to sing it. "I found the trail of the mountain mist, the mountain mist, the mountain mist, I found the trail of the mountain mist, but ne'er a trace of baby." Alphie was in the doorway, with Owen in his arms, cradling him gently back and forth, singing, "I left my darling lying here," and he lifted his head and looked up with a smile on his face. My heart splintered into a thousand pieces and when he saw me standing there with my two arms the one length, looking at him, he must have known for certain, and it was a different face that turned back to his child again, a different face altogether.

I made a quilt for Owen's first birthday out of two old dresses Miss Julia had given me, garments I never would have worn in a million years, the one in white velvet, the other in green silk, and with an old Turkey-red petticoat of my own. I sewed him a pattern: a fish for my father, a star for his, a bird that he might have a light heart always and an oak leaf for a long, strong life. It wasn't easy made, for I'd cut the silk on the bias and had to be careful not to stretch it, and I sewed the whole thing at night, in buttonhole stitch, as carefully as I could, and then onto the whitest bleached flour bags I could get. Peig said it was fit for a prince, nearly too good to put in his cradle, but she must have seen my face fall when she said that, for she got up straightaway and put it over him. I embroidered my initials into the corner of it so you could hardly see, and into the seam at the top I sewed a lock of the lavender Mammy had given me. I wonder where that quilt went.

I think that by the time he was ten or eleven, Peig had worked out that it was no accident that Owen had been left on her doorstep—that he was in fact Alphie's son. He looked nothing like him. If anything, it was my brother Charlie he took after, but thank God no one ever made the connection, what with Charlie being long gone to Canada. The strangest thing, though: he inherited his father's voice. That same low hoarseness, the voice breaking on the highest notes; it began to make itself known when he was leaving boyhood behind. And he took, I'm afraid to say, after his father in other ways. He was selfish and disobedient, and he wasn't good to Peig, who worked her life to keep him and broke her heart over him.

After the castle was closed up, she eked out a living for them both mending nets, kept a few hens, took in washing, whatever she could find. And when the boy got bigger, she got a job in the new creamery, patting out slabs of butter, all the same color, all the same shape—Peig, who had made the best butter in the country. She was a good mother to him, far better than I could have been.

Look, Anna, in that drawer of the cabinet. The only picture I have of him and he's standing, hands by his sides, frowning into the camera. The ink from the photograph is pooled in his eyes and even though his face in it is smaller than the nail on my wee finger, his expression is unmistakable: he is cross at being photographed. His sweater is pulled down low over the waist of his short trousers. No doubt Peig did that, just before the photo was taken. But she hasn't caught his undershirt and you can see the ridge around his middle where it's ridden up and the dimple below it, through his stretched jumper, of his belly button. The sun must have been behind Peig when she took it, for a strange thing this, can you see? The shadow of her head is cast onto his sweater, a stray bit of hair curling up and away. That's all I have of her: a shadow on a photograph. She must have been happy then, that day. It doesn't look like the shadow of an unhappy person's head. She doesn't look unhappy.

I kept him for Peig the odd time she needed to go somewhere, to a wake or a sick relation. When he was small, I used to pick him up and nurse him on my knee and rock him by the fire, and when he was older, I told him the stories Daddy used to tell me, about the way St. Brigid lost her eye, and how St. Brendan crossed the whole Atlantic in a currach. He didn't like the ticking of the clock in the room at night. He liked to chase frogs through the turf stooks, and he loved spuds baked in the embers, the skin black as the coals themselves and the potato coming away from them as dry and white inside as a ball of flour. I've outlived a son and he never knew the love I had for him. But that's the way things were then. That's the way they had to be. At least Conor will know the truth, if you choose to tell him. It's in your hands now.

I can't unwish what I did, because I can't unwish Owen, or Conor. Or your child, Anna, yours and Conor's. I can't unwish yours. You are carrying my great-granddaughter. Oh, it's a girl all right. I know by the way she's lying, all to the front, and the big bony head of her. Before too long, her elbows will be sticking out of your belly like wings, trying to get free. She hasn't much room; she'll be wanting out. I'd have liked to have made a quilt for you, for the baby, but these fingers won't work for me anymore. You'll have to make do with the story instead, pieced together from the scraps of old lives. That's all I have.

Harriet

Grangegorman Prison, Dublin

Wednesday 14 September 1892

Father was shocked at first to learn that Edward was Catholic. Edward was honest, said he believed his father's switch to Rome to have been prompted by political expediency: not long after his conversion Lord Ormond came out in support of the Home Rulers. Edward explained that his father, being a man of sudden passions, had thrown himself wholeheartedly into the new religion, insisted his family do likewise. Edward had still been at Shrewsbury at the time, and was preparing to go up to Oxford, but he had converted gladly and he told my father that he had no intention of reverting. Edward could trace his mother's ancestry back to the Ulster revolt of 1641, when his Catholic predecessors rose up against the planted New English, before a later family member converted to the Reformed Church. So it was not so much a conversion, he explained, as a reversion to the faith that had originally been that of his mother's people. He had a strong affinity with his maternal family. Oranmore had come to him from his mother's father, a gentleman whom Edward is said to resemble in character as well as in looks. I cannot see the resemblance myself. There is a portrait of him hanging in the hall at Oranmore:

a bluff-looking gentleman with a shiny red face and fair hair that curled around his ears, but he did have kind eyes. Edward's religion mattered little to me, either way. Even I, unversed in the interface between politics and religion, could see that my father considered Lord Ormond a fool. Still, Father did not extend the sentiment to Edward, who seemed to have captured his heart. To me, Father put one question: "Will you take him, Harriet?" And I was only too happy to oblige.

Father put no obstacle in the way of our marriage. I cannot help but wonder how he would have felt if his grandchildren were to have borne his name, if I had been a son and not a daughter, proposing to lay aside my cradle religion for the sake of a marriage union. Who is to say? I can only assume that all the other inquiries received satisfactory answers. It was made clear to me that upon his marriage, Edward would inherit his grandfather's estate in Ireland and that he would be expected to live there and manage it. I had no objection to Ireland. Ulster was not Egypt, that was clear; it was but a hop across the Irish sea, but it was far enough. "His being Catholic can be no obstacle to you now, Harriet," my father said with a smile, "not since the restriction has been lifted on the value of horses they may own." It was not such a joke. I would not have entertained for a moment a proposal from a man without stables.

In the months before our marriage, Father grew anxious about my going to Ireland. Stories were reaching us of the activities of the Land Leaguers, of evicted farms lying empty, harvests left to rot, rents withheld. One agent had his ears clipped; cattle houghing was common; there were stories of hunt saboteurs stopping the Kildare hounds, burning kennels, poisoning foxes, destroying coverts. Edward assured us that the tenants in the north were nothing like those in the west and south.

"Ulster has always been different," he said, and then, smiling, "If you want something to worry you, Mr. McIntyre, worry about the fall in tillage prices."

Then, the September before we were due to be married, news reached us of Lord Mountmorres's murder.

"That was in Mayo," Edward said, "miles and miles and a world away from Oranmore. The people there are a different breed from the tenants on my estate." His assurances meant little to a person with no sense of the geography of the place. I might as well have been embarking on a journey to India, such was my ignorance. But I began to catch Father's anxiety, and I believe that even Edward wavered a little: who is to say what can happen when people act as one?

In the end it was his assurances that resolved me to stand firm, although not, I am certain, in the way that he intended. "If you have any disquiet on any account, Harriet," he said, "I will send you home, I promise." Little did he know how much that determined me to have no fear. I had no intention of ever going home again.

We were married at the Oratory at ten on a November morning in 1880, the end of a significant year: Gladstone returned to power in London, Parnell elected chairman of the Home Rule party. Edward had his father's waistcoat retailored to fit him: blue and cream silk, a design of vine leaves and veronica.

"Something old," he said, "to bring us luck."

"Veronica," breathed Julia, "for fidelity; vine leaves for intoxication." Trust Julia to know the language of flowers.

Had Mother had her way, I would have been dressed in gold, beribboned from head to toe, carrying a cartload of roses. It was my wedding, however, and I had chosen a simply cut dress of oyster silk trimmed with pearls.

The London smog was notorious. "You will be covered in blacks before you reach the church," was all Mother said.

Edward sent white roses for the bouquets, and when they arrived Julia came into my bedroom with a spray of mixed heather—purple, red and white. She had had it dipped in beeswax to preserve it. It would have cost her something to have won that battle with Mother. It was perfect.

When she came to visit at Oranmore during my first confinement and saw our wedding picture on the credenza beside Edward's mother's hideous bud vase, she said, "Oh, Harriet, you could put your wedding heather there."

"I could if I still had it," I said.

Poor Julia. She could not disguise her shock. "You have thrown it away? But it would have kept for years . . ." She was almost lost for words. "You could have given it to me if you thought so little of it."

"I have no sentimental attachment to objects that gather dust," I told her.

"And yet you have your butterflies," she said.

I stared at her. How could she make such a comparison? Each time I examine a butterfly I see something I did not see before: the unique pattern of markings, the subtle pigmentation. A butterfly is a window onto another world. A spray of dead heather will always be a spray of dead heather. I allowed her the last word. What is the point in trying to reason with that kind of thinking? We will never understand each other, my sister and I. She made her gesture, I appreciated it, I will not forget it. I do not need to keep the thing to know that it was done.

I was not the choice that Edward's family would have made for him, I suppose. We were not a particularly wealthy family, but at the time they made no real objection. No doubt, they wish now that they had. I had much to learn—about Edward, about Ireland, about the part that religion had to play. I am not sure I know any more now.

Edward enjoyed some fun at my expense. Soon after we took up residence, he read to me from the newspaper that there had been a meeting in the town hall of the Tenant Defense Association to discuss the land question. He was quick to assure me that this did not mean that we were surrounded by Land Leaguers intent upon burning us out. They had spoken openly and condemned agrarian crime; they were supporters of the crown and of the constitution, loyalists to a man, determined to have their grievances heard through proper constitutional means. I asked him to spare me the details and read me the fixtures for the Route Hunt. He did so, mechanically, and then said, "Of course, you cannot ride, for there are sure to be Orangemen at the meet." I threw my breakfast napkin at him. One thing of which I am certain: the only religion among huntsmen and -women is a good scenting day or a bad one, and that, I vowed, would be the only thing to occupy me.

Still, from time to time events reached us that pricked even my armor of indifference. When Mr. Porter, Liberal MP for the county and champion of tenants' rights, was elected solicitor general the following year, the hillsides were ablaze with bonfires lit by his supporters. Until some of those unhappy with the outcome smashed the windows of those establishments that were known to be owned by his followers. Edward passed it off as high spirits at election time, but it was coming a little too close. It seems to me that when people do not wish to confront agitation or unpleasantness of any kind, they distance themselves from it using whatever means are at their disposal.

It was the stance Edward and his father agreed upon when Lord Cavendish and his undersecretary were murdered ten years ago in Phoenix Park. Shocked as they were, they were in agreement: "It could never happen here."

Something did happen. May Day morning last year Julia ventured out unseen. She had hatched a plan with the girls from the Dooey and from Flowerfield. They had agreed to meet at the ruined church between the two houses which Peig had told them was the site of the meeting of three townlands. West Crossreagh, the Glebe and Garrylaban, and the best possible place to collect the early morning dew which they were afterward to use on their faces as a means to eradicate eczema and guarantee eternal beauty. She has no wit: tramping about in mist where anything could happen. She is a liability.

On her return to the castle in the first light, she stumbled and fell and dropped her precious booty. We heard the cries from inside and when we ran out, we could see nothing but the lawn sloping gently down to the wall and the gardens beyond, but still Julia crying out. Paudie ran down toward the sea wall, where a small mound of earth had appeared, and we saw him stop and look, and then just as suddenly disappear, all but for his head and shoulders. Edward ran to him, and Hill, and Feeley, and then, like in some medieval tale, like the earth had decided to give her up, there was Julia emerging intact. By the time I reached them, they were all again visible and we stood, the six of us, staring down into what had held Julia: a freshly cut rectangular hole six feet in length, three feet across, six feet deep. The sides were as neat as a turf bank, the spade marks clearly visible: a perfect grave. I looked at Edward, who stood grim faced; at Julia, whose face and hair and dress were smeared with earth.

"Fill it in," was all he said, and he turned on his heel and strode back to the house.

We all knew what was the source of the threat. A number of Edward's tenants had had their cases heard in the Land Court and been awarded considerable reductions in rent. Awarding a reduction and offering an abatement, however, were two separate issues. The lands were mortgaged. To have done what the Land Court had ruled would have reduced the rents to below what Edward was required to pay in interest. It was an impossible situation and for the first time Edward had turned them down. I began to see the wisdom of Lord Ormond's words: sell the lot and be damned. To me Edward said that the threat was nothing, little more than a drunken prank, a few troublemakers from the village bored and in want of some diversion. The stories that came to us during the Plan of Campaign from the south and west were as of a foreign land: houses guarded by dragoons; landlords attacked with stones and blackthorn sticks; the agent of the Marquess of Clanricarde murdered on his way to church in Galway.

"It will not come to that," said Edward. "The worst is over. We are not the same."

Edward's forebears were lords and barons, dukes and high sheriffs, grand jurors every one. I have dragged him into the courtroom in a wholly different capacity from that which would have been expected. I have done irreparable damage to the Ormond name. Edward never missed Mass, had all the children baptized in that strange little chapel at Portrush. He wanted me to convert and I had no difficulty with it. It mattered little to me whether I sat in the kirk or knelt at the altar rails. I must admit I was curious to experience what the Reverend Mr. Begg had termed "the weekly pantomime for slumbering idolaters." I was not disappointed, although I doubt that he would have been pleased with my response. I was surprised and intrigued by the symbolism of the whole thing, water for washing sin away, oil to anoint, ashes for humility. The alien rituals I observed with amusement and not a little sense of theater: the flickering of candles under the statuary; the washing of the feet; the kissing of the cross; the acrid smell as the thurible swung through the church; the glazed and elaborate monstrance, like a burst sun, on the altar. Looking on the flickering candles under the statue of the Blessed Virgin, my father's voice came to me, quoting from the Confession of Faith. "Religious worship is to be given to God, the Father, Son, and Holy Ghost; and to him alone; not to angels, saints, or any other creature . . ." At Priorwood we observed the service in silence—we were listeners—but at Oranmore the voices of the farm laborers and servants, the shopkeepers and justices, the ladies of the Industrial Society and the village fishermen, all rose together, rose right up into the apse and hung there, heavy like incense, and all of us under the weight of what had been uttered. It did not matter that most of them did not understand the Latin chant. That may even have added to it. For all my cynicism, it did used to move me.

I must have appeared dutiful. The fool of a priest thought me devout and after my arrest took it upon himself to defend me in his homilies. I was speechless when he suggested to Edward that it would help my case if he accompanied me to the readjournment. I suppose that the trial was just another piece of theater for him, a new audience, a different auditorium. I can still see him now, the sheen on his black frock, rubbing his hands, patrolling up and down the anterooms like a cormorant on the rocks at low tide, giving an occasional guttural grunt as a new idea occurred.

If the *Watchman* article, in its implied criticism, was damaging, then Father McGarrity's defense of me was worse again. When the servants gave their evidence at the courthouse in Coleraine, he began thumping the table with his fist and had to be restrained by Mr. Crankshaft, and despite the seriousness of the situation, I could not stifle a laugh. He delivered a sermon the following Sunday in which he publicly objected to the religious makeup of the jurors, there not being a Roman Catholic among them, and accused them all of bias. His contortions to explain my eccentricity had me squirming in my seat. The *Watchman* printed the sermon where he brought up the question of my having ridden to the hunt while I was heavy with child. I could imagine the disapproval rise up into the church and hang above the heads of the entire congregation. I believe he wished to portray me as brave and fearless. "She is always well to the front," I read, "and generally in at the death . . . she is a lady of great determination and power of will, and has never been known to quail when pitted against the most vicious or unmanageable animal." Ordinarily a compliment, perhaps, in hunting circles, but not necessarily attributes that one would wish to have emphasized when on trial for the killing of one's own child. "Brave" and "fearless" belong in the vocabulary of soldiers and kings, and not in that of doting mothers. How was that to help my case? I wished, as the *Watchman* had suggested, that I could muzzle him. I was powerless, though: both Edward and Mr. Crankshaft thought his presence was an endorsement of my good standing. Each time he opened his mouth to speak, I could see the horrid little man from the Cruelty Society scribble like fury in his notebook. And the public liked me less and less.

As if this were not bad enough, the reverend father decided that a letter was the thing, and wrote to the *Derry Gazette*. Perhaps he had been a little harsh, he wrote, in claiming that the jury was prejudiced, but there was no question in his mind that the public had been made so by virtue of what the press had printed. I was, he admitted, "eccentric in some respects," apparently at ease mingling with men in the public marketplace; given to traveling, at times, in the horse boxes with my horses. However, he implied without actually saying it, this did not make me guilty of killing my daughter. Had the child not struggled, he averred, the stocking would not have slipped; had the stocking not slipped, the child would not have died. "If it had kept quiet," he wrote, "it would not have been strangled." Thus says my only public defendant in so many words: she did it to herself. Such defendants I can do without. He disputed that there was a general feeling of indignation against me: "Among the Catholics, at least, there is a feeling of sorrow and sympathy," he stated. He admitted that I was "peculiar." "She is fearless almost to insensibility," he preached (this in my defense!). "Really," he stated, "there appears to be a regular conspiracy against her and her husband, and it is almost entirely on account of their religion." The *Watchman* returned by saying that it was almost refreshing to hear a member of the Roman Catholic clergy defend a landlord. It really would have been quite comic had it not been for the circumstances. It was as a direct result of his histrionics (which went all the way to the ears of the attorney general) that the trial was heard not at the Derry assizes, but at the Four Courts in Dublin, with the solicitor general acting for the crown. Mr. Morell had clashed with Edward's father on a number of occasions. I could not see how such an outcome could possibly benefit my case.

It was only my second visit to Dublin, and in very different circumstances from the first. Edward had brought me down for the castle season, not long after Harry was born, to be presented to Lord and Lady Spencer. On that occasion, we stayed at the Shelbourne, of course, but I was most struck, I remember, by the majestic Bank of Ireland, formerly Parliament House, and its likeness to the façade of the British Museum. It made me think again of all the stunning butterflies housed there, when Edward and I had gone to view them. We attended the State Ball in St. Patrick's Hall and danced a Viennese waltz, to Liddell's Orchestra, I remember, and later Edward tried to teach me a country dance while the orchestra played an Irish jig. We were invited to an occasion in the Throne Room, a much smaller and more select affair, which proved, said Edward, that my Irish jig had made an impression! Edward spent his mornings in his Sackville Street club, from whence he returned each afternoon, having lunched on oysters and champagne; he left me free to wander among the Royal Dublin Society's collections at Leinster House. I recall that on one such day, he said to me, a smile on his face, "What butterfly would you be, Harriet?"

And I said, without hesitation, "A painted lady."

He laughed heartily, feigned outrage, said nothing could be less like me since I was never gaudy or superficial or false but always frank and true, even at the risk of injury to myself. But I refused to relinquish my choice. I would arrive, I said, from North Africa in spring, soar over the castle and settle in the nettle patch behind the garden wall, and sip from the aster and the lavender, and lay my eggs on the thistles and spread my wings and bask in the rare April sunshine when it came, glorious in orange and brown and black. A painted lady could be anyone she wished under her disguise, I told him: the world would be fooled by the mask, but beneath it she would be free.

It was bedlam at the courthouse in Dublin: the hall was packed with people, women mostly, pushing and protesting and insisting on their right to be present for the trial. The police were hard-pressed to keep the entrance clear and to distinguish between witnesses, jurors and those members of the public who were determined to be present. I waited in an anteroom for Mr. Crankshaft to come for me, to escort me into the pew, where I was to sit alone throughout the hearing. It took me a little time to find the courage to raise my eyes and look around. I recall the smell of wood polish, remember seeing the dust motes dance in a shaft of sunlight from one of the high windows, how we all stood to attention when the judge entered, attired in his black robes, powdered wig. I felt every face in the court turned toward mine, the weight of all those glances bent on me. I have never enjoyed public display. The whole process of the trial must be designed to humiliate the defendant. Since one is not permitted to speak, what other reason can there be for being present?

I must admit, my heart stopped when Justice Murray gave his opening address. I will never forget his words: "If death is caused to any person by the act of another the law first says, as human life is sacred, that causing the death of another is murder." It was the first time, I believe, that the word had been spoken aloud, although it had been stuck in all of our throats for weeks. "It lies on the person who has caused the death to show beyond all reasonable doubt that the crime can be reduced to manslaughter." So it was up to me, then, to prove, without speaking or being heard in any way, that I was not a murderess.

Edward had engaged two illustrious counsels for my defense, but out of deference had not sent Mr. Crankshaft away. Mr. McKinney was eloquent on my behalf. He cautioned the jury not to "enter into the spirit of enthusiastic ferocity that was abroad" with regard to my case; reminded them that this was a trial by law and not "a trial by newspapers" or by tea table, a reference no doubt to the hordes of reporters who peopled the public gallery, and to the ladies who had been refused admittance but who were assembled still outside the courthouse. He urged them to "emancipate themselves from prejudice" and to "shut their ears to the poisoned air," to judge me on evidence alone. The evidence he referred to was damning enough in itself. "This woman has been roasted before a slow fire for weeks and months," he said; "she might have strange, hard notions of correction and training for the young mind" but "she has only made a mistake." I grew nervous. He seemed to be falling into Mr. Crankshaft and Father McGarrity's trap: constructing a defense out of my worst failings. Perhaps the best defense *was* silence. Perhaps it was not such a disadvantage that the defendant was not permitted to speak. I began to see the sense of it, after all. He concluded by recommending that the jury restore me to my home and to my children. There is a fine line, I began to see, between defense and condemnation: there was not much the crown needed to do but to repeat his words in Mr. Morell's inimitable sneer.

Mrs. Walsh, the ornithologist's wife, did her best for me and almost got away clear. I seemed genuinely attached to my only daughter, she said, and outwardly affectionate toward her, even though, and here is the rub, "she was a child of very independent will." I believe I have heard that phrase before, a long time ago now, and in reference to myself.

Mother instructed me to wear my nighttime corset in bed. It was only marginally looser than the daytime version, and pinched my ribs and chest to such a degree that I could not turn without whalebone and steel digging into flesh. She said it was for the best. If my waist were molded and shaped at seven, she said, when my bones were young, I would have no difficulty maintaining sixteen inches when I was eighteen, despite what she called my "large structure." She herself had managed fifteen inches in her wedding dress. I felt her eyes on me always at the dinner table, eyeing my portions. She coughed discreetly if she saw me reach for a piece of candied fruit or cheese. What horrors did she imagine would follow if my waist stretched to seventeen inches? I believe I was hungry for the first nineteen years of my life.

Julia had no such restrictions placed on her. "Julia is so fortunate in her frame," Mother would say. "In that respect, she takes after me." Julia, it was felt, needed "building up." She was plied with sugared biscuits and preserves, while I was placed as far away from such delicacies as was possible. Every night, I unlaced the tortuous garment under the covers and slept with it beside me before slipping into it again in the morning. If Elsa remarked on the stays being loose, I said they must have come free in my sleep. I suspect the maid knew I took it off, but she laced me into it every night, as instructed by Mother, and dutifully replaced it with the tighter corset in the morning. Until the night of the thunderstorm, when the rain hammered against the windows and the lightning lit up my little bedroom with flashes of light and I woke, after an uneasy sleep, to see Mother standing over me, leaning on her cane, a candle in her other hand lighting her face in a yellow glow, the covers of the bed turned back to reveal the discarded corset.

"You disobedient child!" she hissed at me. "Do you want to grow up with the figure of a peasant?"

"No, Mother," I said, terrified at the look on her face.

"Get out of bed this instant."

I climbed out, not knowing if I was awake or dreaming. It was a long time since I had seen Mother stand unsupported by Father or by one of the servants, and yet there she was, in my bedroom, apparently able to walk by herself.

She sat down on the bed, put the candle on the bedside table and picked up the garment. "Put it on," she said.

I managed to struggle back into it and pulled the stays as tight as I could.

"Turn around," she said.

I felt a knee in the small of my back and the stays pulled tighter than ever Elsa had managed. A wave of panic rose up in me: my breathing was so much shortened I could not even half-fill my lungs.

"Go and stand beside the wardrobe," she said, and I did so. "You will remain there until morning. I will teach you posture, Harriet." And she stood up, leaned again on her cane. "You may never behave like a young lady," she said, "but I will at least see that you stand like one." Then she picked up the candleholder, turned her back on me and walked out, the candlelight glinting on the silver tip of her cane.

I did not dare move. I stood there, listening to the rain against the window, counting the beats between thunderclaps, watching as the room was suddenly illuminated, and just as suddenly dropped back into darkness, waiting for the storm to pass. My mother did teach me an important lesson. She taught me the importance of armor. She taught me how to construct my own impenetrable cocoon. She taught me how to protect the spirit. She taught me how to hide within myself. I have tried to teach that same lesson to my children, but they have always been stronger than me. If I am guilty of failing to do my duty as a mother then it is in this: I have not succeeded in teaching them how to safeguard themselves from love.

Mrs. Walsh testified to my docile and prayerful behavior in church. The first time I met Mrs. Walsh was at the Dunluce meet; she had never seen a lady ride in a "fig leaf" before and I could tell from her expression that she considered the tailoring distinctly risqué. I decided to meet her with head-on naïveté.

"You do not use the newest safety skirt, Mrs. Walsh?" I asked her. "It is a true innovation. It comes right away at the waist in the event of a tumble. There is no risk of being dragged. I have left several in the saddle, never had one fail me yet."

She was clearly appalled at the prospect of hordes of ladies standing around the fields at Dunluce in their drawers. I'm sure she blamed me for the general decline in the quality of rider at the Route. I heard her mutter to Mrs. Graham that I would be riding cross-saddle next. Alas, no. My audacity never extended to that: a lady could not ride astride and expect to remain in polite society. Not that I am likely to find myself much in polite society now. When I dismounted at Runkerry, I deliberately flashed my ankle at her. I dare say I would not have done so, had I known that my good name was to be put in her hands.

Mrs. Walsh was present on one occasion when Charlotte showed herself to be less than enthusiastic about entering the schoolroom. She was not a child who sat at her studies willingly. I had to admonish her more than once. Mr. Morell found it an astonishing suggestion, however, that a child of barely four years could show independent will and dismissed poor Mrs. Walsh's evidence with one turn of his heel.

That Julia should spend a night in the wardrobe room before the trial was not my idea. It may have been Edward's; Mr. Crankshaft himself may even have suggested it. Whatever benefit the experiment may have been expected to have must have been utterly undone when I saw Julia's face in the courtroom.

For what purpose had she spent a night there, Mr. McKinney asked her.

"For testing it as regards ventilation," replied Julia in an unnatural tone.

"And I suppose the fact of you being here today shows that you were able to breathe?" replied Mr. McKinney, a distinct twinkle in his eye.

Julia looked blankly at him, her face paler than usual, no doubt due to an additional layer of buttermilk and *poudre de riz*. I do not think she was in the humor for satire. The idea of Julia, pale and sickly, voluntarily spending a night in the wardrobe room in April with no fire and no mattress! Did she honestly think it would help my case? What was she trying to do? I laughed aloud. Several members of the jury looked my way.

The prosecution appealed to the jurors' sense of humanity. Imagine what it would feel like for a four-year-old child to be locked in a room without ventilation, light or heat; to be tied like an animal so she could not move; to be left to cry without being heard; to perish there alone.

What is the good in exhorting people to indulge in their vulgar imaginings? We cannot feel what other people feel. The closest approximation one can achieve is through some unrelated experience of one's own, an attempt at a transference of emotion that is entirely unconnected. I do not know what Charlotte suffered and they do not know what it is to be a woman in a dock accused of murdering her child and discussed as if she were not present. It is pointless to waste time pretending otherwise.

What needed to be proven, it appeared—what the jury, if they were to convict me, were required to be convinced of, without doubt of any kind—was that wickedness or evil intention had motivated my actions, and this, then, was the question I asked myself. Had I intended, by binding Charlotte in the manner in which I had, to cause serious injury to her? Did I mean to harm her? Could I have foreseen the outcome? Was it, in essence, a vindictive act? I meant to punish her, certainly. I meant to correct her behavior, without doubt. I did not mean to injure her, not in any way. I was trying to teach her how to save herself.

Mr. Morell, in his summing-up, took exception to my having sat down to luncheon and ordered a bath, knowing that Charlotte was locked in the room in her soiled clothes and had had no food since eleven. There were many more words, sarcasm apparent in his repetition of Mrs. Walsh's testimony of "this mother boiling over with fondness and affection." Were parents to be at liberty, he asked the jury, to hang their children up to rings in the wall, to lock them in dark closets, and to leave them there for hours without care or attention? I opened my mouth and closed it again. Even had I been at liberty to speak, what would I have said in my defense?

The jury took only half an hour. Back in the dock, I watched as they trooped back in, one after the other. The foreman was a small, studious-looking man, with fair wispy receding hair and little round glasses. He stood with one hand gripping the wooden pew in front of him, his other hand holding a sheet of paper, and as I watched and waited for my fate to be sealed, I saw his hand tighten on the pew, his other hand tremble very slightly. When he finally opened his mouth to utter the verdict of conviction, and my heart sank, despite the inevitability of such a return, he added a statement that I had in no way anticipated. He said that in the opinion of the jury, the crime had been committed through a mistaken sense of duty, and as I listened he used a word that had not been much used over the course of the previous weeks. He recommended me to mercy. I thanked him for that, with every pore of my body—not because such a sentiment might shorten my sentence, not because it might sway public opinion even slightly, but because of the human recognition of suffering that it encompassed. Apart from Edward, he may have been the only person in that courtroom who acknowledged it. I think it may have been the first time since Charlotte's death that another human being looked me in the eye.

Maddie

15 DECEMBER 1968

Is it cold out, Anna? There's no way of feeling the weather in here. Did you hear Captain O'Neill's speech? We are standing at a crossroads, he says, and it's up to us to choose: the path of order or the path of violence. The people are to stay off the streets, he says, stop marching and protesting, and that way they'll not get their heads battered in by the police. Well, my head's safe enough in here. There's not much danger of seeing me out with a placard in my hands. But if I was younger, Anna, no speechifying of his would keep me in. Nor you either, I'd say, if it wasn't for the baby. What about the path to justice and the path to injustice? What has he to say about that? Does he think the people are just going to lie down and say nothing? You're lucky, Anna, that you have the house in Victoria Terrace. How would you feel if you were told you didn't deserve a vote because the roof over your head wasn't your own, and you with no way of putting a roof over your head? What sort of justice is that? I know what you think of me—an oul' dyed-in-the-wool Republican, and maybe I am. Maybe I'm a communist too! But I'd like to think I'd stand up for anyone who wasn't getting a fair deal. No matter what color their politics. Peig taught me that, at least.

It wasn't easy going back to the castle after the trial. None of us knew what was going to happen. Miss Julia came back, and the master, but the place was empty without the boys. We didn't know if we'd be kept on: Madge and Cait were already looking around for places in other houses. But by then I knew I was in trouble, and I prayed the master would keep me on. I didn't know where I was going to go or what I was going to do. All I knew was that I wanted to stay near my mother and, if I'm honest, near Alphie too.

I met Alphie once after the time Owen was conceived. On the Strand, it was, early May. I told him and he said: "We'll go. We'll take the boat from Derry as far as Liverpool and after that we'll decide if we want to go any further." As simple as that. A north wind blowing straight down the beach, the sand lifting like a low mist, blasting at our ankles, everything shifting, making you think it could carry you with it if you gave in to it. But how could I? How could I leave Mammy with news like that: a daughter expecting and run away with a married man? As if she hadn't been through enough. And Peig, how could I have done that to her? That would have been a very different kind of life for me: I'd have had a different story to tell. And I just looked at him, and I said, "No," and walked away from him. I didn't have another plan, not then. I didn't know what I was going to do. But I couldn't do that.

Six months after Owen was born, May time again, me and Madge were down on the Peasants' Strand gathering kelp, baskets tied to our backs, shepherds' crowns thrown up by the storm, crunching under our bare feet. Oul' Peter went past and called to us, his horse's straw collar all stuck with buttercups and whin blossoms, and we climbed up to him and he told us the news.

Alphie had gone egg gathering, out near Port Cool. Fourteen men, one behind the other, they had stretched themselves out like a lobster line from the cliff edge, one half of a tug-of-war team, the drop against them. And because Alphie was the lightest and the most supple, he was the one to tie the rope around his waist, pass it up between his legs and go down the side to where the razorbills had been laying. He leaned out against the sky and the thirteen men took up his weight, him leaning out over the sea where it swirled around Lawson's Rock, the thirteen of them leaning back into the land. They fed the rope through their chapped hands and he disappeared over the grass edge, feet, and knees, and head. Then he shouted up that he couldn't get to the eggs for a big jagged bit of rock that was snagging the rope but that it would do for a hand-hold, if he took the rope off. And Denny Campbell, who was the first in the line, shouted down for him to come back up and they'd lower him down the other side of it for the ledges were slippery, but Alphie was already untying the rope, and Denny began to feel the slack and he hadn't time to turn round and tell the twelve men behind him to ease off and the rest of them all landed in a heap, with Denny laughing at them.

He shouted down to Alphie again, and Alphie shouted back that he was there, and that there were plenty of eggs on the rock ledges, and that he'd get one for each of them. So the men sat down on top of the rope on the grass at the cliff top and waited for the tug from Alphie to haul him back up again with the basket of brown speckled eggs, all warm in the May sun. Mackie Logan was ribbing Denny about a girl he was courting, and would he take her to the dance in the hall, and were her eyes still the color of bluebells when you had your nose pressed up against hers? And Denny was clawing up sods and firing them at him and they were all laughing and waiting for the tug on the rope, but it never came.

When Denny went to the edge to shout what was Alphie doing or had he eaten the eggs already, there wasn't a soul to be seen, and they'd heard nothing the whole time, not a shout or a splash, not a thing above the long whistling of the blunt-nosed razorbills returning to the empty rocks.

The boys searched for him for days, shouting his name long

after there was any hope of him hearing it. All along the ledges where he'd been there were egg yolks and broken shells.

Peig got a straw collar and threw it on the water, saying that where it came to rest Alphie's body would be found, but it disappeared out to sea, caught in the current that comes off the rock, and I suppose that's where Alphie went too. I suppose it is, but the way Denny told it, it was like he'd vanished upward, into the air. There was never a trace found of him. It's a hard thing to lose someone but it's a harder thing again not to bury them. Peig never got over it. There was people said after that that they heard a voice calling out by Lawson's Rock, a man's voice pleading to be hauled up the cliff side so his soul could be laid to rest. I never went there, and neither did Peig. But she must have visited every other grave that meant anything to her while she was living, and picked the stones off them. Maybe she was gathering them for Alphie. Maybe she never gave up hope of burying him someday.

Is there anything good on at the pictures at the minute, Anna? Me and Bella used to be mad for the pictures. We went nearly every Saturday night to Menary's on the Parade, and for sixpence you got to be in Hollywood. We saw everything. She liked Shirley Temple so anything she was in we had to go and see: *The Little Colonel* was one, and *Curly Top;* and I liked a good laugh: Laurel and Hardy were the best; and the musicals—Bing Crosby, what a man—and oh, Leslie Howard in *The Scarlet Pimpernel*. I loved that. We never missed.

Then one night, in the summer, we were coming back from a walk around the castle here, back along the Crescent to head down to the pictures, and as we were coming past the town hall, with the music coming out from the seven-piece band and the lights twinkling out over the sea, Bella turns to me and she says, "What about a go at the roller-skating, Maddie?" And I started to laugh at the thought of the two of us, women in our fifties and more at that time, her decently married with grown-up children and me in respectable employment with your mother, and I turned and caught the look on her face and she was daring me, Anna, standing there with the lights shining out over the water and the smell of the seaweed drifting up from the rocks below. So I turned to her and I said: "Fair enough, then, sure we'll give it a try," as if she'd said "Will we slip down to Frizzell's for an ice cream?" or "Will you take another turn as far as the harbor?" And she laughed then herself, and looked a bit scared, but it was her that started it.

So I headed off up the steps to the town hall, and her at my heels, and in we went, not daring to look at each other now, for fear we'd turn tail and run, and we paid our shilling and we handed over our coats and our shoes to the cloakroom girl, as if roller-skating on a Saturday night was the most natural thing in the world to us. We picked up the metal skates and we buckled the leather straps on our feet. I kept my head down and didn't dare look up at her or glance around to see who was watching us. When I had the objects on my feet, I stood up and leaned forward and grabbed a hold of the rail, and she stood up too, and I reached out my hand to her and I said, trying to keep the shake out of my voice, "Are you ready?" and she nodded, and took my hand. Then away we went, the pair of us, me holding on to the rail, her grabbing me by the elbow, hobbling and wobbling and terrified out of our wits, and all the young ones looking over at us, us in our homemade Butterick-pattern dresses, neither of us as slim as we would have liked. We were disastrous at the start, like two newborn calves trying to find our feet, but after a bit we got better at it and learned how to keep steady, and learn the weight of ourselves, and to lean forward instead of back, and how to keep going and get up a bit of speed, and we let go of each other's hands, then, for we were making each other worse wobbling and screeching. Then we were going round, none too steady, but going round all the same, and staying upright to the sound of the band playing "The Music Goes Round and Round," and outside the sea going in and out, and inside the town hall, the sweat tripping us. We laughed till our sides were sore, laughed at the notion of us and what Bella's man would say if he saw us, and what your mother would say, and us supposed to be at the pictures, and us like two dervishes, going round and round the polished wooden floor in the red-brick town hall. And I think, maybe, that's what dying will be like. Frightening at first, and unbalancing, but once you get the hang of it, a hell of a ride.

There are families that misfortune seems to follow, Anna, and ours is one of them. Daddy's family came east from Derryveagh in the 1840s. He told me the story. His father, my grandfather, arrived at his sister's cabin one day and found the door and windows walled up from the inside. He shouted in at his sister and her husband, began to claw the mud out from the door, but his sister shouted out to him to for God's sake turn away. They had the cholera and there was nothing that could be done for them except to lie down together. He kept on clawing at the mud at the door and they kept on shouting out to him to go away and take his weans as far as he could, and in the end he sat down on the stoop, his nails full of muck, and cried every tear in his head while the two of them cried on the inside. He stayed there and talked in to them for three days, with the corncrakes calling out in the long grass, until his people stopped calling out. Then he got up and went home and gathered his family and carried them east and never went back. He came here with hardly a word of English and got work at the curing station in Portballintrae. In my head, I've walked every step of that road with him.

I'm the last of the McGlades, as far as I know. Charlie never came back from Canada, not even for Mammy's funeral. We lost track of each other. Maybe he married, I don't know. He set off one morning for Derry, took a lift where he got it and walked the rest; sold his gold watch, which he'd won at the swimming match on the strand; stepped up onto the *SS Mongolian* and never got off it till he landed in Halifax, Canada. He wrote that as soon as he had the money gathered, he'd send for us both, me and Mammy. He said we'd ride on a carriage and wear green feathers in our hats and no one would ever look down their noses at us. He said that in Canada, if you worked hard enough, you could be anyone. It wasn't like here, where the more you did, the more was expected of you, and no thanks for it either. "Go on oul' horse and you'll get grass," Peig used to say. "That's the most any of us can hope for in this place."

Charlie told us what we wanted to hear and we swallowed it whole. He sent a photograph a newsman had taken of him and the men he worked with on a Canadian railway line. You could see Charlie, clear as day, standing in a drain under the tracks in a dirty shirt and overalls, the point of his pick resting in the ground, his boots and trousers from below the knee soaking wet. In the picture, there wasn't one man smiling. What with that, and the stories that came back from other people, we soon knew what no one wanted to say: that he'd swapped one country of depression and poverty for another.

Thinking of him puts me in mind of the game we used to play, me and Charlie, called Running Like McCartney. Cruel, when I think of it now, but the young have a different word for "cruel": they call it fun. Oul' Harry McCartney lost both his eyes one night in the sand hills when the poteen still he was working on exploded in his face. He knew everybody by their step, or by their voice if they were walking on the strand. We met him one day, me and Charlie, when we were down looking for plovers' eggs. A gust of wind caught McCartney's peaked cap and sent it flying down the strand and he set off after it, his two hands stretched out in the wind, calling his cap like it was a dog that might come back to him. Charlie got it for him, put it back in his hand, and he said, "Thanks, young McGlade," and we watched him stagger on up toward the holy well. And then Charlie said, "What would that be like, do you think? Running blind?" and he took off with his two eyes tight shut and his hands stuck out in front of him toward the Barmouth. The game was, you had to keep the sun on your face and the winner was the one who kept their eyes shut the longest and whose tracks in the sand were the straightest. Charlie loved it; he said you could be anywhere doing anything with your eyes shut, you could be anyone in the whole world, and it was only when you opened them again that you came back into yourself. I never won; I didn't like the sensation much, of not knowing where I was going, what I was running into. I didn't like the dark.

The papers are always full of pictures in the summer months of returned Yankees, all of them in sharp suits and with haircuts like film stars. So-and-so pictured with his brother after fifty years apart. But no one ever came knocking to me, no long-lost relations looking for their ancestors' birthplace. The last letter I got from him was after Mammy died. He was moving, he said, to a place called Calgary. I'll never forget that: the way it sounded like Calvary and how I didn't like the idea of him going to a place with a name like that. He'd write, he said, with a new address, and maybe, he said, I'd come over to visit him. But he never wrote, or if he did, I never got it, and I never went and that was that.

All I knew about it was what Bella told me from the cowboy books she read. Bella was a shockin' woman for the library. She couldn't get enough of the cowboys. She had me tormented, trailing down to the reading rooms with her, picking ones out. I had no interest in them at all, but she could read a book standing at the sink, one hand sunk into the water scraping the spuds, the other hand turning a page, and you'd say something to her about the length the girls were all wearing their dresses, or wasn't it shockin' the price of flour, and she'd be away, out over the prairies, reins in her hand, the wind in her hair, and you'd have lost her for the time being.

She was a great friend to me. There was only one time I felt anything other than love for her. I called for her, as usual, one Friday, to walk down to the harbor and get a bit of fish for the dinner and instead of her being ready at the door, she called me into the kitchen to a stranger: a lovely tall dark-haired girl with eyes black and wide like Bella's. Bella took her by the elbow and she said, "Maddie, this is my Stella," and I knew then she was the baby she'd left behind in Dublin all those years ago. The girl was getting married and she'd asked the Salvationists to find her mother. And I was jealous because I knew I'd never be able to stand with my hand on Owen's arm and say, "This is my son."

Can I ask you something, Anna? When your baby's here, will you bring her to me? I'd like to hold her. I'd like to put my hands on her in a way I never did with Owen or Conor. I never acknowledged them—not to anyone, not out loud—and I'm sorry for that. I'd like to hold her in my arms and announce to the world my claim to her.

Harriet

Grangegorman Prison, Dublin

Thursday 24 November 1892

Our wedding anniversary: twelve years; nine children; one dead. I have matched the queen, child for child. We had an inspection by the visiting justices, who seemed pleased to see that all was as it should be: grim and inhospitable. Julia writes to say she would visit. She says she knows my fangs are all display and she wants to know the truth. I cannot bear to have Julia near me. She is a lightweight. She always will be. I do not want to see her need of me.

Four years ago on our anniversary, Edward bought me Caesar. A cross of an English draft mare and a thoroughbred, at sixteen hands high he is faster and lighter than any other horse I have ever hunted. The day of one of Julia's idiotic bazaars, when the grounds were invaded by dozens of ladies in urgent need of bead-embroidered footstool covers and weak tea from a refreshment tent, I took him out onto the path around the castle. I had never dared try a horse on it before: it is steep and rough and narrow; there are points along it where nothing but air separates the rider from a drop of thirty feet or more onto the rocks; but something about those ladies in their gloves and their pinched mouths made me desperate to try it. It was utterly exhilarating, and worth every sideways glance I earned for it. Caesar was a champion. We made it the whole way around from the start of the path at the Crescent, past Little Ringan and the Gentlemen's Bathing Place at Port-na-happle, where there were several bathers in the water, past the Berrins and the salmon fishery, down past the well at the Strand Head. There is no feeling that can compare to a full gallop on the strand, sand and water flying at Caesar's heels, the clouds scudding by overhead. At the Barmouth we rose a flock of sanderlings, so comic on the shoreline as they ran in and out, trying to catch the tide, but in the air as they appeared above us, breathtaking, a sudden silvering, a shot of happiness.

Anyone with wit knows that ladies are more skillful riders than men: we cannot rely on brute strength or on spurring the horse; we control our beasts with the touch of a hand, a shift in the seat, then fly at a hedge with full speed and a prayer. I do not hunt for conversation; I care little for the pedigree of the hounds, and less for the fox, so long as they go. My aim was always to stay in the same field with the hounds all the way. And Caesar was unbeatable. He went at the solid stone wall of the old deer park at Ballintoy without a second's pause, all six feet of it, and we sailed over it together. He tore through the gorse above Whitepark Bay, leaped a cart road that crossed our path near the Croaghs in one long bound that left many another horse stranded. That is what I hunt for: the soar of feeling; the moment of suspension over a hedge, the flight before the descent; the wish that that sensation could endure. Nothing beautiful lasts.

Edward and I had a game. It began at breakfast one morning, not long after we were married. I wanted the newspaper, for the dates of the hunt, and Edward had his paper knife ready on the breakfast table but had not yet cut it.

"What would you be," he said, eyeing the advertisements on the front, "if you had to find yourself a job?" And he handed it to me.

There was demand, it seemed, for a Smart Girl to become a draper's assistant and I said I thought I would be well suited to the position, since I was, as was required, a good sewer, and felt I could take charge of books and could without much difficulty provide the necessary three references. Edward guffawed; I feigned offense and handed him back the paper with the challenge to find himself a position. He said the Cape Mounted Riflemen would suit him well since they wanted hardy youths who were accustomed to horses, cattle and agricultural pursuits, and would pay him between five and six shillings a day to be shot at, which seemed a reasonable price. I said he could not go, since they required only single men, and his eyes softened and he said: "I am shackled, it is true. I must bear it with patience."

I threw a mushroom, which he dodged skillfully as evidence of how he might cheat the cannonballs. It became our game over the Saturday morning paper. We were, in turn, the sole agent in Ireland for Richardson's bone compound, dentist to the working classes between the hours of nine and ten A.M., a steamboat captain for the *Brittanic,* a plumber (with the most improved sanitary goods on sale), a magnetist, a manufacturer of oil for lamps, a coachman (Protestant, married, teetotaller), a useful companion and lady's help (Edward), and once, famously, I was a harness horse for a dog cart, entirely free from vice and with a good mouth. The game always ended in the same way: in a kiss between the two newly hired workers. I do not recall when it was we stopped playing it. When the children became too numerous—after Charlotte was born, perhaps. We were engaged in it one April morning when Hill brought in the post, including a black-bordered telegram.

In the end it was Mother who outlived Father, but only by a matter of months. Father became ill with a tumor on his neck. He was referred to a London doctor, who rejected the idea of surgery and undertook to remove the offending tissue over a period of weeks, first by blistering the skin with nitric acid and then by lacerating and applying a plaster to the flesh on a daily basis until the whole became infected and could be cut out. He suffered weeks of pain in our house in London, to where Julia had been removed to nurse him and Mother, only to be told at the end that the cancer was in his blood and could not be cured. The dreadful procedure was agonizing and seemed to have accelerated the disease; he died within a matter of weeks. Within six months Mother too was dead.

I never liked our London house, a semidetached villa in Richmond. I could not shake off my sense of its attachment to the house next door, that the layout of our neighbors' house formed a perfect symmetry with our own, as if the architect had merely erected a great mirror on the partition wall to replicate everything exactly: their drawing room adjacent to ours; their kitchen; their bedrooms; the reflected gabled stairway. It made the experience of staying there feel unreal, as if one of us, our neighbors or ourselves, were living a parallel life that held no real substance, was a mere facsimile of the other. The difficulty was in deciding which was real: their existence or ours. When our house was quiet, late in the evening, one could sometimes hear a foot upon their stairs, the creak of a door on their side, the echoes of quietened ablutions. I could never shake off the feeling that the house had been mysteriously butterflied, like those paintings of exotically colored flowers and birds that the children sometimes make with Julia on folded paper: abstract, unreal, but perfectly proportioned. I was happy to leave it on the morning of my marriage to Edward, and I never went back.

We invited Julia to live with us; it seemed the dutiful thing to do.

"Do you think a person can decide to die?" she asked me. "I am quite certain that is what happened with Mother. Once Father passed away, she lost all heart. Her health had never been good, but when he went, she no longer had the will to carry on."

She told me something of what had occurred in the weeks after Father's death: Mother's inability to take anything but toast and water and the habitual salicin for the pains in her joints; her refusal to see visitors or leave the house; her insistence that the coals be wrapped in paper before being placed carefully on the fire so as not to jangle her too-jangled nerves; the long dark story of her declining health. And all the time Julia was telling me, I could not help but see the people on the other side of the partition wall, doing the same things in exactly the same way. I do not know if a person can die of a broken heart, but certainly they can die of self-starvation. It must have been one of the few decisions Mother made for herself in life.

My maternal grandfather was an elder of the Scottish Free Church. He wrote a letter to the *Witness* in 1853 in support of the Reverend Mr. Begg, calling for the overthrowing of the Catholic college of Maynooth, insisting that only true Protestants should be sent to Parliament. Julia found the cutting among Mother's things, wrapped in muslin, smelling of lavender to keep away moths. Such talk of fire and brimstone and the sulfurous fires of hell conserved in scented fabric. What would he say if he could see me now? He would be turning in his roomy graveled grave. And be unsurprised that I ended here; evidence, he would no doubt say, that if one sleeps with the devil one will rise with horns. I never met him. Mother never spoke to him after she married Father, and she never spoke of him to me, but I cannot help but feel that I have inherited something of his direct opinions. There is much to be said for a vision of the world in black and white: it is so much safer than having to consider shades and variations of color and tone; it is a kind of protection against overexposure to too much pigment.

Mother never told me a single intimate thing, nothing that I could form into an impression of her as anything other than a permanent invalid. There was some link missing between us, something she saw in me that made her want to keep her distance.

The little I know of her life before marriage I have learned from Julia, to whom she spoke freely after Father died. She must have had some spirit at a time, for she told Julia that she had married Father against her own father's will. He had made a match for her with another young man, one which she had entertained for a while. Then she met Father, at that time a brilliant young theology teacher of the Free Church College at Aberdeen, but when he came out in defense of Samuel Davidson, who stated, among other things, that the Pentateuch was not written by Moses, he immediately set himself up in opposition to her father. I can see why that would have ended any contemplation of a marriage in my grandfather's mind. Clearly there was no place for "private interpretation" in his worship. My father had a dictum: "Docility is our first duty," he used to say, "and freedom of thought is the next." I sometimes find it difficult to reconcile the two, but it was behind his philosophy always.

Unusually among his peers, Father encouraged us to read all kinds of academic literature, including (to the shock of many of his friends) Mr. Darwin and Professor Huxley and Professor Newman. He had no difficulty, he said, in reconciling the concept of evolution with his faith: it was neither shock nor contradiction to him to believe that God could create species that were capable of self-development.

"Let Man's mistaken vanity, his foolish contempt for the material world, impel him to struggle as he will, he strives in vain to break through the ties which hold him to matter and the lower forms of life." How can such words by Professor Huxley, once read, ever be forgotten? No woman who has writhed in the agony of childbirth would dispute our link to the animal world. A rational mind is of little value when one is laid helpless with pain on one's back, ankles shackled in stirrups, having lost control of bladder, bowel, reason. We are at our most primitive in bringing forth children.

Julia and I had an hour of Bible reading every day. I was entranced by the Psalms, the surprise of the vitriol in them: "The wicked go astray from the womb. They are wayward as soon as they are born, speaking lies. Their poison is like the poison of a snake; like a deaf cobra that stops its ear, which doesn't listen to the voice of charmers, no matter how skillful the charmer may be." Is there redemption to be found, then, in the voices of charmers? Can a person be saved through words? Is this my deliverance, this little book that the priest has left for me?

It is difficult to reconcile that rebellious impulse of Mother's with the mother I knew, but it must have been there, under the folds of silk and lace. No one can change that much. Perhaps that is the reason they made no real opposition to the union between Edward and me. From Free Church to Catholic is something of a leap, it is true. "But for all that," said my father, "we are all dissenters, and I would rather see my grandchildren reared in some faith than in none at all." Or perhaps it was a relief, to have me off their hands. They never seemed to know how to deal with me. The rules that applied to Julia did not apply to me.

Julia loved Oranmore, threw herself wholeheartedly into the entire romantic ideal of Ireland. Edward told her that the partition walls had originally been constructed of peat, for heat retention, and later lined with brick. She was delighted with the idea, and never once complained of the cold thereafter. It was exactly the kind of thing one would dismiss as nonsense in Ireland only to discover that it was true. I never fully inhabited Oranmore the way I had Priorwood. Perhaps that is true of any house one comes to as an adult: it does not occupy a person, nor a person it, in the way of one's childhood home, where one knows every creak on the stair, every knot in the breakfast table, the exact and velvety smell of the drapes in a closed-up room. Children see more than adults. As grown men and women we are too engrossed in what we say to one another, in what the next move is; we are not enough in the present. Children carry a superior knowledge: they are closer to the roots of things, of what is implied and not said. They can sniff out decay, taste treachery before it comes. Perhaps that is why Charlotte never trusted me. Perhaps she knew all along what was coming. Perhaps, for her, it was simply a matter of waiting.

Julia was fascinated by the stories of banshees and fairies. If I ever lost her, I knew she could be found in the kitchen, prattling to the servants and keeping them back from their work. Every season of the year is marked in a bizarre mixture of the pagan and the Christian, which the priest tolerates, if not openly encourages. There is an excuse for everything: the fire not being lit, or the cows not being milked, or the corn not taken in, or the sheets not going out, and inevitably it is to do with a saint or a fairy or a goblin and the terrible tragedy that will befall us all if their demands are not respected.

Not long after Julia came to live with us, early September, the afternoon mild, midges as thick as rain under the holly and around the late fuchsia, infesting the house with tiny V-winged dots, Edward announced that an outing was what was needed: a spot of blackberrying and a picnic to the standing stone at Carnalridge. The boys were delighted, of course, as was Julia. She had been talking to the servants and had a mind to photograph the White Wife. And on the way, Edward said, we would stop by the Mass rock, much overgrown now, but that Julia had expressed an interest in seeing. Edward described to Julia how the people would arrive there in their dozens with bundles of straw on which to kneel, and how the priest would stand with his back to the congregation, reciting the Mass, with lookouts posted on the outlying land. Julia was suitably impressed, admired the landscape, the bravery of the people who, despite fear of capture, turned out every week to worship their god. I never once pointed out the irony—that in all likelihood it was Edward's ancestors who were complicit in the oppression of his adopted faith. Edward had embraced Catholicism wholeheartedly, as if three hundred years of Protestantism had been a short deviation in the otherwise straight road of his family's religious history.

"There is nothing like the threat of opposition to bring out religious zeal," said Julia, and despite myself, I smiled at her. I had not realized she possessed any perspicuity at all.

Julia wanted to see the prayer tree too, which Peig had told her about. She made us smile with her poor attempt to mimic the accent. "It's where you go when there's something that you wish for, and the tradition is that in order for your prayers to be heard, you must leave a clootie, something precious to yourself—not valuable, you understand, but personal."

It was an extraordinary sight: a hawthorn tree by the well at the Strand Head, the worst place for a tree, battered mercilessly by the wind, entirely devoid of leaves or haws, even in May, but in their place budded tattered red ribbons, sorry scraps of clothes, shreds of paper, pieces of crockery gouged into the trunk. Where the bark had partly closed over these odd articles of faith they looked like they might have grown there, strange dark tumors in the flesh of the tree, each one of them fixed there by a prayer and the fervent, frantic wishing for something. All the debris from other people's lives, fluttering in the sea breeze, exposed in the desperation of love and wishing. Prayer: the universal poultice. Apply it to all fears and ills and it works not at all on the object but has a miraculous effect on they who offer it up. I think it is one of the most hopeless and most moving sights I have ever witnessed.

The boys had all brought something to leave and when Julia had helped them tie their scraps to the tree, I saw her pull a ribbon from her own hair, reach over and knot it to a battered branch.

"What did you wish for?" I asked her. "A happy marriage? Or a new photographic exhibition?"

She eyed my stomach, swelling for the sixth time. "A girl," she said, and smiled. "It would do you good, Harriet." And off she went, chasing Morris and Gabriel around the tree. Sometimes, I think Julia truly felt she had wished Charlotte into being that day. Perhaps she did. Who is to say where the personality of a child comes from? And Charlotte was trying; perhaps Julia did have some part to play in her character.

Death is so very straightforward when compared with the complexities of living. I did not go to Charlotte's funeral. Her body was coffined after the inquest, and the coffin left in the hall, covered in a black velvet pall, bordered in white cambric, until the burial ground in Bushmills was got ready. The funeral was a small and lonely affair: I watched them leave from the drawing room window, the attendant in a white sash, carrying a staff tied with a love ribbon, the horses bearing white plumes. Edward did not give notice of the arrangements. We had no strength for the platitudes of our neighbors, no patience for the hordes of curious tenants who would, no doubt, have turned out en masse to gawk and stare and reputedly pay their respects. And, since death has been decreed to be a strictly male affair, there was no question of the attendance of any of the female members of the household. So there were no mourners but Edward and Harry, home from school, a special dispensation for a dead sister. Harry favors Edward: he will always try to do the right thing. And everything was properly done; Edward saw to that.

If I had been asked before I would have said that grief was a question of sadness, a matter involving tears. I did not know anything of the horror involved, the nagging nausea at the neck of the stomach, like an early pregnancy. I did not know that it was looking around at everyone and everything important in one's life with the horrifying knowledge that there was more pain to come: that every one of them has the potential to cause agony; that despite one's very best efforts, one had laid oneself open to loss.

Maddie

1 FEBRUARY 1969

It's good to see you, Anna. I've missed you. But you're wise to stay in when the weather's the way it's been. Bitter cold; British Summer Time doesn't seem to be having any effect. And you've picked a good day to come. "Every day after Brigid's Day," Peig used to say, "is longer than the one before by the length of a rooster's step." Spring is on its way, the lightening of the days. Have you ever made a St. Brigid's cross, Anna? The one Brigid's Eve we were all at the castle together, I taught the weans the way Mammy had taught me. You start with a straight reed. Then you pinch a second one in the middle and bend it around the first one, to the right. Then you turn it, against the clock, as it were, and you pinch another one and you bend it over to the right and you keep doing that, again and again, holding the whole thing tight in the middle until it's all finished. You can't use reeds that are too fresh and that have too much spring in them; it's better to cut them a day or two before. But they can't be too dry either, or they'll not bend but break. You need to be able to feel the sap in them. I always thought it was an odd, lopsided thing, the St. Brigid's cross, the way the top never met the bottom and the right never met the left and the rushes all ended in different lengths. But the middle, the very center of it, is always the same. As if that was the whole point of it: like you needed the rushes to frame what had always been there, what you couldn't see without them: a perfect square of air. Within fourteen days of making it, Charlotte was dead.

Daddy used to lay people out. It's a strange thing when you think of it. I asked Mammy how it'd started, and she said his father used to do it, so I suppose people just kept on coming to the house. The knock would come to the window in the middle of the night sometimes, and he'd speak out to whoever it was, and sigh, and get up. At the door he'd shake the relative's hand and say, "Sorry for your trouble," and then he'd lift the old canvas bag from beside the hearth and set off. I didn't think much of it before, but when I saw little Charlotte, lying on the mistress's bed, her lips blue, a strange mark on her throat, I thought of him and of all the dead bodies he had touched, gently massaged into a thing a grieving family could look on. And I wished, not for the first or the last time, that he could be there again.

Do you remember, Anna, the day you and Conor took me out? July 1959, you wrote me it in your letter. A day of sparkle and glitter, you said. I can see it like it was yesterday. I was on the Cliff Walk, watching you swim, and you slipped through the water like an eel, hardly breaking the surface. You had your arms by your sides, your two knees together, and under the green gauze of the sea your body dipped and gathered. You could have been a current, a strand of weed.

Then you came back, the pair of you, dripping with seawater, and lay down on the grass to dry. And you said: "When was the last time *you* felt the sea on you, Nanny Madd?" and your gray eyes twinkled, and I smiled back, and you jumped up and shouted to Conor, and the two of you took me by the hands, laughing, down to the shore. You slipped off my shoes, peeled down my stockings. At the water's edge you took me by one elbow, Conor took me by the other, and between the two of you, you oxtered me in over the rippled sand until the water licked my ankles. I leaned on you, arched my feet, rose up on my toes, and I couldn't help but laugh as the cold slapped my shins and soaked the hem of my good summer skirt and took the breath from me. You walked me in further. "Tell us when to stop, Nanny Madd," said Conor, and a wave caught on my knee and then on my thigh and the shock of it made me laugh even more and I didn't tell you to stop. You kept your eyes on my face the whole time, "Further, Nanny? Are you sure?" and I swallowed my fear and I said, "Yes, the whole way in!"

To be weightless was what I needed. To lose the burden of creaking joints and bulging veins, to float. You kept walking until we were waist-deep in water, then an Atlantic wave that had begun to gather itself a mile out, beyond Crab Rock, came roaring in and hit me in the kidneys and knocked me sideways. You held me tight, took me right in, until the water buoyed me up, and I felt light and thin and faint and I thought—I really believed—that lying on my back with the whole ocean under me and the whole sky above, that I might just drift away, like that could be a way of ending.

"Don't tell the matron," I said to you afterward. "She'll say we've lost the run of ourselves. She'll never let us out again." And Conor laughed and said maybe we should make it an annual outing—celebrate the twelfth in the sea every year—but we didn't do it again. You and Conor went to England not long after that. And I didn't know if I'd see you again and I tried to tell you the story of what happened but you didn't want to know at that time. It was too hard a thing to hear. "It'll keep," you said, "Nanny, it'll keep." So I kept it. And now I can let it go.

What can I tell you about your mother that you don't know? She loved skies; she used to collect them. Everywhere she went she fell in love with one and she would bring it back and tell it to me. In the yellow house where you were born, she used to stand by the window with you in her arms and look out over the sea and tell you what the day was doing; she used to sing you the sea and the sky.

What was it Peig used to say? "A boat leaves no record when it passes through water." Well, your mother left you something. She left you all the love she could, and now I'm leaving you something too. It'll not be long now till your baby's in the world and I haven't told you everything yet. But it's a strange and a hard thing to tell, Anna, and I don't come out of it well, and I don't relish the telling of it. It's not something I've ever talked about, not to another living soul. The knowledge of it pulls at me the way the sea tugged that day at the hem of my skirt, twisting it around my wet legs, hobbling me. It won't let me go on and it won't let me go back. It won't let me go.

Harriet

Grangegorman Prison, Dublin

Monday 23 January 1893

Edward writes to say that we now have oil streetlighting on the Coleraine Road, a sight to behold. So now we will be able to see the full extent of the gloom.

Julia has come regardless, in the most astonishing gown, a fine gray silk, respectfully buttoned up to the throat, terrified, no doubt, of picking up some germ. The shape, however, was anything but respectful: loosely cut, smocked at the waist, puffed at the sleeve. It was the oddest combination, somewhere between Greek peasant and rector's wife. I do not believe she was wearing a corset, but I suspect her of using a "gay deceiver"; she really is terribly vain. I remember eyeing her once, just before we left for the Dawsons' (her bosom was distinctly conical under her magenta silk), and she colored right up to her ears, and then dashed out of the room on the pretense of having forgotten her shawl. We were not the kind of sisters who could have a conversation about undergarments; that was not the way Mother raised us.

As a special privilege (I have been uncommonly well behaved, it seems) they allowed us to meet across a rough wooden table, with a warder standing a little distance away. It was a relief to talk in such a way. Irony does not travel well when shouted through a grid.

"Good God!" I cried when I saw her. "Is that what ladies are wearing?"

"It is what I am wearing," she said. "There is no need to be so rude, Harriet!"

Not a good start. I was thinking (but did not say) that there may be some advantages to being here if that is what passes for fashion on the outside.

"How are you?" she said.

"As you would expect," I answered.

"You look thin."

"It is not the Savoy."

"How are they treating you, Harriet?"

"The same as everyone else, a little worse perhaps."

She fidgeted with her purse, an abomination in matching smocked gray silk. "Do you have a room, a cell, to yourself?"

"Oh, yes," I said. I was almost enjoying this little exchange. "They are keen on privacy here."

"Well, that is something. I mean, there are many things you can bear, Harriet, but encroachment is not one of them."

I stared at her. "What do you want, Julia?"

"What do you mean?" she said.

"Why are you here?"

"To see you, Harriet."

"After all this time? Why now?"

"I have been thinking about you. I did mean to come sooner, but I have been busy . . ."

"Busy?" I believe I laughed. "How? At lectures? Demonstrations? Invitations to musical soirées?"

"There have not been many invitations."

"No," I conceded, "I suppose not. Still, I would have thought your interesting suffragist friends would have been supportive. They are forever threatening prison. Do not they approve of me?"

"It is not the same, Harriet."

"No?"

"No."

"No, I suppose it is not."

We sat looking at our hands, neither of us knowing what to say.

"How is Florence?" I asked her.

"Oh, she is bonny," she said. "Such a contented child, Harriet. She hardly ever cries. And so long, not at all fine boned, and quite dark now. She is going to be like you."

There was a pause while we both reflected on this.

Then: "Do you get the papers?" she asked suddenly.

"No," I said. "Such privileges must be earned. Besides, I have tired of reading about myself."

"Mr. Gladstone has reintroduced the Home Rule Bill. Edward will be pleased. With any luck, you could be released to a new Ireland."

I believe I snorted.

"Is it the truth, Harriet, what the papers have reported? Is that what truly happened?"

"What do you care?"

"Harriet . . ."

"Why do you want to know?"

"I have always felt your treatment of the children to be harsh but I would have defended you to the last. I believe you punished them so they would learn responsibility, however misguided that was. I could never have thought you capable of cruelty for its own sake, no matter what you did. And yet what you did to Charlotte . . . I feel that I no longer know who you are."

"Why should that be important to you, to know who I am?"

"So I will know if there is anything of you in me."

I burst into laughter. I could not help myself. "Oh, Julia. You are not the same. You could never be like me, no matter how hard you tried."

"Then there is something to be celebrated," she said.

"I do not know why you have bothered to come."

She looked at me for a moment and then she said, "Why do you make it so difficult for people to help you, Harriet?"

"I do not need your help," I said.

"I went to look for the key," she said. "I found the apron in the usual place, but the key was not in the pocket. Why do you bait me so? Is it worth it to you now?"

I did not speak.

She picked up her gloves. "Mama knew you better than you thought. She said you would never look for affection, but that did not mean you did not need it every bit as much as the rest of us, or possibly more. You will never thank me for it, I know, but you will always be my sister, Harriet, and despite everything, I love you." Then she did the most extraordinary thing. She leaned across the table, placed her hand on my arm and kissed me on the cheek, and as she did so, I felt her slide a paper into my sleeve. And then she left.

My mother must have felt entirely unfooted by the secret she had kept hidden her entire life, the secret revealed by the paper Julia gave me. It was a letter addressed to my mother, and it simply read: "Do not go through with this marriage, Olivia, I beg of you. We can have a future together. Do not choose him because of his position. I would never publicly disgrace you, you must know that, but I beg you not to use that knowledge against me. I would be a father to our child. I would be a husband. I love you." The letter was unsigned but it was dated 18 April 1861: a few days before my parents' wedding; seven and a half months before I was born.

My dream comes back to me, the one in which my mother tried to tell me something. Was that what she was trying to say? That I am not my father's daughter? Is it possible to dream something that you did not already know? Is that what was missing when they looked at me? Is that what was there for them both when they saw Julia? I will never know the truth. When I think of my mother now, the look I see in her eyes is one of distrust. She must have thought me capable of betraying her to the world, but how could I have done that, when I did not know myself what I might betray? What a blunt and useless instrument is the truth when divorced from knowledge and from opportunity.

It makes sense of Julia and me, the differences between us, although if I had been asked to name which parent we shared I would not have chosen Mother. I have nothing of hers that I can detect and Julia is so much her daughter. Julia has never appreciated the hunt, the thrill of the chase. She is heading steadfastly toward Mr. Salt and the Humanitarian League. I would not have been surprised had she appeared with her hair cut like Lady Dixie and wearing a knee-length tartan. Once at breakfast, when Edward and I were preparing to go out to meet the Route, she lifted her head out of a volume of Mr. Blake's to deliver one of her well-rehearsed "statements."

"So," she said, "you are off now to hunt down and savagely kill an innocent animal that you and your fellow hunters have taken pains to conserve and protect for months for the express purpose of being able to hunt it now." She did not pause for breath.

"How very succinctly put," said Edward, smiling. "Harriet darling, are you ready for the blooding?"

And off we went, Edward in his red coat, leaving Julia frowning over her kedgeree. When I went into the morning room on my return, I found her book of poetry on my writing table, left open at "Auguries of Innocence." "The caterpillar on the leaf / Repeats to thee thy mother's grief. / Kill not the moth nor butterfly, / For the Last Judgement draweth nigh." I actually laughed aloud. Then I looked up Tennyson for her and left the page open at *"In Memoriam,"* on top of her Blake so she could read: "The seasons bring the flower again, / And bring the firstling to the flock; / And in the dusk of thee the clock / Beats out the little lives of men." The next morning, Blake was gone, and nothing more was said. Ridiculous sentimentality, to pine for nature. There is no human mother more cruel nor more resilient than she.

How strange and yet believable to find that I have been part of an elaborate masquerade since birth. Mr. Darwin says that in the natural world, the mocking abandon their own dress for the dress of those they imitate; that the imitators are rare; that the mocked abound in swarms. He says that the two invariably inhabit the same region. (For what would be the point in pretending to be something else if you then put yourself where none of those things were?) I have no ability for counterfeit; that has been my weakness. I have failed in turn to act the dutiful daughter, the quiet wife, the adoring mother. I thought I could play all these parts and still retain something of myself, but I was wrong. Perhaps if that realization had come sooner, I would have fared better. It is impossible to say.

If Mr. Darwin is right, if species of animals and plants do become modified over time, might it be true that such a change could come upon a person in the course of one lifetime? If I find myself at variance with the opinions of all those around me, if I find the position I am expected to occupy in the world too narrow a place, if I am inappropriate, would I do well then to change? Could I alter my appearance so as to blend in? I am neither behind nor ahead of my time but, somehow, at odds with it, an anomaly. I suppose I could smile and nod and coo as required; I could say I prefer needlework to the hunt; I could learn to quill, could bring myself to contemplate a flower arrangement and banish my customary look of boredom. I could adapt to survive, be green among foliage and yellow next to pollen. In a plant, in an animal, mimicry is considered evolutionary; nature selects for survival those individuals that have the capacity to adjust. But only imagine the state of such a person's soul.

Have I ever felt the need for another person? Mother, Edward, the children, Julia, they all needed me. I have been content to listen in on their lives, but have I been a part of them? It would be an act of kindness to release Edward. It is not such a hardship for me to be alone. The real endurance is to be trapped in a room with other people. I am happiest when I am by myself, with the cabinet that houses my little scraps of sky.

Why do I write this? How strange to contemplate the shape of one's own handwriting on the page: its intricate loops and tangled links, like a knotted chain. Is it to pass the hours, to keep a record, to remind myself to appreciate every minute of every hour I have outside of here? Or so as to be heard? And if so, by whom? What I know is, I need to write it. I need to make a mark, need to lay something down. I feel like a sculptor must feel, making a cast out of plaster of Paris, laying down layer upon layer of soaked linen strips in the hope that some recognizable form will emerge. The danger, as with the writing of it, is that the gypsum will set too quick to be molded: the flaws will be all preserved. Perhaps that is just as well. It is, perhaps, the counterargument that I am constructing. I call upon myself, Harriet Ormond, daughter, sister, wife, mother, horsewoman, lepidopterist: witness for the defense.

The truth is, I killed a child, my own. The last thing I can remember having in my pocket is a key that I dropped and that was the beginning of the unraveling of everything. If the key had stayed put, I would have gone back and opened the door and let Charlotte out and she would be alive and I would not be here now, without any pockets at all. What would have been the ending then? How else could I have been stopped?

I took the carriage to Coleraine, into Stewart and Hamilton to see if they could mend my riding boots, which had split up the back on the last outing with the Route. I was politely told that the boots were useless. I got back late for luncheon, where the children were assembled but for Charlotte. Julia was out on a visit to one of the Flowerfield girls, getting up an outing, no doubt. The governess explained that she had sent Charlotte up to wash her hands and, when she did not come down, went up to find that she had soiled herself and put her directly into the wardrobe room. I had lunch with the children. Morris complained of a cough, I remember, and I gave him a spoonful of syrup of ipecac and sent him back to the schoolroom and then went up to Charlotte. There was little light in the wardrobe room but her eyes had adjusted quickly. She had pulled out some old clothes from the press and gotten into an old dress of mine. Actually it was my green one, the one I was wearing when Edward and I first met. I had kept it in the hope that I would wear it again; of course it never fitted after Harry was born. She had taken off her own dress and stuffed it full of petticoats and stockings and propped it up so it looked like a headless child sitting lolling in the chair. She was talking to it, wagging her finger, telling it how naughty it had been, chastising it. Everything she had touched was filthy from her own mishap. I scolded her severely and put her own dirty clothes back on her and told her that if she insisted on behaving like a dirty animal she would be treated like one and I tied her hands up with one of the stockings and attached it to the ring on the wall to prevent her running around the room and I closed the door on her again and locked it.

I hung my apron on the hook at the back of the nursery door. I went about my usual business of the afternoon. I was in the morning room when I heard Julia return about three o'clock. I went up a little later, reached into the pocket for the key and found it was gone. I was certain that Julia had taken it. I imagined her going quietly up the stairs, turning the key in the door, speaking softly to Charlotte, offering her a drink, going as quietly as she had come. I left the apron there, so she could return the key unobserved by me. It was, I thought, the latest episode in our silent agreement. She would ensure that Charlotte was well; I would maintain the dignity of the one who had punished her. When I went back some time later and the key was still not returned I began to doubt her. The apron was hanging too high for any of the boys to reach, and besides, they had been in the schoolroom with the governess the entire time. None of the kitchen staff had any reason to be above stairs, but I mistrusted the girl, Maddie. I discouraged any communication between the servants and the children, but Charlotte had become a pet of hers. There was that incident on the beach when she had disobeyed my orders.

I went down to the kitchen but the girl denied having seen the key. I could not say if she was telling the truth. What to do? Confront Julia, an admission that I knew about her tampering, risk upsetting the balance? It occurred to me that perhaps the key had caught in my dress and fallen out between the nursery and the morning room. Peig began to talk to me about dinner and sent Maddie out to the greenhouse to gather some parsley. When I finally got away and retraced my steps I found it, on the spiral stairs, where it must have lain all along. That was when the dread hit me. Charlotte had been alone in the punishment room for three hours.

Maddie

13 FEBRUARY 1969

St. Valentine's Day tomorrow, Anna, and not a single card, not even from John Roddy, the oul' goat. You needn't be laughing. Everybody needs a bit of loving, even at my age—especially at my age. Aye, loving maybe, but not sleep; the old need little of that. I lie awake in the dark at three and four and listen to the plumbing. It worries me, the sounds it makes. I don't think they replaced the half of those old copper pipes. I hear them groaning and the water plumping above my head and under the floorboards, and I remember stories of burst tanks. But when I ask them about it the nurses say there's nothing to worry about, like I was a wean worrying about monsters under the bed. That's what it is to be old: no one takes you seriously. Worrying about things that are never going to happen—that's what's expected of you.

I've been lucky, Anna. Your mother's family was good to me, a warm bed in the yellow house for as long as I wanted it, and I was happy there, till I got the cold from going out to the line in a shower with no cardigan and my lungs caught, and I ended up here again.

The castle has changed hands that many times. The family moved out during the Great War, the place was all closed up, the gardens planted out with vegetables. And when the Second World War broke out, it was commandeered by the troops, trees torn up, the grounds covered in Nissen huts, unrecognizable.

Then in 1942 the Americans arrived. I can still see the coils of barbed wire along the beach, the soldiers crouching behind antitank guns in the sand. So odd to see that: strangers on the strand, defending us against the enemy. Owen signed up, early on, gave us all a shock; an odd thing for him to do, to sign up for a British war. I don't know if it was the newsreels that set him thinking; maybe he thought it would be glamorous. Or maybe it was that old wanderlust that he got from his father, that feeling that there must be more to life than this. I kept my distance from him for the most part. It wasn't my place to stick my nose in his affairs; I didn't have the right. I watched him court Greta and marry her, and I waited for news of Conor and I celebrated the arrival of my grandson in private with a cup of boiled water and a drop of Bushmills and a spoonful of sugar to sweeten it. I made Conor a quilt too, like the one I'd made for Owen. I gave it into Greta's hand. I could tell she wasn't interested; old-fashioned it must have seemed to her, I'm sure. She probably never put it over him. She never passed any remarks about me making it. Nobody pays any attention to an old woman who puts her time in sewing for other people's babies.

When I heard that Owen had volunteered, I kept an eye on the papers for news of the Coleraine Battery. He must have been one of the oldest recruits; it's a wonder they took him on at all, but he was a driver for Shivers' at the time and knew how to handle a heavy vehicle and I think that stood in his stead. Of course, Greta's father had been in the First War and likely enough put a word in for him with the officers. He became a gunner in the Sixth Light Anti-Aircraft Battery, was recruited above Bobby Love's seed shop in New Row. I read in the paper how they were entertained in the town hall by the Boys' Brigade Silver Band;

how they all sang "Tipperary" and "Hang Out the Washing on the Siegfried Line," and were praised high and low by the president of the Rotary Club. Then there was a final dinner in the Strand Hotel, just below here, and on the twenty-eighth of November 1939, they paraded down the main street in Coleraine, on their way to the train station, and I stood with the rest of the sisters and wives and mothers, hidden in the crowd, and waved him good-bye.

He did look smart in his cap, cocked to the side, and the shine on his buttons and the buckle on his belt, and that white strap coming down his right-hand shoulder, under his arm. And that was the last time I saw him. Nearly a year after that, Bella called at the door in Victoria Terrace and said there was word that the Sixth LAA Battery were on board the *Dominion Monarch* on their way from Liverpool to Freetown and that the ship was in the Irish Sea, passing Rathlin. We got up onto the Green Hill, the pair of us, to see if we could see any sign of it, but it was blowing a gale and we could see nothing but gray seas and white water. He was killed at Halfaya Pass, the seventeenth of June 1941. I'll not forget that name: Halfaya Pass. It doesn't sound like a place to die at all. It sounds like a place where you'd go for the scenery.

I loved him, I suppose, but not in the way a mother should, for I never had anything much to do with him and no one ever knew he was mine. No one but Bella. The night before the news came that he was lost, two cats took up station outside my window and the pair of them went on yamming the whole night. Have you ever heard that, Anna? I'm not talking about when they're in heat and you would hear the female cat screeching round the whole country. The two of them stood facing each other, and the one would open its mouth and say something: yam, yam, yam; and the other would stand and listen and then answer it back. And that was the way they went on, the whole livelong night, till I was ready to put my toe in them. I got up at the finish-up and threw a teapot of water over them. The oul' people would have said it was the banshee, but it was no banshee, just two cats talking. And then Owen was dead.

It was Bella I went to. She opened the door to me, her hands covered in flour and the house full of the smell of sodas on the griddle. I said, "Owen's dead," and she nodded and took me in and sat me down and held my hand in hers with the flour and the buttermilk sticking to them, until I'd cried every tear that was in me.

Oh, I've lived too long. The young ones shouldn't die before the old. It's not the right order of things. Charlotte is seventy-seven years dead today. Impossible to think of her as an old woman of eighty years and more. When I think about it now, about the way things were back then, I think I must have lived three lives. It's all so long ago.

Some ghosts are so quiet you would hardly know they were there. This morning I woke with ten more minutes of night in the sky, the moon tinting from behind a cloud, not a star to be seen. There's a bough that hangs broken from one of the elms in the avenue. It's landed in a crook in the lower part of the tree and it rocks like the rib from the keel of a boat, or a cradle, one solitary bone of a branch, blackened by rain, keeping me awake, rocking bony lullabies the whole year round. And then a draft at my back, a shadow over the chimney breast, and when I looked, there was Charlotte at the end of my bed. People think that the dead leave quickly but Charlotte died in a windowless room, behind a door with the key turned in the lock. There was nowhere for her to go and she is here still. Little wonder. The living need to let go of the dead, and how could the mistress ever have let go of her? She'd have had to let go of guilt. We both would. And guilt's a sticky thing, sticky as sap, hard to rid yourself of.

In the sky this morning, there was one small curl of pale blue to the east, and it was the space between his forefinger and thumb when Alphie used to make his hand a spyglass and peep through, one-eyed, monstered, and say he was a pirate, Calico Jack, come to steal a princess. Charlotte would scream and run straight at my knees, catch in my skirts, trouser me. Alphie steadied me by the elbow and said, "Charlotte, don't annoy Maddie, now," and winked at me and turned away.

The air and the light today are as thin as a cobweb: a sky that would break your heart. A glimpse of what could be. Down on the shore in the early morning light, a fox scavenging for sand eels in the low tide. Peig never liked to see a fox on the beach. There was one there the day Charlotte died.

"That's before something," she said. And she was right. Everything, from then on, was after.

About four o'clock, Peig sent me up to empty the hot water bottles and flush down the toilets, and when I opened the nursery door, there was a chair behind it that scraped back across the carpet when I went in. I put it back against the wall and it was then I heard sobbing from the wardrobe room. I went to the door and spoke in and it was Charlotte who answered me. I tried to quieten her, for there was nothing else I could do. I headed back down to the kitchen and there was nobody about so I took the spiral staircase, and near the bottom, at the bend in the stair, I found a key on the step. I knew it was the key to the wardrobe room, and I knew Miss Julia was out of the house. I picked it up and stuck it in my hair, under my cap, and went downstairs to get Charlotte a drink of water. Outside the schoolroom, I passed Morris, going in, wheezing, a sly look about him as usual, something glinting in his hand, under his sleeve, blue glass. He knew I shouldn't have been on that stair. He was probably storing that up to use against me. When I got to the kitchen, Peig wasn't there, but she'd left the spuds soaking for me in the scullery. I heard a step, and I stuck my hands in the water of the sink, for fear it was the mistress coming looking for me, but it was Alphie saying the mistress wanted a sea bath, and would I give him a hand in the cellar.

In the dim light, Alphie took off my cap and unpinned my hair and combed it out with his hands. He said it held all the colors of the stars, the dead ones and the living, and when he did that, he combed every thought out of my head except the one: that I wanted him, that I chose to have him.

A while later, the mistress came into the kitchen and asked if anyone had seen a key. She looked me straight in the face and I looked straight back at her and said, "No." I went looking for it as soon as she'd left and I found it after a while on the cellar floor. I slipped back up and left it on the stairs. We read in the papers that she told the inquest she had it in her pocket the whole time. Why did she say that? In her mind, was losing a key as criminal as losing a child? I forgot about her, Anna. I forgot that Charlotte was in the wardrobe room.

Harriet

Grangegorman Prison, Dublin

Monday 3 April 1893

These are the borrowing days, wet and cold: the days March stole from April to teach a lesson to the old brindled cow. Edward told me the story: how the cow boasted that the severity of March could not kill her; how March took nine days from April and with its foulest weather slayed and skinned the poor old cow. I laughed when he told me this. I was carrying Harry, our first, and my belly was tight and swollen already and he came round the back of the chair where I had been sitting at breakfast and he leaned over and kissed me in the hollow of my throat where he knew, after months of exploration, I had no resistance, and his hair brushed my cheek and I closed my eyes as he cupped his hand under my stretching stomach. Then the door opened, Julia's voice before we could even see her, saying it is sure to brighten up, it always does in April; we will go for a walk, a gentle one, and she does not even hear the sound that her shoes make as they crunch over the shattered fragments of a moment that lay scattered everywhere about the room.

These are the pictures that form under my closed eyes when the pain makes a fist that clenches and unclenches inside my head.

Edward writes to say that he heard the new bells at St. Patrick's Church ring for the first time and it was a charming sound. He says it will not be long now till I hear them too. This is the last night I will spend here. Edward comes for me tomorrow. He seems to be of the opinion that I am going back. He must know that that is not possible, that the time for new beginnings is past. I have a chance, I suppose, to try again, to make a new life with Edward and Florence and the boys. But it feels to me that the time for love is past. Who would believe me now?

I have no mirror, but I do not need one to see all the places where life has touched me: the red welts around my waist where the band of my skirt tightens when I sit; a lobster pinch between my breasts; the dead-skin stretches on my belly; the permanently swollen knuckle of my right-hand thumb where Caesar kicked me once; my body history; my identifying marks. We harm ourselves: the attrition that is life happening, a gradual weathering; a loss of moisture and roundness replaced with cracked skin and folds of flesh. The inevitability of it: why do the old not warn us? Or is that all they do, judging with their eyes while we hear nothing?

The sky is losing light. Night grows up from the ground. From the cobbled yard, it creeps up the walls, thickening, darkening even the lighter of the stones, pools and gathers in the mortar, fills in all the joins and cracks. It completes the boundary wall, stands poised at the top to do battle with its old enemy, the sky, so that it feels like night is not the onset of darkness but the rejoining of masses that have been temporarily separated by the day. A thrush starts up, insistent trill. What possesses a bird to sing at dusk? To ward off the dark? I will never forget how it felt to pass under those walls, to walk through that great door that still had something of the manor house about it; to know that I would not step outside again for a full twelve months.

In the last days, I have noticed a difficulty. I see other people (a warder or an inmate, there are no others) make a gesture or mouth a phrase that I recognize as my own. Parts of me are being stolen, right in front of my eyes. No one here will acknowledge it, and I am powerless, since to do so myself would surely result in an accusation of madness. Soon there will be nothing left of me but the mask I wear here, and what will become of me then? How can I take it off if there is nothing of me left underneath? I am afraid I have forgotten my face.

This is not my prison. I carry it with me. We devise cages of our own choosing. I will never say, "It was not so bad," never dilute the fear and the dread and the horror of it, because it was, every bit as bad, and worse. I will never say, "It is over now," because it will never be over. I will never say, "It is long in the past," because it is not. It is the hole in the present and in the future, in my every day and in my every day still to come. I will never say, "It is extraordinary what the spirit can endure," not because that is not true, not because it is not extraordinary what the spirit can endure, but because to speak it, to set it down in words, is to belittle the extraordinary achievement of the spirit.

Just say, you struck out one night across a field, away from lights on a night without moon or stars. Just say, you stayed close to the hedge where the dark pooled under branches and small noises quickened your steps. Just say, you stopped then, and let the night settle on you like a blanket. Imagine if you let the dark seep into your ears, up through your nose and your mouth. Imagine if you let it slide down your throat, down into your chest, let it fill your lungs, fly into your veins and your fingers and toes until it filled all of you, every last inch of you. Who would you be then, standing there, full of the liquid dark? Would it really be so bad? Would it, say, be worse than the dread of it? Could you take it on yourself, all the things that could happen, all the dangers that might befall? Could you do it? Life is fluid. We are the ghosts of all the people we might become, peering forward to try to catch a glimpse of what could be, our future selves staring back at us, at who we might have been, never were.

Last night, a figure walked into my cell, through the locked door, past the foot of the bed and up to my side. It was a woman, I think, darkly dressed, her face cowled in a black hood, but with an impression of pale hair at the edge. I tried to say, "What is it?" but my throat was dry and no words came out. She turned after a moment and walked away, something blue in her hand, a bottle I think. As I struggle to recall it now, it seems to me that she reached down and touched my forehead, made some kind of sign upon my brow, and I thought it was Charlotte grown, come back from some future life to extract an impossible promise from me. I think I made her one, because I woke up saying something, my voice thick with sleep. I cannot be sure that this is what happened. I cannot be sure it happened at all.

All day I've been trying to reach for it, what it meant. What comes back to me is Robert Templeton's superb South American collection, his *morpho* and *prepona* butterflies. I saw them, on loan to the Royal Dublin Society, that time I went to Dublin with Edward. I spent hours gazing on them, struggling to try to describe that agonizing color, even to myself: how it altered when a visitor passed the window and a shadow fell across them; how the texture seemed at once compressed, like so many layers of fine metallized tissue, and at the same time translucent, pearlized markings clearly visible behind. As if the source of the color were hidden somewhere; not pigment but light itself, solid and at the same time vaporous, shifting, like a secret one knew once but can no longer recall, something on the borders of memory, of understanding, of enlightenment, of love. One felt as if one were peering at a ray of phosphorized sunlight through blue water, utterly bewitching and unattainable, a yearning for something one does not understand.

Maddie

28 FEBRUARY 1969

So, Anna, this is the latest. The Russians and the Americans can put men into space and bring them home safe, and we can't walk from Belfast to Derry without half killing each other. We're a backward race, there's no doubt about it. I don't think there'll ever be any saving of us. We're as bad as each other. The captain says, "There's green and there's orange; and there's places the one can go and the other can't, and if only people would abide by that, we'd all live peacefully." So that's to be the way of it, then. We're to be like the blacks and the whites in America: as long as we don't mix, all will be well with us.

What have you brought me? Snowdrops: pearls of spring. It's true then, the winter's over.

A year or two after I was born, Mammy told me, the town was overrun by geologists, who got very excited about the things that people had been stepping over for years: tools made of flint, hammer stones, part of the antler of a red deer that had been used as a grubber. The wind had been playing archaeologist, it seemed, and had dug out the sand pits above the Big Strand. And they had decided, the men from the geological section of the British Association, that at one time, centuries before, the river Bann had emptied into the sea about two miles further inland than it does now. Imagine that, Anna. That means that when you stand on the sand dunes and look over the river to Castlerock, you're standing on land that was underwater, land that's been given back by the sea. It makes you wonder how anyone—the master or his father or his grandfather—could have had the nerve to put their name on it. The sea's just as likely to take a notion of having it back again, and what will it matter then whose name is on the map? Nothing lasts.

Don't be afraid of what you might have inherited, Anna, of what you are capable of. Have faith in yourself. You are Harriet's daughter as much as Florence's and there is no shame in that. If she could, this is what I think your grandmother would say to you. Make friends with the dark in you. It is not your enemy. Open your mouth to it, drink it in, talk it out, know it. It's as much a part of you as are your nails and your knuckles and your tongue. And you're not alone with your dark; none of us is. Know this: old Nanny Madd knew you before you knew your own self, before you knew how to be, how to act, how to pretend, and she loved you, for everything you are. That bell you hear, Anna, when it rings for the Angelus, the howl of the sea at night, those sounds that are in your ears are in my ears too. Those vibrations that we haven't touched or held or owned, but that have traveled through us both, they're what connects us to this place. They are what gives us the right to stand here and say this is home, this is where we belong, and not be afraid. This is my wish for you: that you'll never feel dread at the swell of a baby in your belly; that God will always be between you and all harm.

The sea is our constant, Anna. What else is like the sea? When the sun shines on it, it's the green of the bottle that the ginger wine came in, and when a cloud passes over, it's the gray slate of the schoolroom, flecked with chalk. There are days when it looks brimful, like it couldn't hold another drop without spilling over, or like it's forcing the sky to shrink to make room for it. It's hard to believe, from up here, that the sea is liquid—that if you kicked off your shoes and rolled up your stockings and waded in, the whole solid self of you would push that mass of water aside.

I know where I'm going when my time comes. On my way back to my mother's cottage, I'll stand on the cliff top and watch a streak of sunlight trace the spine of Binevenagh and dance off the white villas at Castlerock. I'll fix my eye on the blind eye of the Bishop's Temple at Mussenden. I'll be a water-gazer again. I'll stop at Burnside, and turn and look down the road behind me and wait for the racing sun to catch me up and close my eyes until I feel its heat on my face, and turn back and walk on only when it has begun to chase the clouds on up ahead. I'll turn my head to better hear the crickets sawing in the long grass and as I walk along I'll rise wrens warbling out of the hedges. I'll put my hand on a stone in the wall on the sea walk and I'll feel the weight of every hand that ever rested there. I'll smell the smoke that climbed the chimneys. I'll feel the rain that spat at them, the sea that licked their feet, the wind that wrapped around them, the ice that crept up between the stones. I'll be home. I know just how it will look.

People said that Bella could see things, things that other people couldn't. One time, I remember, her man took us out on his boat over to Greencastle. It was a fine September day, with the sun shining and the waves high. When we got across the lough, we had tea from a can and fruitcake and fraughans, and we went for a walk around the village. On the way back again, the wind got up, though the sun was still shining, and when we hit the open water round the Barmouth, the boat began to dip low in the water and then climb high up on the waves. Each time a wave hit, we got a soaking. There was no such thing as a sheltered spot. Bella was at the side, cowering down—not that it was any drier there—and I was standing in the center of the boat, feet planted apart. I could feel the waves as they hit, and the dip and rise under my feet, and I started to feel like it was me that was guiding the boat, the strength in my legs that was powering it, my feet balancing it on the water; like nothing could harm me. Another wave hit and my mouth filled with salt spray and I laughed and looked over and waved at Bella to come out and enjoy the ride. She was looking toward me with a look of terror on her face. Not terror of me, I was sure of that, and not terror of the sea either. But there was something in her face. God knows what dark angels she saw at my shoulders, willing me on, pushing me toward the bow. Whatever they were, they weren't strong enough then. My feet were planted, steady, but my mind, my mind was standing on the prow yelling, "More! More!" ready to jump right down into the shock of the cold water, to join whatever was powering that sea, ready to fly to the dead.

Bella believed that the dead moved around within their dead lives. She thought them capable of revisiting the parts of their days they'd lived and the parts they hadn't. She said the walls between this life and the other were thin, and if there was a need, a wish to make amends, a wish to hear the truth, an urge to forgive, then a way could be found between the two, a way could always be found.

If I hadn't gone with Alphie to the cellar, if I'd remembered the key and gone back up and brought Charlotte a drink and not forgotten her, there'd be no diary and no story to tell. My whole life I've had two lives to live: my own and Charlotte's. For her, I lay down on the sea and let it carry me and looked up and fell in love with the sky. For her I swallowed my terror. I took off my mother's turquoise brooch and slipped it under my mattress because I wanted not to be safe for one day and that was the day with Alphie in the cellar. Because of me there was Owen, and then Conor, and because of the mistress, there was Florence and then you, Anna. And now because of all of us, there's a new life, child of my heart. Charlotte is waiting, Anna. She is here now. Don't look like that; the good have nothing to fear from the dead. She wants her life back. She's owed one, by her mother, and by me. I am father and mother both to her—because of what I know, because of everything I've seen and done and never said, never uttered, until now. I can see her kicking. She's ready.

Will you sing me the sea, Anna, will you, will you sing me the sea?

AUTHOR'S NOTE

The Butterfly Cabinet is a work of fiction inspired by real events that occurred at Cromore House, the home of the Montagu family of Portstewart, on the north coast of Ireland in 1892. On the evening of 13 February, the family doctor was called to the house, where he pronounced three-year-old Mary Helen Montagu dead by asphyxia. At the inquest that was held in the house the following Monday, the child's mother, Annie Margaret Montagu, gave evidence that on the Saturday, she had tied the child's hands with a stocking to a ring on the wall of "the wardrobe room," locked the door and left her alone for three hours. The assembled jury returned the verdict that she did "feloniously kill and slay the said Mary Helen Montagu" and returned her for trial at the Derry assizes, bail having been accepted. Following a magisterial inquiry at Coleraine Police Barrack, which was adjourned to Coleraine Courthouse, fresh charges were brought under the Act for the Prevention of Cruelty to Children regarding the treatment of three of the family's other children. Several servants gave evidence. Following accusations of a biased jury, the case was eventually heard on Monday 3 April at the Four Courts in Dublin, where Mrs. Montagu was found guilty of manslaughter and sentenced to twelve months' imprisonment. She gave birth to a child in Grangegorman Prison in the summer of 1892 and was released in April 1893.

ACKNOWLEDGMENTS

Sincere thanks to: the Arts Council of Northern Ireland and to Damian Smyth, to the Creative Writers' Network, Belfast, and to mentor Damian Gorman; to the Tyrone Guthrie Centre at Annaghmakerrig; to the staff at Portstewart and Coleraine Public Libraries and the newspaper archive at Belfast Central Library; to Gregory O'Connor, archivist at the National Archive in Dublin, and to the Ecos Centre, Ballymena, for access to the butterfly collection on loan from the Ulster Museum. Thanks also to: the staff at Flowerfield Arts Centre, Portstewart; to the Flowerfield, Ballycastle, and Jane Ross writers' groups; to Heather Newcombe and the facilitators at the Let Me Take You to the Island writing festival on Rathlin, especially Joan Newmann, Kate Newmann and Ted Deppe.

Thank you to my brilliant first readers, Una Kealy, Bridgeen McAlister, Alice McGlone and Zoë Seaton, and for listening on the beach, Sheena Bannon and Joan Grier-Mulvenna. I wish to acknowledge Sharman Apt Russell's inspirational book *An Obsession with Butterflies* and Hugh Kane's selections from the *Coleraine Chronicle* in *The Flood Tide* and *Ebb and Flow*. Huge thanks to my UK editor Mary-Anne Harrington and to my U.S. editor Wylie O'Sullivan, both of whom have eyes that see differently to other people's; to my agent Clare Alexander; and to Anna Stein of Aitken Alexander Associates, New York. Thank you to *Zoetrope: All-Story* magazine and particular thanks to the NEELB mobile library service (c. 1975–1985) for bringing the books.

ABOUT THE AUTHOR

Bernie McGill was born in County Derry in Northern Ireland in 1967, the youngest of ten children. She received her BA and a master's in Irish writing from Queen's University Belfast. For twelve years she managed a professional theater company, and more recently has worked as a part-time teacher and lecturer (in English, creative writing and Italian) and occasionally works as a freelance fund-raiser for the arts. In 2008 her story "Sleepwalkers" won the *Zoetrope: All-Story* Short Fiction Contest. Other short stories have been shortlisted for a number of awards (Bridport, Seán Ó'Faoláin, Michael McLaverty, Brian Moore, Orange/Northern Woman) and published in *Brand, Fortnight, Verbal* and *Northern Woman* magazines and in *The Belfast Telegraph* and broadcast on BBC Radio Ulster. Her work has also been anthologized in *My Story* (BBC/Blackstaff, Belfast, 2006) and in *The Barefoot Nuns of Barcelona and Other Stories* (Greer Publications, Belfast, 2005). She has been a recipient of an Arts Council of Northern Ireland Individual Artist Award on three separate occasions. In 2006 her stage play *The Weather Watchers* was produced and toured throughout Ireland. In March 2010 her script for the musical production *The Haunting of Helena Blunden* was produced and toured Ireland. She is married and has two children and now lives by the sea in Portstewart, Northern Ireland.

ABOUT THE AUTHOR

The Butterfly Cabinet

A NOVEL

Bernie McGill

Reading Group Guide

Author Q&A

ABOUT THIS GUIDE

The following reading group guide is intended to help you find interesting and rewarding approaches to your reading of *The Butterfly Cabinet.* We hope this enhances your enjoyment and appreciation of the book. For a complete listing of reading group guides from Simon & Schuster, visit www.community.simonandschuster.com/.

Introduction

When Maddie McGlade, a former nanny now in her nineties, receives a letter from the last of her charges, she realizes that the time has come to unburden herself of a secret she has kept for decades: What really happened on the last day in the life of Charlotte Ormond, the four-year-old only daughter of the big house where Maddie was employed in her youth? *The Butterfly Cabinet* unfolds in chapters that alternate between Maddie's story—as told to Anna, Charlotte's would-be great-niece—and the prison diaries of Charlotte's mother, Harriet, who was held responsible for her daughter's death.

Topics and Questions for Discussion

1. How did you feel about the dual-narrator structure of the book? Did you want to hear more from Anna? Were there any other characters whose narration you would have liked to read as well?

2. What parts of the book took you most by surprise? What were your favorite moments?

3. Who do you think was the most conflicted character in the book? Why? How about the most tragic?

4. Maddie said to Anna, "Everyone should have a person in their life to tell them stories of their birth" (p. 7). Who is that person for you? What are some of your favorite stories about you as a child?

5. Who do you think was the more reliable narrator, Harriet or Maddie? Why?

6. Harriet describes her parenting philosophy, stating: "It is a kindness to teach them as soon as is possible that they cannot always do as they would, without regard for others. It is for their own safety and their own self-preservation" (p. 149). Do you agree? Do you think Harriet adhered to this method of parenting? Why or why not?

7. Harriet states, "I watched with relief as Harry and then Thomas and James were sent off to school, regretted only that the others were too young to go" (p. 151). How does this confession affect your perception of Harriet as a mother? Do you feel any sympathy for Harriet?

8. Discuss the relationship between Harriet and her mother. What behaviors did Harriet learn from her mother? In what ways do you think Harriet's mother influenced Harriet's personality and parenting style?

9. Maddie wrote about the legend of Molly Bradley: "There was always a point behind those stories we were told. Dark warn-

ings as to what could happen to a girl who didn't guard herself: keep your coat buttoned up tight; stay out of the dark of the hedges; don't talk to the tinkers, they'll turn your head; be wary of men" (p. 128). What were the purpose of these stories? Based on what you read, how did these stories influence Maddie? Were you ever told any kind of "cautionary tales" as a child?

10. Do you think Maddie was in the right when she wrote the letter to the Cruelty Society? What do you think you would have done in the same situation?

11. The press acted as a Greek chorus of sorts in Harriet's trial. At one point, she described the papers as saying, "There is still one law for the rich and another for the poor" (p. 71). Do you think Harriet was treated differently because of her social status? Do you think a similar distinction between "rich law" and "poor law" exists today?

12. Consider Harriet's conclusion that "The whole process of the trial must be designed to humiliate the defendant. Since one is not permitted to speak, what other reason can there be for being present?" (p. 174). Discuss the differences between the judicial system Harriet went through and the one in place in America today. Do you think the modern American system is any more fair or more kind than the one that Harriet experienced?

13. Reread the paragraphs starting with "I took the carriage to Coleraine, into Stewart and Hamilton . . ." on page 210. In revisiting Harriet's side of Charlotte's death, do you see any moral wiggle room in her account? Can you sympathize with Harriet at all?

14. Harriet's trial for Charlotte's death set out to determine, as Harriet described, whether "wickedness or evil intention had motivated my actions" (p. 179). Harriet went on to say, "I meant to punish her, certainly. I meant to correct her behavior, without doubt. I did not mean to injure her, not in any way. I was trying to teach her how to save herself" (p. 179). Do you believe Harriet?

15. The final opinion of the jury was that "the crime had been committed through a mistaken sense of duty" (p. 180). Do you agree? If you were on Harriet's jury, how would you have ruled?

16. Maddie asked Anna, in reference to her taking the key to the wardrobe room, "Is a lie always something you've said that's not the truth, or can it be something you've never said? Can a lie be a truth you've never told, not to anyone? Not in the confessional, and not in the witness box? Is it any defense to say you were never asked?" (p. 125). Do you think that, in keeping the key story secret, Maddie lied about her culpability in Charlotte's death? How do you personally define a lie?

17. Harriet often described her life in fairly despondent terms, writing, for example, "My whole life spent in the way of myself: working in my own shade, not able to crawl out from underneath it, obliterating with my own being what I have been striving so hard to try to achieve" (p. 52) What do you think Harriet was striving to achieve, and what was she fighting against? What do you think was the source of Harriet's profound unhappiness?

18. Consider Harriet's love of butterflies. Why do you think Harriet was so drawn to the creatures? "How hard the smallest of creatures will try for life," she writes (p. 139). Do you see the butterflies as a metaphor for something or someone else?

19. Harriet described the wallpaper she bought for the sitting room where she kept her butterflies as "an extraordinary design of white dove and gilt cage with a background so dark as to be almost black. Unexpectedly, when . . . the light caught it near the window, the narrow bars of the cage all but disappeared, leaving only the gilt base and the bird apparently freed, about to take flight, while in the darker corners of the room the flickering firelight picked out the gilt and showed the bird to be exquisitely caged" (p. 52). What symbolism do you see in this passage?

20. After Maddie told Anna about how Harriet died—she fell from her horse—Maddie added, "Since we're in the business

of telling the truth, Anna, I'll tell you this. Feeley said she was the best horsewoman in the country, and no horse that he knew of would dare to throw her off if she didn't want to be thrown" (p. 139). Do you think Harriet committed suicide?

Enhance Your Book Club

1. Visit a butterfly museum or butterfly zoo with your reading group, and see if the butterflies inspire you in the same way that they did Harriet: "The colors, the markings, the scales on the wing, each one different, each one unique: the wonder of nature transfixed," she writes. "[Butterflies are] a piece of earth made heaven-bound. To look at a butterfly is to remind us of what we are and of what we will be again" (p. 121). After your trip, do you see Harriet any differently?

    a. Visit en.wikipedia.org/wiki/Butterfly_zoo#United_States or www.butterfly-houses.com for lists of butterfly zoos in the United States, or Google "butterfly museum" or "butterfly zoo," followed by your hometown, to find local alternatives.

    b. If you can't visit a butterfly museum, go to the photo gallery at www.butterfliesandmoths.org/gallery to see a wide variety of beautiful close-up photos of butterflies.

    c. You can also visit the American Museum of Natural History's butterfly website at www.amnh.org/exhibitions/butterflies/cams.php# and click on "Click to View Our Live Butterfly Web Cam" to check in with the tropical butterflies at AMNH in real time.

2. The theme of passing stories down from generation to generation is central to *The Butterfly Cabinet*. Reach out to an older family member or friend and ask them for a story that they want to pass down to you. If you have contact with younger generations, reach out to them and tell them a story from your memory that you want to keep in the family. Or, if you

prefer, write out a family story—either one you've heard or one you want to share—and bring your writing to your book club. Once you're all together, share your stories!

3. Though *The Butterfly Cabinet* in its entirety is fictional, the author used a true story for inspiration. Do a bit of research on the real-life story and the historical backdrop that inspired *The Butterfly Cabinet* and bring your findings to the book club. Possible topics include, but aren't limited to, Cromore House; the Montagu family; Annie Margaret Montagu; the history of the Act for the Prevention of Cruelty to Children; Grangegorman Prison; the history of lepidopterology; and women's rights in late-1800s Ireland. Refer to the Author's Note for more ideas. Once you're together, discuss how the real-life story differed from the fictionalized one. How did your understanding of the novel change after connecting it to concrete historical events?

A Conversation with Bernie McGill

You've written plays as well as short stories and novels. How has your experience with playwriting (and with watching your plays unfold in front of you) affected your fiction writing?

Writing for the theater, in my experience at least, is a much more collaborative process than writing fiction. During the making of a theater piece, there are a number of voices in the room, there's more input from other creative people, all of whom have an investment in the final made thing. When it comes to writing fiction it makes you very aware that the choices you make are your own. I always read my fiction aloud; I need to hear what's being said to gauge its authenticity. I think theater writing makes you a more spare fiction writer; it makes you aware of how much you can show and how little you need to tell. It makes you realize how redundant most adjectives are and how important nouns and verbs are, the real nuts and bolts of writing. And I think it helps you to focus on what happens. You need to treat your potential reader with the same respect you'd grant an audience member, ask yourself, "Would an audience sit through this?" If the answer's no, then you know what to do. Get the scissors out and start cutting.

YOU WRITE ON YOUR WEBSITE ABOUT GLEANING THE EDITORIAL SERVICES OF A FUSSY ANNAGHMAKERRIG TABLE LAMP AT THE TYRONE GUTHRIE CENTRE, A WRITER'S AND ARTIST'S RETREAT. DO YOU FIND YOURSELF AT THE MERCY OF ANY OTHER UNORTHODOX EDITORS DURING THE WRITING PROCESS?

There are a number of techniques that we use in the writing groups I work with to "test" our writing, questions such as "Does this passage move the story forward?"; "Where does this incident take us?"; "Is this piece of writing absolutely essential?" I am guilty of being seduced by the poetry of language, I become attached to a piece of writing because it sounds good, but you do have to remind yourself that you're telling a story, that you need to keep the reader with you at all times. My UK editor did a fantastic job on the first draft of *The Butterfly Cabinet,* and many of her edits could be paraphrased thus: "Beautiful piece of writing, what's the point of it?" I use the second part of that phrase now when I'm writing to help me focus.

PER YOUR WEBSITE, THE ORIGINAL TITLE OF *THE BUTTERFLY CABINET* WAS *THE LEPIDOPTERIST*. WHY DID YOU CHANGE THE TITLE? WERE YOUR EARLIER DRAFTS MORE FOCUSED ON HARRIET—THE LEPIDOPTERIST—AND LESS ON THE SYMBOLISM OF THE BUTTERFLY CABINET?

The Lepidopterist was always a working title; before that the book was called *The Sea Diaries*. I always thought it was a little inaccessible as a title; in general I try and avoid Latinate phrases and go for the more direct Anglo-Saxon choice. But it got me through the first draft. Harriet was always the main protagonist of the book, Maddie was invented to act as a foil to her, but she ended up having an important role to play, not just in the telling of the story, but in the story itself. The story is fairly evenly divided up between the two narratives. I think it was my agent who suggested *The Butterfly Cabinet* as a title, either her or my editor, and I liked it, so we went with it. It changed the book a little—the cabinet became more prominent, and I had to come up with an explanation of how it had ended up in Maddie's possession, but it's fun trying to work those things out.

ON YOUR WEBSITE, YOU TALK ABOUT THE PROCESS BY WHICH YOU DECIDED TO RELOCATE YOUR FICTIONAL STORY AWAY FROM THE CASTLE WHERE THE REAL-LIFE INSPIRATION OCCURRED. WHAT PARTS OF THE HISTORICAL RECORD—THE NEWSPAPER ARTICLES ABOUT HARRIET, THE PRISON DETAILS, OR THE MAID WORK, FOR EXAMPLE—DID YOU ADOPT MORE DIRECTLY?

It's very hard to say what percentage of the book is fictional and what percentage is more closely tied to fact. In broad terms, the events surrounding the child's death follow the testimonies as related by witnesses at the trial. According to the newspaper reports, the child was put in the wardrobe room by the governess because she had soiled herself. The mother was out of the house at the time, and when she returned she went in to the child, tied her by the hands to a ring on the wall, went out, locked the door, put the key in her pocket, and left her alone for about three hours. When she returned, the child was dead. These events were related by the mother at the inquest that was held in the house the following day. Harriet's backstory is a complete invention, as is her obsession with butterflies, and Maddie is an entirely fictional character, although in some ways, she is a kind of collage, inspired by the servants who gave evidence at the trial. The prison details and the maidservants' work came from reading social histories of the period. I wanted to make those two worlds as authentic as I possibly could. I also visited the National Archive in Dublin to read the original prison records for Grangegorman. It was really strange to see the mother's name there, written by someone who had actually known her and would have dealt with her on a daily basis. That was far more chilling than reading about her in the newspapers. It made it very real to me.

HOW DID YOU LAND UPON THE IDEA OF TWO NARRATORS (PLUS A FEW BRIEF LETTERS FROM ANNA) FOR YOUR STORY? DID YOU EVER CONSIDER ADDING MORE VOICES?

It was very important to me that we heard Harriet's story. As I said above, she made a statement at the inquest, hours after the child's death, which was recorded and reread on several occasions, and printed in the newspapers. It was a fairly bald, emotionless statement of fact and it makes for very uncomfortable reading. She comes across as a fairly cold individual. But I think that was what intrigued me most. As far as I understand it, the law at the time was such that neither the defendant, nor members of the defendant's immediate family, were permitted to give evidence during a trial, so these printed words by the mother are the only words of hers that we have. I wanted to know what she would have said, had she been given the chance. There were questions I wanted to ask her, and this was the only means I had of having her speak. There was no question in my mind that Harriet should be allowed to talk for herself.

As for Maddie, I was looking around for someone who could offer another version of events, and for a while I became interested in the idea that that other character might be a reporter working on the case. I eventually rejected this idea, though, because I wanted that other person to have an insight into the workings of the household, both before and after the child's death. For a while, I entertained the notion that the other narrator might be Julia, Harriet's sister, but I became more and more drawn to a servant's voice. I wanted someone who would contrast with Harriet in terms of their social standing, their upbringing and education, and who had that duality that servants often had: someone who was an integral member of the household but who could be a witness to events, almost unseen. Other voices do come into the story—Edward's, the children's, the other servants'—but all filtered through Harriet and Maddie. I'm always interested in how people's versions of events will differ from one another, how we all put our own spin on things. That relationship between truth and interpretation is very engaging, I think.

Which character would you most want to be friends with? Why?

I think Peig sounds like a good soul, and Maddie as a young woman would have been fun to know, and you could have had a good old flirt with Alphie. I think Harriet's the kind of woman you would avoid at the school gates but gossip about endlessly with your friends. "Did you hear what she said to Mrs. So and So . . . ?"—that kind of thing. She'd be very unapproachable, immaculately turned-out, her domestic life would run like clockwork. You'd never have a good word to say about her but your ears would prick up every time her name was mentioned, which would be often. She'd be much maligned and much spoken about.

How did you originally stumble across the historical research that gave way to Harriet's character? Did you know immediately that you'd found a book idea, or did the idea resurface later in your mind?

I came across the story in a local parish magazine, just a short article about the big house up the road and the mother who'd been imprisoned for the killing of her young daughter. It lodged in my brain. I pass the entrance to the house regularly, and every time I did it sent a shiver up my spine. My own children were fairly young at the time, around five and seven. I couldn't stop thinking about what had happened there, so short a distance from my own home, albeit more than a hundred years before. Around that time, I'd been awarded a grant from the Arts Council of Northern Ireland to write a collection of short stories. I decided to start with this one. My idea was to write about ten stories, roughly ten years apart in time, leading up to the present day, but I couldn't get away from this one story. Everything I wrote led back to it again. I was working with a mentor, a writer named Damian Gorman, and he suggested that there might be scope for a novel. It was a frightening idea, but after a bit of persuasion, I decided to give it a go. The research was quite time-consuming, but I kept coming across aspects of the story that held me—at the time of her imprisonment, the mother was pregnant with her ninth child. The child who died was the only daughter in the family. I'm the youngest of a family of ten children, seven boys and three girls. I'm sure it had some bearing on my interest.

Did the butterfly theme come from historical research or from your own construction of Harriet?

The butterfly theme was an invention of my own. I had read that the mother was a keen and skilled horse rider, a huntswoman, and a renowned horse breaker. This passion of hers seemed to fit very neatly into the image of her as a strict disciplinarian, but I was looking for something a little more poetic. I had been reading about the Victorians, about the legacy of Darwin, the rise in interest in the study of the animal world, the apparent lack of squeamishness around collecting, preserving, studying insects and much larger animals. That image of the collector's cabinet is, I think, quintessentially of that era. I began to wonder if Harriet was a collector and if so, what that meant. Was she someone who could only appreciate the beauty of the thing when it was still? I thought that if that were true, that that was both chilling and sad, and that seemed to fit with who I thought she was.

You write on your website, of Harriet, "I wasn't trying to justify what she'd done, I didn't particularly want to identify with her, but I did feel compelled to try and understand the motivations of that fictional character she had become." By now, at the end of the writing process, do you feel you understand her motivations? Are there parts of her as a character that you still don't understand?

There are, absolutely, parts of Harriet that I don't understand, that I'm wary of understanding. I did want to get inside her head, but I didn't particularly want to dwell there. It was, as I've said before, a dark place to be. I'm glad I don't have to be there anymore. There are things I admire about her as an individual. When she made the statement at the inquest about locking the door and putting the key in her pocket, she essentially damned herself from her own mouth. She was saying, "I, and I alone, am to blame." She wasn't allowing room for speculation, which is, of course, what caused me to speculate when I was writing the book.

You write in your website bio, "I love the contract that's made between writers and readers/audiences: when people sit down, individually or together, and conspire to believe in what is openly, transparently, not true." What messages or emotions do you hope to convey to your readers in this particular shared conspiracy of belief?

I always look for emotional truth in fiction, for characters that you can believe in, who do things that you may or may not agree with, but which you can understand. I think that's the real joy of fiction and the theater, and if those made-up people doing made-up things can cause you to look at the world a little differently, be a little more tolerant, a little less judgmental, then I think the art form is doing its job. Sometimes we need a medium like that, or a mirror, or a filter, we need to look at make-believe in order to get a clearer perspective on our own world. I love George Eliot's definition, in *The Mill on the Floss,* of metaphor: "we can so seldom declare what a thing is, except by saying it is something else." We seem to need to pretend, sometimes, that a thing is something else in order to appreciate what it is. You should always come away from a story or a book or from the theater a little changed, I think, in your outlook, a little cheered, or a little more enlightened, or a little better informed, or a little more sympathetic; otherwise what's the point?

Do you have any ideas for, or beginnings of, a second novel right now? If not, what do you plan to work on next?

I'm tentatively working on a second novel set on Rathlin, a small inhabited island off the north coast of Ireland. It was the site, in 1898, of some of the first wireless experiments conducted by Marconi's engineers. Even nowadays, the island is occasionally cut off in bad weather. I love the idea that this relatively remote and isolated place, which didn't have electricity until the early 1990s, was the site of such experimental technology at the end of the nineteenth century that people were able to send and receive messages between there and the mainland without the aid of cables or wires. It must have seemed like magic was at work. I'm fascinated by that idea that your words can travel beyond you, specifically in the context of a community that knew all too well what it was to be isolated from the rest of the world.

Before your writing career took off, you worked as a theater manager and events coordinator. Would you consider going back to the theater, or are you firmly and happily entrenched in the writer's path now?

At the moment, I seem to be a fiction writer, but I'd love to write again for the theater. It is a magical place, even, maybe especially, when you know what it looks like from behind the scenes. When I was a student I worked as an usherette in the Queen's Film Theatre in Belfast. We used to view the same film six, seven times or more, and even though the film never changed, even though what was showing on the screen was essentially fixed, the experience was never the same twice because the audience took on a different personality for each screening. Imagine how much more exciting it is to experience a theater piece, often in a different performance space, always in front of a new audience, and where the actors respond directly to the exigencies of that space and those people every time. It is wholly live, it is never, ever the same twice, nor could it possibly be, and that's what's most exciting about it. There are some stories that work better in the theater, that need to be seen and not told, and when I next find one, that's where I'll take it.

